By the same author

A Matter of Time

The Diarist

Themah Carolle-Casey

The Diarist

Copyright © 2018 Themah Carolle-Casey

Themah Carolle-Casey asserts her moral right to be identified as the author of this work in accordance with the Copyright, Designs and Patents Act 1988

This is a work of fiction. Names, characters and incidents either are the product of the author's imagination or are used fictitiously, and any resemblance to actual persons, living or dead, business establishments, event or locales is entirely coincidental.

All rights reserved. No part of this publication may be reproduced, stored in or introduced into a retrieval system, or transmitted, in any form or by any means (electronic, mechanical, photocopying, recording or otherwise), without the prior permission of the publisher.

ISBN-13:978-1537414270

Cover Photo : istock.com/sasiistock

Cover Design: Themah Carolle-Casey

For the people and stories of the Valdarno that inspired this book

*For us to go to Italy and to penetrate into Italy
is like a most fascinating act of self-discovery*
D.H. Lawrence

The Diarist

ENGLAND

1

Kate placed the diary on the kitchen table and, staring at it, pulled out a chair and sat down. She knew at a deep level that once she opened it there would be no turning back, her life would be changed. The strength of her curiosity soon outweighed any resistance, known or otherwise, and she reached towards the book with outstretched fingers that stroked its soft, leather cover. She sighed, pulling it towards her, resistance was futile, it was already written and, in that moment, the past, present and future merged and became one.

She had bought the cottage on a whim. Well, not exactly a whim, but in retrospect it had happened quickly, and she was not known for having an impulsive nature. It was not that she was unhappy, not at all, she loved her house, had been happily married and raised a family there. She had not planned to move, it was more an invitation. In fact, she had only known about the cottage by accident, a friend of a friend who had mentioned it in passing; someone he or she knew had bought it, renovated it and, due to a change in circumstances, wanted to sell. As soon as Kate saw the photo she knew she wanted to live there. It was the quintessential country cottage. Flower beds edged a path that led to the front door where roses arched and continued their climb above the windows on either side. She could almost smell their heady fragrance.

Suddenly her home of thirty odd years became large and unwieldy. The children had left home and were now busy building their own lives and since her husband's death a couple of years ago, there was an emptiness, echoes with nowhere to go haunted her on a daily basis. As she looked at the sale details for the cottage she could see herself walking in the front door and happily living there. She phoned the vendor immediately to arrange a viewing for the following Monday and showed the details to her daughter when she visited that weekend.

"What do you think, Emma?" she called from the kitchen.

"Think about what?" Emma asked as she sat down at the table next to her mother.

"This cottage...., oh damn, I've lost it," she sighed, frustrated by her impatience with the new laptop. "It's so sensitive. I hardly touch anything and it zooms off all over the place."

"It's alright, mum, you'll get used it," Emma smiled.

"Ah, here it is, see, doesn't it look just perfect?"

"Well yes, it's very pretty but I don't see why you want to move. I thought you were happy here."

"Oh Ems, I have been and I am, but I don't know, I'd like something a bit smaller, more manageable – both financially and physically. You understand don't you?"

Kate realised, of course, that it had been Emma's home as well, filled with memories of her growing and her father. She was not the only one who would be letting it go.

She remembered it as if it was yesterday as she stood in the porch facing the front door knowing that at some point she must turn the key in the lock and cross the threshold into what had once been their home, now hers. She knew now that it was final, there was no going back. The future stood before her, long and empty. Not only had she to grieve the man she had loved for the past thirty years but also her dreams. Dreams of a future, a future together, not the void she now saw as inescapable. She had always believed they would grow old together, endearingly old together and that had now been snatched away. He had been snatched away.

"Come on mum, let me ...." Emma raised her hand towards the lock.

"No, no, it's alright, I can..." Without looking at her daughter, Kate turned the key and together they entered the house. Even though it was only an hour or so since they had left to go to the crematorium, to Kate it felt like forever. Time had changed since John's death, it had stopped.

She felt a sudden pang of selfishness as Emma walked beside her to the dining room where everything was laid out for the imminent guests. Whilst she had been deprived of the love of her life, Emma had lost her father.

It's odd, she thought, all her beliefs about life and death were now lost to her and what had been easy philosophies in life were now nowhere to be found. She must pull herself together she thought as she heard voices drifting into the house from the drive and David, her son, directing people. Oh dear, more sympathy and commiserations, she felt overfull already. Still, she took a deep breath and turning to Emma forced a weak smile. "We'd better go to the front and meet them."

They had met in Paris. She was in her final year of a Modern Languages degree and in Paris for a long weekend to absorb some culture and practise her French. He was there for the weekend doing research for his Master's in English Literature into writers that had lived there. They were young, hedonistic and believed they could make a difference. Their romance continued beyond Paris and after graduation they each found jobs in London. Their lives evolved over a few short years to marriage, babies and mortgages, though not necessarily in that order. As they outgrew the flat they had struggled to buy, they uprooted their family life to Bath, taking advantage of its increased value that enabled them to buy a substantial house close to John's new job at the university.

At first Kate missed her life in London, the buzz, the culture, but she soon delighted in the fresh air, open spaces and being able to spend more time with the children. As the children grew and became independent she longed for something more than the occasional teaching and translation work that had sustained her through their childhood. Before she was able to fully explore the possibilities John's heart had stopped and life as she knew it had come to an abrupt end.

Several months passed as she became accustomed to the new rhythms of her life. Her daughter had flown the nest long ago and was busy feathering her own and her son, David, was teaching in Asia. At first Kate found the solitude both a blessing and a curse. The freedom to do what she wanted when she wanted was a joy until something went wrong and she realised there was no one to blame any more, only herself. It was a chastening and self revealing time as she slowly emerged from the grief of her losses and, little by little, began to appreciate life once more.

Gradually, she worked her way through the house. She cleared all the pictures and ornaments she had never liked, took any clothes she no longer wore to the charity shop, and, after sorting through years of accumulated paperwork, had a bonfire in the back garden. Finally she set about decorating, painting the walls in shades of white and using soft furnishings to bring in colour. By the time it was finished she had taken tentative steps towards reinventing herself and her home.

On viewing the cottage, she offered the asking price, which she thought was fair and put her house on the market the same day. She accepted the first offer and it was done and dusted within three months.

Moving day arrived accompanied by excitement and apprehension. It took longer than she anticipated to not only pack everything, but to downsize from a substantial four bedroom house to a small three bedroom cottage. As she veered between exhaustion and elation there were times she questioned why she was doing it at all.

Many of the larger items of furniture would either not fit or were totally unsuitable and, in exasperation, Kate called a local auction house to remove the offending items for sale while she went in search of more appropriate alternatives. By the time she closed the door and said goodbye to her old home and its memories, she felt lighter and freer than she had for years.

When she arrived at her new home, her eyes first scanned the front garden then the cottage itself as she claimed ownership of this new chapter in her life. She was pleased to have a short time alone to savour the moment of transition. Once inside she walked from room to room inhaling the clear and open space. It was only the kitchen that still retained anything from the previous owners; an oil-fired Aga, which she was overjoyed to now own, and a wide pine dresser that had probably been built into the wall years before and a sacrilege to break up and remove.

She heard the sound of footsteps on the path outside and was relieved to see the John Lewis van had arrived. She had arranged for the delivery to dovetail with the removal van and prayed they would not overlap. By her calculations she should have at least an hour before the removal men arrived, by which time her new furniture would be in place and the path clear for the arrival of her remaining furniture and possessions.

She watched as her new life took shape. A new bed and wardrobe disappeared upstairs followed by two new sofas that were allocated to homes in the living room. A pine table and chairs were taken to the kitchen, together with her additional purchases of rugs, bedding, cushions, throws and, most important at the moment, a new kettle. Kate rinsed it, filled it with water and went to the car to get the mugs, tea, milk and biscuits she had brought with her. After thanking and saying goodbye to the delivery men, she made tea, sighed and sank into a chair to await the arrival of the rest of her belongings.

A knock at the door shook her from her reverie. Her mind raced through possibilities as she walked the short length of the hall. When she opened it Kate was met by a woman, probably in her forties she thought, who had a disarming and friendly smile.

"Hello, I just wanted to introduce myself, I'm Annie and I live next door. I know, moving's hell and if there's anything .... well, I'm sure you have it all organised. Just let me know if you need anything, tea, coffee, a glass of wine. Anyway, welcome." Annie eventually paused for breath.

"Oh, thank you, that's very kind. I don't think there's anything at the moment," Kate replied thinking there was a freshness about Annie she liked and hoped they might be friends, "but I may take you up on the glass of wine later. I'm Kate, by the way."

"Great," Annie beamed. "I'm just next door. Anytime." And she turned and left.

Before Kate could close the door, the removal van pulled up outside and the next hour or so was spent directing furniture and boxes. Once the men had gone, Kate closed the front door and leaning her back against it, surveyed the chaos. It was a strange feeling, this in between time, she thought. Leaving one world behind and entering a new one yet to be discovered. Taking a deep breath, she walked along the hall to the kitchen and opened the first box.

Her mobile rang. It was Emma.

"Hi mum, how's it going?"

"Oh Ems, hi. Well, the removal men have just left ...."

"Do you want me to come ...."

"No Ems, thanks, I'll be fine. There's no rush, come and see me when it's all done." Kate said, realising it was something she wanted to do on her own.

"Ok, but if there's anything …. you will let me know?"

"Yes, of course darling. Now, I must get on and … thanks."

The natural light was fading and Kate was surprised to see how much she had done. The kitchen and living room looked almost normal save for an odd box secreted behind a chair or discretely placed in a corner. The sun was setting and as the walls turned from gold through ever deepening shades of pink, Kate felt a warm satisfaction wash over her. She went upstairs to make the bed before surrendering to the need for food and relaxation.

The fridge contained the bare essentials. She had ensured she would have enough to get her through the evening and breakfast then, well then, she would explore the village shop and locate the nearest supermarket. Tonight she had the joy of a pizza which she put into the Aga's oven and opened a bottle of Rioja. The warmth from the Aga and a few sips of red wine were comforting and soporific, and the energy that had sustained her throughout the day soon dissolved as exhaustion took over.

Meanwhile in the cottage next door, Annie was thinking about her new neighbour.

"Penny for them?" asked Ben.

"Oh, I was just thinking about Kate, you know, our new neighbour. She seemed …well, friendly."

"What, you mean you've been round already? Really Annie, the poor woman has only been here a few hours," he sighed but there was a warm affection in the tone of his voice.

"Oh, I only popped round to say hello and welcome, I didn't stay or anything. I just thought …."

"And I just thought," Ben said embracing her from behind and lowering his cheek to hers, "that I might like to take my wife out to supper, what do you think?"

"Mmmm, I'd like that. Where shall we go?"

"Well, I've heard good things about that pub just outside the village. It's under new management, we could give it a try."

"Ok, do you think we should ..."

"No," he said firmly, pre-empting her suggestion, "not tonight, let the poor woman unpack and settle in."

"Alright then, give me five minutes and I'll be ready."

As Annie went upstairs she remembered when she and Ben had first moved in and, despite having lived in the village for almost twenty years, they were still considered newcomers. It wasn't that the other residents were unfriendly, far from it, it was just that time had a longer rhythm here when it came to local families and their homes and she began to imagine introducing Kate to village life.

By the time Kate was ready for bed she felt a hollow exhaustion, maybe it was the wine, she thought, and flopped into bed before her mind could take it any further.

She woke early and it was still dark as she gradually became aware of unfamiliar surroundings. Then she remembered the previous day, the goodbyes, the moving, her new life and she felt in the dark to switch on the bedside lamp. A mistake, she thought as she looked at the boxes waiting to be unpacked. She felt as if she had been up for a week, her eyes dry, her limbs weak. She turned off the light and pulled the duvet round her in search of oblivion.

When she woke again, it was to a bright sunny morning. She rubbed sleep from her eyes and determined she must sort out some curtains. The unfamiliarity was less disturbing in daylight and she got up eager to create order from the chaos. It did not take her long to finish unpacking and find new homes for everything.

The Diarist

By the the end of the day, the last packing box was folded and designated for recycling, and it looked as if she had lived there for years. She filled the rooms with fresh cut flowers from the garden and thought about how she would dry the hydrangeas once the blooms were at their best. A ray of happiness touched a corner of her heart as she sat down at the kitchen table with a cup of her favourite earl grey tea.

It was getting late and she still had shopping to do so she went to open the dresser drawer in search of pen and paper to make a list. It stuck and, despite tugs and wiggles, refused to move. Odd, it had been fine yesterday. There must be something wedged, and she went in search of a means to investigate further. She returned to the kitchen with a wire coat hanger which she opened out hoping it would clear the length of the drawer. After more wiggling of the wire hanger and the drawer, Kate heard a clunk and the drawer, freed from the obstacle, shot out towards her. She took out a pen and paper for the shopping list, then bending down, opened the cupboard beneath the drawer to find out what had been causing the problem. It was dark and difficult to see behind the china to the wall so she reached in, fumbling with her fingers for the offending item.

"Ah, got you," she said folding her hand round it. She drew it out with care. It was a book, no a diary, and standing up, she placed it on the dresser shelf above the drawer. Closing the cupboard and ensuring the drawer was now opening and closing without hindrance, she decided to forget about the shopping list and grabbed her bag and car keys. She had a vague memory of a supermarket a few miles away, thinking it was probably too late for the village stores, which was confirmed by the closed sign on the door as she drove past.

An hour or so later Kate walked up the path to the front door, laden with carrier bags filled with essential food and supplies. Behind her the light was fading and deep pink-edged clouds offered the promise of a sunny day to come. As she put away the shopping her eyes fell upon the book she had found earlier and left on the dresser. She picked it up again, but her curiosity was postponed as her hunger took precedence.

She made a quick *spaghetti peperoncino*, a simple dish of olive oil, garlic and chilli that her Italian father loved and one she had learnt to make from an early age. She added some salad, poured a glass of Rioja, sat down and took stock of her day. She was pleased with her progress and able to relax now that the unpacking was done save for a few boxes which she had relegated to the spare room.

Her thoughts wandered to her new neighbour, Annie, and she decided she would knock on her door in the morning, invite her for coffee. It would be good to take a small step into this new life but before she could follow the thought any further she was pulled by a more mundane one, to do the washing up. When she had finished, she curled up on the sofa and watched some uneventful television, leaving the book, still untouched by her hand or mind, on the dresser.

2

Morning arrived with the promised sun shining from a clear cobalt sky. Kate woke and stretched as she tried to recall vestiges of a dream that still clung to the edge of her memory. She had a sense of another time and place but it dissolved into mists beyond her reach. She shook her head to clear it, showered, dressed and went downstairs to the kitchen for breakfast.

She made coffee and opened a bag containing the special treat of an almond croissant. I could get used to this, she thought, but better not. John's sudden death had invoked a heightened awareness of the fragility of life and she now gave more thought to what she was eating but not to the exclusion of enjoying treats when she fancied something.

Kate sipped her coffee, enjoying the silence interrupted only by occasional birdsong. She smiled as she embraced the moment, happy in her new home. She stood up to put her mug and plate in the sink when she remembered the book on the dresser. She picked it up and, feeling a wave of dizziness, held on to the back of a chair before putting the book down on the kitchen table.

She sat down and stared at it. Being a rational person her mind raced, searching for an explanation. She could find nothing in her experience that made sense of what had just happened or the sense of knowing that was now overpowering her. She reached out and pulled towards her the slim, leather-bound volume with the word 'Diary' etched in gold in the faded green cover.

The urge to put the book down and go out was strong but less so than her curiosity. She turned back the cover to reveal a name, Hettie Forbes, 1952, written in even manuscript. The pages were thin, akin to airmail letter paper and the writing covered the pages in a regular, italic hand.

The first entry was not until April with a short paragraph on the twelfth.

'I have decided to go to Italy and I will do my best to keep an accurate record of my trip. I believe it is important to know the truth, not just for myself, but for the family. I have booked my ticket and will leave next week on Wednesday.'

Kate held her breath as she read and turned the page to the next entry.

'Ma is not happy about my trip. She thinks it an utter waste of time. Maybe she doesn't truly want to know what happened, or perhaps she is just concerned for me. It doesn't matter as I will not change my mind.'

Intrigued, she continued to the next entry, resisting the urge to fast forward to Hettie being in Italy. As she entered Hettie's world, back to a time before she was born, before her existence was a wish or desire, she stopped. Oh, I don't think I can do this now, she thought and closed the book. It felt like an intrusion and one she was now unsure about making, if at all.

She wandered out into the garden, cataloguing the plants in her mind, calling herself back to the present, to her home, to herself. Oh dear, she thought, what's wrong with me, it's only a book, well, a diary. Why does it feel so important? Maybe I'm more tired than I thought or, I suppose, it could be the stress of moving. I mean they say it's one of the most stressful things in life. She heard a car pull up outside and went back into the cottage and looked out to see that it was her neighbour, Annie, returning home. Maybe I'll invite her for coffee .

Annie was only too delighted to accept Kate's invitation and within half an hour they were sitting in Kate's kitchen exchanging brief histories. Annie waxed lyrical about Kate's ability to create a beautiful home so quickly and Kate modestly explained that it had not been so difficult considering she had got rid of so much before the move.

It turned out that Annie had lived next door for nearly twenty years. Her husband, Ben, and she had moved there after deciding that city life in London had become too much for them and the village offered the peace and quiet they sought as well as being close to a station with direct trains to London.

They discussed the pros and cons of life in London and what they each missed. Kate's mind kept wandering to the diary and she wondered if she should tell Annie about it but instead asked her who had lived in the cottage prior to her.

"Oh dear, it's hard to remember," frowned Annie as she searched her memory. "It was let as a holiday cottage for years, people coming and going all the time. Then it was empty for a while until, oh what was his name, tall man, moustache, I hate moustaches, erm no, it's no good. Anyway, he bought it, did it up and at the last minute, just before he was about to move in, he sold it and here you are," she grinned, before adding, "wait a minute, I think it might have been when we first moved in, there was an elderly lady living here. Yes, I remember now but she moved not long after that. Oh, what was her name, Amelia, no Alice, that was it."

"Oh," said Kate almost disappointed not to have heard Hettie's name. "It must have quite a history. You know, its age and that."

"Yes, I imagine it has. Maybe we should investigate?" Annie queried with a raised eyebrow and soft giggle. "You know, the person you need to speak to is Betty, she's lived here forever and knows everything there is to know about everyone, well almost, anyway I can introduce you if you like, we have a book group that meets once a month and ...."

"That sounds great, I'd love to," Kate enthused thinking Annie may not stop. "Oh, I'm sorry, I didn't mean to jump in like that," she added realising it was not an actual invitation.

"Oh no, that's okay, I was going to invite you to the next meeting which is Friday morning, if you're free of course?"

"Oh, yes please, but will that be ......?" Kate wondered if there was some formality that Annie might be ignoring in her eagerness to include her.

"Don't worry, it'll be fine. As you've just moved in, everyone will be keen to meet you. There's usually five or six of us who are regulars and a few odd ones who drop in when they can make it, but I'll ring round and let everyone know. And, you must come to the pub one night, that's always good ......"

Kate half heard Annie wax on about some of the local characters and how holiday homers were changing the nature of the village, and at the same time realised how non-existent her social life had been since John's demise. A shadow flitted over her as she returned her attention to Annie's words.

"Are you ok? I'm sorry I know I do go on a bit sometimes, Ben always..."

"No, not at all, I'm fine," Kate said, thinking how perceptive Annie was to have caught such a subtle and fleeting change in midst of her flow. "What time on Friday?"

"We meet at ten and I think this month we're at Betty's, so that's perfect. I can knock about a quarter to, if that's okay, it's not far."

"Thanks Annie. Do I need to bring anything?"

"No, just you. Not first time anyway. Now is there anything else, I mean, are you finding your way round? There's the village shop, which is good for basics but not always open, and there's a supermarket a few miles up the road, oh and a wonderful farmer's market every Friday."

"Yes, I found the supermarket last night, thanks."

"Right, I'd better go and let you get on. Thanks for the coffee." Annie stood up to go. "Look why don't you come round for supper, say tomorrow about seven? I think Ben's home tomorrow but even if he's not…"

"Thanks Annie, but …"

"No buts, unless of course, you have a hot date," Annie grinned.

"I wish," Kate laughed and, relenting, agreed she would see Annie at seven.

Alone again, Kate replayed Annie's visit in her mind. She's like a breath of fresh air, Kate thought, happy that she was making a new friend. It wasn't that she didn't have friends, she had, though some had drifted away after John's death, mainly because they were more his friends than hers, and others gave up when she either ignored or repeatedly declined their invitations. There were a handful that she had known for years, whom she spoke to now and again on the phone or the occasional Facebook visit, but they were scattered around the country.

In moving away from the life she had known and, until recently shared with John, she felt she was reclaiming part of herself. She began to remember things that she had put on hold, to do sometime, one day, forgotten until now; dreams lost and displaced by newer dreams of love, marriage and children. Any small, creative impulse had escaped her when John died and as distant memories called, she began to feel the presence of her muse beckoning her.

She picked up the diary and opened it at the next entry.

Ma now refuses to talk to me about it. Anyone would think I was still a child and she keeps telling me that I don't understand. She's right, I don't understand. I don't understand why she's being so difficult, why she doesn't want to know what happened. Yes, maybe it is foolish, but at least I will know I tried to find the truth. I can't believe that's it. Missing. No body. Nothing. Anyway Aunt Issy says I can stay with her so I won't be alone, in fact it may even be fun, if one can have fun of course.

The words and Hettie's thoughts petered out and what was this about someone missing and there being no body.. Maybe she was interrupted, thought Kate and, intrigued, she turned the page to the next entry.

Only two days to go. I think I have everything I need now. I will take the train from Victoria to Dover, then the boat to Calais and the train through France, into Italy and on to Florence. I feel nervous and excited at the same time and I know I'm doing the right thing despite whatever Ma thinks. Oh Charlie, what happened? I wish you could tell me.

Who was Charlie? Was he the one who was missing? Kate noted that the entries were short and tried to imagine what it must have been like for Hettie at that time, going against her mother's wishes and following her own trajectory. Maybe she snatched minutes here and there to write in the diary. There were no indications as to how Hettie otherwise spent her time. She had the impression that she was an independent, young woman, somewhat feisty, determined, and possibly with resources of her own to be travelling to Italy so spontaneously. She looked at the kitchen clock and, realising she was hungry, got up and

The Diarist

opened the fridge to investigate.

She found some buffalo mozzarella and prosciutto, lightly toasted two small pieces of sourdough bread on which she then rubbed garlic and drizzled extra virgin olive oil before covering with the cheese and ham. As she ate she thought of Hettie going to Italy and of the wonderful food she would find there. How exotic it must have been, long before supermarkets and the easy access to foods from around the world that were now commonplace. Hettie's excitement seemed infectious and Kate was already picturing what she would pack in her own suitcase if she was going to Florence.

She pulled her thoughts back to the present, made a fresh pot of coffee and decided to go for a walk, clear her head and allow her thoughts about Hettie and the diary to settle. She wondered what she should do about it, if anything.

After finishing her coffee, she grabbed a cardigan and went out to a soft spring afternoon. The sun was not yet at full strength and she felt its gentle warmth on her shoulders as she headed in the direction of the village centre where there was a primary school, a church and the stores which also incorporated the post office.

Kate set off along one of the drove roads, edged by open fields and leading to woodland in the distance. Breathing deeply she appreciated the beauty of the open landscape and, turning round, smiled at the way the village nestled, almost hidden, within it. Again, she felt that inner sense of knowing that she was in the right place. Immediately her mind turned to the diary. What was she going to do about it? Was there someone it should be returned to? At that thought, a wave of guilt passed through her, as if she had intruded on something private. She kept walking wondering what else she could have done. Was she only trying to ascertain who it belonged to or ......, or what, was she prying? Well no, that wasn't my intention, she thought, or maybe she hadn't thought. She decided she would not look at it again until she knew more about who might have left it there and hoped that Betty would have some answers when she met her the day after tomorrow.

She felt a chill as the sun was occluded by gathering clouds and realised she had reached the wood. Turning round she retraced her steps to the village and mused on what she was going to do now that she was here. Whilst she could probably manage for a while without working, she knew she would have to do something, if only for her own sanity. Before she could explore her options she felt the beginnings of the threatened shower as an odd drop of rain fell and, quickening her pace, pulled her cardigan tighter and headed for home. She ran the last fifty or so yards as the heavens opened and was glad to reach her kitchen and the warmth of the Aga.

Running upstairs she removed her wet clothes and, exhilarated by the walk and getting ready for supper with Annie, indulged in the luxury of another shower.

3

Friday arrived sooner than Kate had imagined. She had spent an enjoyable evening with Annie and Ben and Thursday had disappeared in a whirl of emails and phone calls as she caught up with essential and procrastinated correspondence and put out tentative feelers for future work projects. She had managed to resist any pull of curiosity to look at the diary and now she was about to meet Betty who may be able to help her locate its owner, she felt rather foolish about her previous thoughts about it.

The doorbell rang. Kate picked up her bag and went to greet Annie ready for immersion into village life.

"Hi, you ready?" beamed Annie.

"Sure, let's go," Kate closed the door behind her and followed Annie out into the road.

"Ready to put a toe in the water of village life?" grinned Annie.

"Oh," Kate smiled, mirroring a diluted version of Annie's infectious grin, "I'll do my best."

"Well, I think instant immersion is best and what better way than a book club!" Annie laughed and Kate could not help joining her.

"I'm sure you're right, is it far?"

"No, about five minutes. Do you mind walking?"

"Not at all, I'd rather walk."

"Ok, so I'm not going to say anything about anyone,

you can have a blank canvas to paint your own judgments ..."

"You're too kind, Annie," Kate said with a touch of irony and they both laughed again.

They soon arrived at Betty's bungalow which was set back from the road behind a high box hedge that Kate thought must have taken years to grow tall and thick enough to achieve such privacy.

The next hour passed in a haze of new faces and names. After welcoming Kate they discussed the book they had read during the last month before stopping for tea, coffee and biscuits. This was the part Kate had been dreading but was surprised how easy conversation came to her in the warmth and friendliness of the group. Betty was a delight, diminutive at under five feet with a youthful enthusiasm that shone through mischievous crinkled blue eyes. Annie manoeuvred Kate and the conversation in her direction.

"Annie tells me you're interested in finding out more about the history of your cottage, is that right?"

"Yes, I'd love to know more, who lived there etc.," Kate enthused.

"Well dear, it was a holiday home for years before that man bought it - sorry, can't think of his name - and, well we all thought he was going to move in after spending a small fortune doing it up, but he put it up for sale and we never saw nor heard anything from him again. And, here you are, and very nice too if I may say. Another biscuit dear?"

"Do you know who lived there before that?"

"Oh, that would have been Alice. Lived there for years, I think an aunt or someone before that. Probably in the same family for years. I tell you who would know is old Bernard, just up the road from you on the corner. You may have seen him, though he doesn't get out as much as he used to. I'm sure he'd love to talk to you about it. Would you like me to introduce you?"

The Diarist

"Yes please, Betty, if it's not too much trouble."

"I'll be in touch. Right, we'd better get on with things," and Betty stood up and clapped her hands once before saying, "Let's clear away and see what we want to read next month then."

Later, as Kate was eating her lunch she reflected on the morning and in particular her conversation with Betty. She wondered about Bernard and whether he would be able to add anything to the history of the cottage and its residents. The diary still sat on the dresser and she felt the pull of Hettie's world and, again, she imagined herself preparing for a similar trip to Italy. Shaking her head, she stood up and walked over to the sink to do the washing up. She looked out of the window on to the garden, grounding herself once again in the present as she considered a trip to a garden centre and what plants she could buy to give new colour and life to the drab borders. Remembering she had seen one on her way to the supermarket she resolved to go that afternoon.

Startled as the telephone ringing broke the silence, Kate took a deep breath, picked it up and pressed the green answer button.

"Hello?"

"Hello Kate, it's Betty. I hope I'm not disturbing you but I just wanted to let you know that I bumped into Bernard only half an hour ago and he would be delighted if you'd like to pop in any time. He says he's home most afternoons. Like I said, it's the cottage just up from you on the corner. Rose Cottage. You can't miss it, it has the best garden in the village."

"Oh, thank you Betty. I'll do that. And thank you for this morning I really enjoyed it."

"Well dear, I'm glad you enjoyed it. I do hope Bernard can shed some light on the cottage for you."

"Yes, see you again soon I hope."

"I'd like that very much. Hope Bernard can be of help.

Well, goodbye, dear."

"Goodbye, Betty and thank you."

Kate left the washing up and headed off to the garden centre where she lost herself in the world of ready-made, colour schemed, bedding plants. She soon found her heart was not in it and, unable to choose anything, thought she would call in on Bernard on the way home.

She parked her car outside the cottage and walked back up the lane following Betty's directions to Bernard's cottage. When she reached it she took a moment to marvel at the glorious garden at the front and the well-tended vegetable plot that ran along the side towards the back of the cottage. He must have very green fingers she thought as she walked up the lavender lined path to the front door. Before she could knock the door opened and she was greeted by a man larger than she had imagined, in a checked shirt with rolled up sleeves and braced corduroy trousers. His whiskered face was amiable and his soft brown eyes crinkled into a smile as he held out his hand in greeting.

"Ah, you must be Kate. Betty said I should expect you. Come in." And after a firm handshake, he showed her into a cosy living room dating back to the 1930's that looked out on to the front garden.

"Can I get you a cup of tea, Kate?" he offered.

"That would be lovely, thank you," she replied.

"Make yourself at home, I won't be long," and he left her while he went to prepare a tray of tea and biscuits.

Kate looked around the room, admiring the well-kept Art Deco furniture and the memories of his life encapsulated in the display of framed photographs on a walnut sideboard.

Bernard returned with the tea tray which he placed on an oval coffee table between the two armchairs either side of the tiled fireplace where Kate now sat.

"I'll just let it brew a bit. Now, how can I help you, Kate?" Bernard asked as he sat down in the other armchair.

The Diarist

"Well, Betty said you might be able to tell me something about the people who used to live in the cottage. I know it was a holiday cottage for a long time and before that there was someone called, oh ...."

"Alice," Bernard confirmed.

"Yes, Alice. But that's all I know."

"Ah, tea should be ready - milk and sugar?"

"Just milk, thanks."

Bernard poured tea into two china cups and offered a plate of assorted biscuits. "Please, help yourself."

Kate thanked him and helped herself to a shortbread.

"Now, let me see, where were we? Oh yes, Alice. Well, I'm not sure I can tell you much, she was a bit of a recluse you know. She didn't get involved in village life in any way, just kept to herself. I seem to remember there was a sister and think she inherited the cottage from an aunt or some relation."

"Do you know the name of the sister?"

"Er, I'm not sure Kate. I do remember thinking the family must have been fairly well off as she spent a lot of time in Italy."

Kate's heartbeat increased as she made connections to the diary and wondered if she should mention it to Bernard. Before she could say anything Bernard continued.

"What about the deeds, would they help?"

"Oh, the cottage is registered and the Land Registry don't keep the deeds any more so there was nothing with the papers when I bought it. My solicitor said he'd make enquiries for me but doesn't hold out much hope."

"Mmmm," Bernard scratched his whiskery chin. "Well, if I remember anything I'd be happy to let you know. Here," he said handing her a notepad and pen, "write your phone number and email for me so I can contact you. Something may come back to me."

Kate took the pad and pen and did as Bernard asked, surprised that he had a computer let alone knew about emails and immediately chastised herself for having such ageist thoughts.

"Thank you," she said as she handed the pad back to him. .

"Well, I hope you'll be very happy in the village Kate, and any time you feel like a chat, just knock on the door."

"Thank you, Bernard. I'll do that, and thanks for the tea."

Bernard walked to the gate with her where they said their goodbyes and Kate returned home realising another day had gone and she was no closer to solving the mystery of the diary. Maybe I'll have to read more if I'm ever going to find its owner, she thought as she walked into the kitchen.

"Damn it," she said and picked up the diary. Confused by the strength of her curiosity she wondered if this was how obsessions began and, if so, what it said about her. This was not the joy she had envisioned on moving here and she questioned what path she had stepped on to when opening the little, leather-bound book.

"Oh to hell with it!" she cried, poured herself a glass of wine and put a ready meal in the oven before once again pulling the diary towards her and opening it where she had left off.

I leave tomorrow and Aunt Issy is going to meet me at the station when I arrive. Ma hasn't changed her tune and is now warning me against all manner of things. She doesn't seem to have a very high opinion of Italians or maybe, just maybe, she's a little bit envious of Aunt Issy having married one and being happy. Dear Charlie, I wonder what you would make of all this. I will find out what happened to you, find you, I know I will, whatever Ma says.

Kate considered Hettie's last sentence. She turned back a page or two and reread a previous entry. So, Hettie

The Diarist

believed Charlie was alive, but who was Charlie? Husband, father, brother, lover? Why was her mother so against her visit to Italy?

Kate picked up a pad and pen from the dresser and started to make a list of questions on one page and what she knew so far on another. This consisted of Hettie going to Italy to stay with her aunt, Issy, in search of someone called Charlie, against her mother's wishes. Then there was Alice who had lived in the cottage and how did she fit into all this? And what was Hettie's diary doing in the dresser? How did it get there and how come nobody had found it before now? Her head whirred with questions and, as yet, no answers.

Kate heard the timer ping and got up to take her supper from the oven. Transferring it to a plate she poured another glass of wine and sat down to eat surrounded by the diary and pieces of paper. Just as she finished eating the phone rang.

"Hello Kate. It's Bernard. I hope I'm not disturbing you."

"Not at all, Bernard ..."

"Good," he interrupted, "I've remembered the name of Alice's sister. It was Henrietta."

"That's wonderful, Bernard," Kate said smiling at the touch of triumph in his voice. "Thank you."

"I was wondering, would you like to come over for coffee tomorrow, say about eleven? I may be able to find out a bit more by then."

"Yes, of course, Th....."

Before Kate could finish, Bernard said, "Good, see you then. Goodbye." And he put the phone down.

Kate leaned back in her chair and thought that maybe there were some answers after all. Damn, she thought as she remembered that she had arranged to see Annie in the morning. She quickly called her to apologise and rearrange, only managing to extricate herself after promising to tell all when they met later. She made a note to ring her solicitor in the morning before going to see Bernard, and ask if he had heard anything about the deeds.

After washing up she settled in front of the television in an attempt to distance herself from the diary and the questions still circling her mind. She wondered what John would have made of all this and became acutely aware of how much she missed his presence, being able to share her thoughts with him and feel his reassurance even if he didn't share her views. She sighed as she resigned herself to the ongoing sense of loss and grief. There were times in the old house when she thought she had caught a glimpse of him, smelt his aftershave or heard his distinctive chuckle and whilst the intensity of longing for him had eased, it was still there.

She watched a couple of forgettable programmes and unable to engage with them or retain any memory of them decided it was time for bed.

Kate woke from a deep sleep to the dissolving fragments of a dream, of John, of Florence. Unable to grasp and make sense of it, she showered and dressed and went down to the kitchen. She filled the little coffee pot and put it on the Aga, then looked out at the garden, hoping for inspiration. Her garden had always been not only her joy, but also her sanctuary, the place she went to find herself when overcome by the vagaries of life. The garden before her now awaited her personal touch to create something new, add more colour and texture, to claim it and make it her own, and provided an interesting mirror to where she stood in her own life.

By the time she had finished breakfast and completed one or two chores it was time to leave for her visit to Bernard. She tried to contain any anticipation or expectation as she walked along the road to his cottage. As she opened the gate Bernard turned round from the corner of the garden where he was dead heading some roses. He placed his secateurs on a nearby windowsill and walked over to greet her.

"Ah, good morning, Kate, I'll go and put the kettle on. Will it be tea or coffee?"

"Er, a cup of tea would be lovely, thank you."

"Well, come inside and make yourself at home, I won't be long."

Kate followed him into the cottage and sat down in the living room while Bernard made the tea. He soon returned with a tray of tea things and a plate of biscuits.

"Now let me see, where were we? Oh yes, let me pour the tea and I'll tell you what I managed to find out."

Kate studied him as he poured the tea and offered her a biscuit. She took the cup and saucer from him and declined the biscuit.

"So, you have news?" she said.

"Yes, yes, I have, though I don't know if it will be of much interest to you. I was talking to a friend of mine who lives on the other side of the village and he remembered the family. Seems he was one of the few people Alice ever spoke to. They would sometimes sit next to each other at church. Of course, not being a churchgoer myself ... anyways, oftentimes she would exchange a few words with him after the service and there were odd occasions he says when she was almost friendly and they would chat as they walked down the lane. Maybe he reminded her of her brother .... sorry, I'm getting ahead of myself. Apparently, he did glean that there was a brother, Charles, reported 'missing in action' around 1943 I think he said. And, it was her sister Henrietta, who some years later, went off to Italy to find him. Now, as to the cottage, that was gifted to Alice and her sister by an aunt who had married some Italian and gone to live in Italy. Even then it was only a sort of holiday home, somewhere for them to go to get away from the city, London that is. I don't think the sister spent much time here at all and Alice only spent more time here in later years. It's not much I know, but a start." Bernard offered hopefully.

Kate could barely contain her excitement as Bernard's words confirmed the diary entries.

"That's wonderful, Bernard. Thank you. I wonder where I can go to find more information. Do you have a surname? Maybe I could trace the brother."

"Oh, that would be Evans and I imagine there'll be records online. You could try the National Archives, I think they hold all the available records now."

Again, Kate was surprised by Bernard's extensive knowledge of the internet.

"Right, I'll take a look." Kate said before tentatively adding, "Bernard, do you think your friend might speak to me about it?"

"I don't know, Kate. He's not as he was but I'll have a word and let you know."

Kate thanked him, finished her tea and excused herself by saying she had to get back for a phone call. Doing her best not to be in an obvious rush she told Bernard that he was welcome to visit any time he wished and that maybe he could give her some advice on the garden.

She walked briskly back to the cottage and went straight to the kitchen where she picked up the diary and turned on her laptop. While she waited for the laptop to start up she took the pen and paper from the previous evening and quickly added the names that Bernard had given her. She felt a surge of adrenaline as she typed 'national archive' into the search engine. However, once she found the website her mood fell as she tried to find the relevant page to begin her search. She soon discovered that it would not be as straightforward as she had hoped and without more information it could prove more difficult than she had anticipated. With reluctance, she admitted she would probably need help.

"Damn, damn, damn," she said as she pushed the laptop away from her. She had never enjoyed technology and it had always been on a need to know basis and now here she was needing to know more. She looked at the diary and wondered if she would be able to get the help she needed without mentioning it. Of course, she would offer the names Bernard had given her and say she was exploring the history of the cottage, no need to mention the diary at all.

Kate decided she had better eat something before fulfilling her promise to see Annie and tell her about the visit to Bernard. Maybe this would be the perfect opportunity and she felt sure that Annie would be very resourceful when it came to searching on the internet. She began to relax a little and feel hopeful once again.

Annie was positively effervescent as Kate regaled her with the morning visit to Bernard and could not get to her office quickly enough to start searching for the Evans family.

"How exciting. I wonder what we'll find."

"Well, I don't know about exciting. I just thought it might be interesting to know who used to live here."

"Yes, yes, of course, but who knows what we might dig up. Look, a few months ago I started researching my family tree and you have to join various websites to get any information. I didn't get very far, but we could start with looking at the register for births, marriages & deaths for each of them. Now, who have we got? Alice, Henrietta and what was his name?"

"Oh, Charles ….."

"What about dates? Any idea when they might have been born?"

"Not really, only that Charles was 'missing in action' in about 1943. I suppose we'll have to work back from there. Mind you, I don't know how old he was then."

"Well, let's start at seventeen and work upwards," Annie suggested and started filling in boxes on the screen.

The next two hours sped by but with little success and Kate was losing any will to continue.

"Shall we call it a day. Maybe Bernard got the name

wrong or something or perhaps we're just not meant to know ...." Kate said in a quiet, resigned voice.

"Oh Kate, don't give up so easily. Maybe you could check the names again with Bernard?" Annie said by way of encouragement. "Ben won't be back for a couple of days and I haven't got a lot on so I'm happy to help."

"Ok," Kate smiled, buoyed by Annie's enthusiasm, "I'll speak to Bernard again and let you know."

"Great."

Kate spent the evening trying, unsuccessfully, not to think about the diary, Bernard, Annie or anything to do with the previous inhabitants of the cottage. By the time she went to bed she had played out a myriad of scenarios in her mind of what might have happened to the Evans family and, exhausted, immediately fell asleep.

When she woke the next morning, it was from more dreams of Florence, so visceral that she felt she had been there. Strange, she thought, she had not been to Italy, let alone Florence, and yet there was a feeling of intimacy she could not explain.

As she enjoyed her ritual cup of coffee that completed her breakfast, she remembered her conversation with Annie and their futile attempts to trace the Evans family. A knock at the front door interrupted her thoughts. It was Bernard.

"I hope you don't mind me calling unannounced as it were, Kate. I'm not disturbing you am I?"

"No, not all Bernard, come in. I've just made coffee, would you like some?" Kate said, wondering what could have caused him to call round so quickly.

"Well, if it's not too much trouble, that would be lovely, thank you," and he followed her into the kitchen, bending his head slightly to clear the low lintel.

Kate quickly cleared the kitchen table of her papers, including the diary.

"Milk or sugar?"

"Just milk, please Kate."

They sat down at the table each nursing their cup of coffee.

"I'm afraid I owe you an apology, Kate. Remember yesterday, when I told you about Alice and her family. Well, I got it wrong. They weren't called Evans at all. I thought it might be my hearing, you see, doesn't always work as it should. Anyway, I hope you don't mind but I couldn't resist having a quick look on the internet to see if I could find them, but of course I couldn't because I'd got the name wrong. Anyways, when I went to get my paper this morning, I saw my friend so I asked him again and it turns out he got it wrong. Said he didn't know what he was thinking and the name was Forbes."

"Oh ….."

"I'm sorry about this my dear, but I wanted to let you know as soon as I could so you didn't waste any more time."

"Er, that's very kind of you, Bernard. Thank you."

"Now, while I'm here, would you like me to take a look at your garden, I'm sure I can find some cuttings and such for you, that's if you'd like some of course."

"Oh yes, that would be lovely. It all seems a bit overwhelming at the moment." Kate said, relieved to have some help.

Kate led the way into the garden and after walking round the perimeter they sat down on a seat that gave them a good view of the whole. Bernard made some suggestions and Kate eagerly accepted his offer of cuttings and arranged to call to collect them that afternoon. By the time he left she felt less daunted and was actually looking forward to getting her hands dirty, but first, now she had the right name she couldn't wait to get back to her laptop.

Kate hoped it would not take long to find the information she sought and signed up for 30 day free trials at what seemed to be the two main sites.

Armed with the correct details it did not take long to find the possible birth years for Alice, Henrietta and Charles. She soon calculated that at the time of writing the diary, Henrietta, Hettie, would have been twenty-one. Her mind raced, imagining all manner of possibilities. Did she have to wait until she was twenty-one? Had she come into some money, from a trust maybe, or a legacy? Is that what enabled her to make the trip against mother's wishes? And, why was her mother so against it?

If the references she had found were correct, they were all born in London. She felt uncomfortable with her lack of experience and the uncertainty that accompanied it and decided to call Annie who seemed more at ease with the technology of search engines and the like.

Annie, as always, was only too happy to help and suggested that Kate join her for lunch after which they could see what else they could find out. Kate closed her laptop and for some unbeknown reason, picked up the diary and put it back in the drawer where she had found it. As she did so she wondered why she felt so protective of it but could find no rational reason. Dismissing the thought she went next door where Annie was setting the table for lunch.

Annie saw Kate approach the front door and shouted for her to come in.

"Hi, come in, come in. I've just put on some soup so it shouldn't be long. I'll warm some bread and there's cheese on the table."

"This is great Annie, thanks."

"Been tearing your hair out, have you?"

"You could say that. I just don't seem to have the right kind of mind for it, or maybe I'm just too impatient."

"Oh, join the club. I used to be just like that, it's just practise ….."

"Annie, I can't imagine any amount of practise will ….."

"You will, don't worry. Trust me."

"Hm, I admire your optimism."

Not put off, Annie grinned. "How about a small glass of wine, I've only got red I'm afraid."

"Ok, why not." Kate said submitting to Annie's ebullient good humour.

Over lunch Kate brought Annie up to date as she told her about Bernard's visit that morning.

"Well, that explains why we couldn't find anything, and you say you've had some success with the new name?"

"Ah, I think I've found their birth dates. I'm not sure they're the right ones though." Kate replied with a frown.

"Mmm, let's have a look after lunch and see what we can find. More cheese?"

It turned out that Kate had found what seemed to be the right records and Annie suggested they calculate the years and look for any death records for Charles. Kate found herself holding her breath as they waited for the results to come up on the screen. Nothing.

Next they searched in the war records where they did find a listing for a Charles Francis Forbes that confirmed he was 'Missing in Action'.

"Oh, does it say where?" Kate asked, eager to find out more.

"Hold on, I …... ah, here we are ….. no, that's not it. Ah, looks like a place called Laterina."

"Never heard of it, have you?"

"No, let's look it up. Here it is, it's in Tuscany, near Arezzo, sort of south of Florence."

"Oh," Kate said, "what do you think that means? Did he die there?"

"I'm not sure. It could do I suppose. I thought 'missing in action' meant they either couldn't find or identify a body. I can keep looking if you like?" Annie offered. "There might be more details somewhere, it's just finding them".

"Oh no, Annie, I couldn't......"

"Don't be silly, I'll enjoy it. Have you heard anything from your solicitor yet about the deeds?"

"No, I meant to call him this morning but what with Bernard coming round I forgot all about it. I'll do it when I get back."

"Ok, I'll call you later if I find anything else."

"Thanks Annie. Look why don't you come over for some supper. I mean, if Ben's still away although you're both welcome of course, if he's back....." Kate felt she was babbling and was grateful when Annie interrupted her.

"That would be lovely. No, there's no Ben until tomorrow or the next day. What time? Can I bring anything?"

"No, just your brain," Kate said with a wide grin. "Shall we say about seven?"

"Great. See you then."

The rest of the afternoon seemed to disappear in an instant. Kate rang her solicitor only to speak with his secretary who told her that he was with a client and she would ask him to call her back.

When she turned on her laptop there was an email from Bernard. Again apologising for his inability to contain his curiosity, he explained that he had looked up Charles Forbes and had come across the same records she and Annie had found. However, having vague memories of the war and his family's stories of their adventures, he had searched further and discovered there had been a POW camp near Laterina. He posited that maybe young Charles had been captured, held there and then escaped. He thought there should be records of this if it was the case and he would let her know if he found anything further.

Well, Kate thought, it all seems to be happening around me. The phone rang and it was Mr Regan, her solicitor. He explained that he had not heard anything about the deeds and he would send a chasing letter if she wished. Kate confirmed she would like him to do so, thanked him and put down the phone.

She looked back to Bernard's email and it was his mention of Italy and the POW camp that caught her attention though not in relation to the diary this time. Her father was Italian and had been in one of those camps in Scotland. She wondered what it must have been like, so far away, not knowing what was going on at home. Her father had said that he was treated well in the camp but refused to talk about his family in Italy, only saying that he had none.

Over the years she, and her brother, had given up trying to find out. All she knew was that he had met their mother, married her, stayed and opened a café in Edinburgh. When he retired her brother, Luc, had stepped in and it was now a thriving Italian restaurant. Suddenly she felt sad she knew so little about her Italian heritage, not even the language. The one thing her father had retained was his love of food which he had passed on to both his children. Sighing, she realised she had better turn her thoughts to preparing supper for herself and Annie. It had been quite a day and Kate was aware of an ebb in her energy. She shrugged off any thoughts of giving in to the slump, tempting as it was. It was not so long ago that she would probably have succumbed, but that was then, and she determined to enjoy the evening as she put together a simple mushroom risotto and steamed vegetables.

Annie arrived just after seven with a bottle of wine in her hand.

"I thought I'd bring the rest of the bottle, if that's alright?"

"Of course it is, come in and sit down."

The kitchen table was already laid, Kate asked Annie to pour the wine while she made some last minute touches to the risotto before dividing it into two bowls and bringing them to the table with a bowl of steaming vegetables. Once seated their conversation returned to where they had left off earlier that afternoon and what direction they should follow next.

"I had an email from Bernard not long ago. It seems he is also eager to find out more about the Forbes family and has discovered the same record for Charles. He also said there was a POW camp near Laterina and had his own theories as to what might have happened to him."

"Oh Kate, I think we might be getting somewhere, don't you? By the way this risotto is delicious."

"Thanks. I don't know. I called my solicitor and he hadn't heard anything about the deeds so said he will chase them. I mean, if we had those then we'd know, wouldn't we?"

"Well, we'd know who owned the cottage, but that's all. I'm sort of intrigued now and would like to know more, wouldn't you?"

"Er yes, I suppose so," Kate said, thinking about the diary and how it had set her on this path and still she did not mention it to Annie. "Anyway, we can hypothesise until the cows come home. Where's Ben gone this time?"

"Oh, he's just in London for two or three days, meetings, editing, that kind of thing. He'll probably be off again soon on the next project."

They chatted for another hour or so before saying goodnight and promising to keep each other updated on any developments.

Alone again, Kate loaded the dishwasher and felt suddenly drained of energy. As much as she wanted to find out more about Charles and his disappearance, she decided on a hot drink and an early night. As she got undressed her mind travelled back through the day, filing and sorting words and images. When her head touched the pillow she pulled the duvet round her even though it was not cold, and fell into a deep, undisturbed sleep.

4

The next day arrived accompanied by a grey sky and morning shower. Kate realised she had forgotten to collect the plant cuttings from Bernard the previous afternoon. It seemed to have got lost amongst Annie, Charles and the search for his past. She opened her laptop and clicked on Bernard's last email and then reply. She thanked him, apologised for her forgetfulness and said she would collect the cuttings as soon as she could. Probably not today, she thought, as she looked out of the window at the rain that was becoming more persistent. Like most gardeners, she was happy for the garden, its need for water satisfied, but not so keen when she wanted to get on with other things.

Unable to do more research she retrieved the diary from the dresser drawer and sat down at the kitchen table. She opened it and turned the pages to the next entry.

At last, I am on my way. The boat crossing was not as calm as I would have liked but I seem to have survived without too much discomfort and am now ensconced in a little hotel near the station in Paris. Early tomorrow morning I will take the next train to Florence and will be met by Aunt Issy. I can hardly wait to be there, in Italy, closer to finding out what happened to Charlie. I haven't said much to Aunt Issy in correspondence about my reason for visiting save for taking a holiday and to see some of the wonderful works of art on offer in Florence. I think it best to wait until I'm there so I can gauge how she might react to my wish to find him or, at the very least, what happened to him. Of course, I do not know if Ma has written to her about my visit other than to confirm various details. Since they are not close I do not imagine she will have done. I hope not. No doubt I'll find out tomorrow.

Yes, at last, Kate thought, it's moving on. As she read Hettie's words, she felt as if she was sitting beside her. Quickly she turned the page to the next entry.

Oh my, Florence is beautiful. So much to see, to swoon over, digest and, oh dear, words almost elude me completely. Aunt Issy is being wonderful. I think she guesses there is more to my visit than I am sharing with her but she is not pressing me to say anything. I know I will have to speak of my quest very soon but for the moment I am content to immerse myself in the magic of this remarkable city, its culture, its beauty and, oh, I really do not understand Ma's dislike for it all. This morning we had coffee at the Caffé Giubbe Rosse in the Piazza della Repubblica and I could almost hear the poets and artists discussing their dreams, passions and politics, their ideas

Hettie had stopped mid sentence and Kate rushed to turn the page hoping for an explanation.

Here I am again. Another day full of beauty and joy. Aunt Issy took me to see the Boboli Gardens. It was made even more wonderful by a dresden blue sky so clear and high, I thought how London paled in comparison and wished I never had to return there. Oh dear, I don't think I really mean that but I am so in love with Florence. There seems to be so much to see and do and, dear Charlie, I haven't forgotten you. Did you come here? Did you fall under the spell of its beauty? If you did, I feel sure you would understand. I haven't spoken to Aunt Issy about you, not yet. I will, I just have to find the right moment. She is being so kind and Uncle Vittorio is absolutely charming, I don't understand why Ma is so against it all. Anyway, I will speak to her at the first opportunity.

Again, Kate had to restrain herself from turning the pages and rushing headlong into Hettie's future. She heard the click of the gate and saw Bernard heading towards the front door armed with a tray of cuttings and some larger plants he had divided from some in his own garden. Kate quickly returned the diary to its home in the dresser drawer and went to open the door for him.

"Good morning, Bernard." Kate welcomed him and was happy to see that it had stopped raining.

"Yes, morning Kate. I thought I'd just pop these over between showers. They say there will more later." They both looked up at a potentially deceptive blue sky. "You never know, we may see a rainbow," he chuckled.

Kate would normally have been annoyed if someone turned up without warning, but Bernard had a warmth and openness she found a comfort and was happy to see him.

"Oh, wouldn't that be lovely! Come through, I'll put the kettle on, if you've got time."

"Well, I don't want to take up too much of your time, but I wouldn't say no if you're putting it on for yourself."

Kate took the tray of cuttings from Bernard and they walked through to the garden and put everything in the greenhouse.

"They'll be alright in here while you decide where to put them." Bernard said and followed Kate back to the kitchen.

"Thank you so much, Bernard, it's very kind of you. Coffee alright?"

"That'll be fine, Kate. You know, I've got so much in

my garden now, I'm sure I can find more when you're ready."

"Oh....."

"And if you do decide on a veg patch, I've always plenty of seeds. Now, any more luck with this Charles what's-his-name?"

"Er, no. I don't really know where to look next. I did phone my solicitor though and he's chasing the previous owners about the deeds, but I'm not sure how much use they will be if I should get them."

"Well, I suppose they'll just tell you who owned the property and when. Maybe if you went to Italy, there might be records ...."

"Oh Bernard, I don't know, that would seem a bit ....."

"A bit what? Couldn't you do with a holiday? It could be an adventure." Bernard grinned and winked as she put a mug of coffee on the table in front of him.

"Yes, a holiday would be great, though I'm not sure I want to spend my time chasing someone I don't know."

"Ah Kate, you never know where things may lead you," he said raising one eyebrow.

"You sound as if you speak from experience," Kate said returning the look.

"Maybe," and Bernard hid a mischievous grin as he drank his coffee.

After he had gone Kate mused on Bernard's words. The thought of a holiday appealed to her and she could afford it now that she was not burdened with the cost of running a larger house. But Italy was not somewhere she had considered, not until now. She felt a surge of excitement as she imagined herself walking the streets of Florence, following in Hettie's footsteps. Would the same places still be there? Stop it, what are you thinking? A holiday was one thing, but following a diary written by someone she did not know, well, wasn't that a little bit crazy?

The Diarist

Maybe crazy was good sometimes. It was just that she was not someone who did things on impulse. Mind you, she thought, I suppose I did buy this cottage on something of an impulse. She looked at the dresser drawer containing the diary, then at her laptop. Maybe I'll just take a look. I mean I don't have to book anything, do I? She sat down at the kitchen table and switched on the laptop.

Kate looked at the screen wondering where to start. What am I doing, she asked herself while she waited for the icons to come to life in front of her. She clicked to connect to the internet and typed in 'holidays florence italy'. Overwhelmed by the choice, she closed the laptop in frustration. She stood up and walked out into the garden. The grass was still damp from the rain but she was oblivious, driven only by her need to clear her head and think. She found being outside, whether in a garden, field or woodland, calming and if she sat for long enough the chaos settled and everything fell into place. After a few minutes her tumbling thoughts separated and a gradual sense of order ensued. The idea of a holiday began to take shape as a normal and natural thing to do. Moving was a stressful experience no matter how positive it may be, and Kate realised that she had not had a holiday since ….. when was it? It was not long before John died, she remembered now, they had gone to this lovely little place in the South of France, even considered retiring there. She caught her breath as a single tear escaped and rolled down her cheek; another dream lost. Yes, the time was right for a holiday and Italy seemed as good a place as any, whatever her reasons for going. Of course she could take the diary and then it would be up to her if she followed Hettie's story or not. Convinced by her own reasoning she decided she would first pick up some brochures from the travel agent to get an idea of what was on offer.

Eager to get on with it, Kate grabbed her bag and got in the car without thinking where she might find a travel agent. She started the car and headed for the nearest town adding a few other things to her objective such as joining the library and finding a hairdresser – essential if she was going on holiday. Her spirit rose as she surfed this wave of new found optimism.

With an air of joyful efficiency she gathered brochures from the travel agent, joined the library where she took out books on Florence, decided she would ask Annie if she could recommend a hairdresser and dentist, and was home in time for a late lunch.

Armed with an avocado and tomato sandwich and the holiday brochures, Kate returned to the seat in the garden that she had left only a couple of hours earlier. As she poured over the images of Florence she could see herself walking along the streets, standing next to the *duomo* and visiting the Boboli Gardens. Oh dear, I have to do this, don't I? Now her mind was made up she went inside and, once again, opened the laptop. This time she typed in 'last minute holidays florence italy' and waited for the search engine to do its work. They all seemed very similar until one caught her eye that flew from Bristol which she thought would be so much easier than having to go all the way to Gatwick. There was a choice of hotels and she decided to go for a slightly more expensive one situated in the heart of Florence not far from the famous *Ponte Vecchio*. If I'm going to do this I may as well enjoy it.

The next flight was the following week so she now just had to decide how long to stay. She clicked the 'Book Now' button and chose the eight days option. After completing all the required details, she entered her payment details and, taking a very deep breath, pressed 'submit' and before she could release her breath, it was done.

Sitting back in her chair, Kate watched as confirmation emails arrived and she tried to quell a rising panic as her mind began to list all the things she needed to do. Bernard of course would not be surprised, but there was Annie and her daughter, Emma, what was she going to say to them? She wondered why she felt the need to justify her actions, if that was what it was. Was it a result of being married for so long, a habit that still continued or did it have roots earlier in her life. It was not that John expected explanations, far from it, now that she thought about it. It was more that she felt she owed them. As this new understanding settled she relaxed into it and wondered why it had taken so long.

She grabbed pen and paper and made a start on a list of the things she would need, such as check if her passport was valid and was relieved to see it had another year to run when she managed to find it. Impressed by her organisation, she continued to add things to the list and very soon the afternoon had disappeared.

After a light supper and her head still full of, will I need this, what will I need to wear, and repeating lists of euros, insurance, hair cut, and more, Kate switched on the television hoping to escape her overcrowded thoughts. When that did not work she rang Emma thinking it would be one thing she could cross off her list.

Emma surprised her by being totally supportive of the idea and enthusing that she had not had a holiday for such a long time, it would do her the world of good, and it was the best thing she could do after the stress of moving house. She even offered to take her to the airport. Somewhat nonplussed, Kate thanked her and said she would let her know.

So, this was really happening. Somehow her conversation with her daughter had not only given it the seal of approval, but a greater sense of reality than she had felt a few minutes earlier. She, and her life, seemed to be changing beyond recognition. How and when did this happen? Kate retraced her steps over the last few weeks in search of an event that had effected this change. A moment of recognition, that was it – it all started when she saw the photograph of this cottage. Before that? Hm, she thought, before that she had dragged herself through long grey days longing for relief from the tedium that enveloped her. She was more at a loss than unhappy as she adjusted to an unwanted singularity. Now a fog was clearing and she could feel the warmth and light of the sun filtering into her life once more. She allowed the thought to wrap itself round her and surrendered to its care.

The spell was broken by the telephone ringing and she jumped up to answer it as if waking from a dream.

"Hello," she said in a sleepy voice.

"Oh hello mum, you ok?"

"Oh, hi Ems, yes fine, just watching tv. What is it"

"I was just thinking if you email the flight details I'll sort out picking you up etc."

"Are you sure? I mean I ……."

"Mum, it's fine. I'd like to do it, ok?"

"Ok, I'll do it in the morning, I don't think I could bear to look at the computer again today, and thanks Ems," Kate smiled even though she could not be seen.

"No worries. Love you."

"Love you too." Kate put down the phone and made a note to email her daughter in the morning.

5

Night became morning as Kate woke in the same position in which she had fallen asleep, unaware of time passing between. The sun's rays shed golden motes of light that settled on her eyes as she blinked away the remains of dissolving dreams. As memories of the previous day dawned she sought a sense of order to quell the uncertainties that began to seep into her thoughts.

She left the bed and headed for the shower. She looked at her reflection in the mirror. Did I really do this? Italy, Florence ..... oh dear. Then she smiled, unsure at first but liking what she saw. Mmm, the new me then, let's go.

Showered and dressed she went down to the kitchen to make her ritual coffee. While she waited for it to brew, she made toast, topped it with marmalade and, satisfied it was ready, poured the coffee.

She looked at the list she had started and opened her laptop, accepting with some reluctance that it might be a good idea to make friends with doing more online. First, she searched for travel insurance and, bewildered by the plethora of choice, wondered what she had done in the past when she realised it was something John had always dealt with.

Frustrated she checked her emails and saw the booking confirmation from the holiday company which stated that travel insurance was included. Feeling foolish but grateful she had not gone ahead, she searched for the best currency exchange rates for euros. Having managed to find this, with growing confidence, she entered her location and discovered where she could buy them locally. Ah, maybe I'm getting the hang of it after all, she smiled.

Next was to speak to Annie. Kate picked up the phone and called her.

"Hi Kate, I'm just making coffee, want to join me?"

Kate hesitated at the thought of another coffee, "Ok, that would be lovely, only a small one for me though, I've not long had one."

"Great, see you in a minute."

Annie greeted Kate with a wide smile and led the way to the kitchen where a cafetière sat on the table with mugs, a jug of milk and a plate of biscuits.

"I've been experimenting," Annie waved her arm in the direction of the biscuits, "you will try one won't you? I mean, if you'd like one."

"Thanks Annie."

They sat down and Annie poured the coffee.

"So," Annie began.

"Well, I just wanted to let you know that I'm going away next week for a few days ….."

"Ooo, where …."

"Italy, Florence, about a week." Kate wondered why she felt embarrassed telling Annie.

"Is this anything to do with the research you've been doing about the cottage – wasn't there something to do with Italy?"

"Well yes, and no, that's not why I'm going," she said, uncomfortable with the lie. "It just seemed a good idea. I mean, a holiday after all the stress of moving and I've never been to Italy and everyone says how beautiful it is, so ….."

"Oh, you'll love it, Kate. Of course, everyone's right, it is beautiful, seductive and, have a biscuit, please try one." Annie encouraged, lifting the plate in Kate's direction.

"Ok, thanks. I was wondering if you'd mind keeping an eye on things for me. House plants, post not sticking out of the letter box, that kind of thing."

"Yes of course I will. Happy to. Just come back with a hunky Italian." Annie giggled.

"Annie! I'm not sure about 'hunky' ...."

"You know what I mean Kate, enjoy it, have some fun."

Kate looked at Annie through a frown, unsure what to say.

"Look, have a wonderful time and don't worry about anything here. How are you getting to the airport?"

"Emma said she'll take me and pick me up."

"All taken care of then. Have you decided what you'll wear? Or, you could shop when you get there – all those beautiful clothes. Ah," Annie sighed into her chair, "I wish I was going to Italy."

"I think Ben would ...." Kate stopped herself, surprised by the sudden need to protect her holiday.

"Miss me?" Annie continued. "Of course he would."

Relieved to be saved from a potentially awkward moment, Kate sought safer ground.

"I suppose it could be quite warm, I do hope so."

"Probably, but I think you'll just love it whatever the weather. Do let me know if you want to go shopping though." Annie's mischievous grin was infectious and Kate thought that might be a good idea after all.

"Ok, I will. Right now though, I'd better get back to my list. Thanks so much, Annie. I'll let you have a key before I go and, er, I'll be in touch about the shopping."

"Pleasure Kate. See you soon."

Back in her kitchen, Kate retraced her conversation with Annie and wondered if she had noticed her hesitation or if, in her usual way, she just rushed in guessing the end of the sentence. Oh well, I can't dwell on it.

Kate spent the rest of the day going through her

wardrobe and thought that maybe she could treat herself. She had forgotten to ask Annie if she could recommend a hairdresser and decided to take pot luck.

Then there were her parents. She had only seen them once since John's funeral and although she tried to phone them at least once a month she did not always succeed in doing so. She supposed it would be best to let them know she was going away and wondered what they would make of her going to Italy, particularly her father. Well, I can't worry about that now and added 'call *maman'* to her list.

ITALY

1

As the plane soared away towards the Channel Kate smiled, barely able to believe she was on her way to Italy and finally released from the last few days of phone calls, shopping, and last minute plans. She touched her bag, reassuring herself that Hettie's diary lay safe inside. She had not looked at it again, choosing to wait until she got to Florence when she could, if she wished, combine Hettie's journey with her own. She had still not mentioned it to anyone and could find no reason for not doing so apart from every time she thought she might tell Bernard or Annie the words refused to be said.

The plane rose over the snow capped Alps and Kate's mood swelled with appreciation for the opportunity to see such raw beauty. So many of the passengers seemed oblivious to it, maybe they flew so frequently it had become normal, but Kate could not imagine ever tiring of its majesty.

The captain's voice broke the magic as he announced their expected time of arrival and temperature at the airport and she was overwhelmed by a mixture of exhilaration and trepidation.

It was early afternoon when the plane landed, the sun was high and Kate welcomed the heat that reflected off every surface. She was soon swept along through the usual airport rituals of collecting luggage, and passport control before being met as she stepped out on to the concourse and driven to the hotel in the heart of Florence. She took in and was enchanted by everything en route. She loved the tall elegance of the cypress trees, the primal energy emitted by the mountains and even the row on row of factories and industrial sites failed to disenchant her.

Her heart picked up a beat as she saw the famous Florentine skyline in the distance and it was not long before she was checking in to the hotel that would be her home for the next eight days. It had a timeless elegance and she absorbed every detail of the reception, bar and restaurant as she was shown to her room, which was more than she had imagined.

The room was spacious with a large bed, contemporary décor and furnishings. Kate was delighted to see that the view, through tall draped windows, overlooked the River Arno and the renowned Ponte Vecchio. The marble bathroom provided everything she could wish for and more, including luxurious toiletries, a bathrobe and slippers. She twirled round in a little dance of joy before locating where to unpack her things. Despite her eagerness to explore the city she felt tired from the journey and instead immersed her aching limbs in a relaxing bath, revelling in the luxury. As she sank deeper into the water she felt not only the journey, but years of tension ebb away. She tried to remember the last time she had truly relaxed and tears surfaced and rolled down her cheeks as she slowly came home to herself. Tears of grief, tears of joy flowed freely.

She stepped out of the bath and into the shower to wash her hair then, exhausted by the tsunami of emotion that had overwhelmed her, she wrapped herself in a large white towel. Curling up in an armchair she contemplated the view over the Arno, embracing her newly found budding independence from the past.

Her inner life was changing faster than she could keep up with and she saw this holiday as the perfect opportunity to absorb this evolution. As she looked out of the window

The Diarist

she sighed. She was actually here in Florence, the city of art, romance and shops and with the idea of shops she decided to get dressed and at least have a quick look before dinner.

There was still warmth in the air as she left the hotel and walked in the direction of the famous Ponte Vecchio. As she turned on to the bridge she saw it was edged on either side by rows of glittering jewellery shops and would later learn of its fame for gold and gems. She turned and walked in the opposite direction, enchanted by the number of independent shops and, in particular, one that sold only gloves, in every colour imaginable. Turning from the main street she explored the twisting back streets with their bars, restaurants and more specialist shops. As she admired the architecture she breathed in a sense of timelessness, of walking in ancient footsteps.

Her thoughts turned to Hettie and she wondered if maybe she had walked here, what her thoughts would have been. She would go to the places she had read about in the diary tomorrow. In fact, she would not look at the diary again until she had done that. That way she could follow Hettie's journey as it unfolded, step by step. Feeling suddenly hungry she retraced her steps back to the hotel.

Morning arrived bursting with sunshine that penetrated the heavy curtains reminding Kate that she was on holiday. After luxuriating in the knowledge that the day was hers to do with as she wished, she showered, dressed and went downstairs to enjoy her breakfast seated on the terrace overlooking the river. She loved the way the buildings reflected on the water below a high cobalt sky that gave a greater sense of light and space.

She left the hotel and bought a small street map and found the Piazza della Repubblica where Hettie had been taken for coffee at the Caffé Giubbe Rosse. She made her way along the already tourist filled streets, acutely aware of the assault on her senses of the beautiful architecture at odds with the many stalls selling cheap leather goods and souvenirs.

It did not take her long to find the Caffé Giubbe Rosse and she was astonished to see it still there, as Hettie had described it.

She sat at a table inside, wanting to get a sense of the place and ordered a cappuccino. Taking the diary from her bag she opened it and re-read Hettie's entry about her visit. Resisting a strong curiosity to read more, Kate remained on this page. She wanted to take each day of Hettie's visit in line with her own but then thought this could be a foolish idea, she had only eight days and she did not yet know how long Hettie stayed.

She turned the page. In her eagerness to see the *Caffé*, she had forgotten that she had already seen this page describing when Hettie had visited the Boboli Gardens. As for the *Caffé* itself, it may once have been a place where new movements were born, but now it seemed to Kate to be an empty tourist shell, an expensive attraction, its creative and reactionary atmosphere only a memory, lost to an unavailable past.

She contemplated going to the Boboli Gardens when an elegant middle-aged woman stopped by her table.

"*E libero?*" she asked, indicating the seat opposite Kate, who assuming she was asking if the seat was free, nodded

"Forgive me," she said in slightly accented English, "you are English?"

"Yes, I am," Kate replied wondering what was going to follow.

"I wonder, may I join you for a few moments?"

Again Kate nodded. She was an attractive, well dressed woman and Kate could see no objection to her request.

"Thank you," the woman said. "I am Simonetta Morelli and although this is a place it is not normal for me to visit, today I felt compelled to come inside as I crossed the

The Diarist

Piazza."

Kate held her breath, curious yet apprehensive, and merely said, "I see."

"Please, I do not wish to disturb you but I have found that at times like this one, I can sometimes be of help to a person. You are here on holiday but I think there is something else, *no*?" Simonetta said with a slight rising inflection that left Kate unsure whether it was a statement or a question.

If she had been less charming Kate thought she would have been nervous but, far from it, she felt a calm knowing wash over her as Simonetta spoke.

"Er yes, I suppose there is," Kate replied, "but how .... why ..."

"Please do not worry. I do not wish to frighten you. As I said, sometimes I can be of help and I would not be here if you did not need some help," she smiled.

"Well, I don't know if I do or not. I mean, I'm not really sure why I'm here at all and ...."

"I'm sure it will all become clear. Maybe if you can tell me a little about the book," Simonetta said, looking at the diary.

"Oh this? It's just something I found. A diary, written by someone who came to Florence." Kate said.

"It was written some time ago by someone searching for .. .er *come si dice,* how do you say .... a sibling?"

"How do you know that?" Kate said suddenly uneasy.

"Ah, it is something I cannot help, a kind of gift I suppose, but nothing for you to worry about. Now, how can I help you?"

"You mean you're clairvoyant?" Kate asked, thinking of an aunt who had a similar such gift and remembered how she would talk to people who were not there, dead or otherwise. As a child she had found it disconcerting yet was curious to know more but her mother had always intervened saying it was all nonsense. As a teenager Kate discovered that she would know things before they happened but gave it little attention thinking it was normal and by the time she was an adult had forgotten all about it as hormones and life took over.

"Yes, among other things. As I believe you are also?" Again the rising inflection indicating a question.

"Not that I know of, I mean ...."

"I think you have forgotten, is that not so?" Simonetta said with a gentleness that instantly dismissed Kate's burgeoning fears. "First, can you tell me about this diary, you say you found it?"

Kate found herself telling Simonetta about buying the cottage and finding the diary. About Hettie's search for her missing brother and how now she was here in Florence, following in Hettie's footsteps.

"I see." Simonetta looked thoughtfully at the diary then up again to look Kate directly in the eye. "And what do you hope to find here?"

"Er, I don't know. I...er... hadn't really thought about it. I just seem to have .... I don't know why but I had to come." Kate began to feel uncomfortable.

"Like a calling?"

"Well yes, sort of ...."

"*Eh*, I think you have a connection here, someone in your family?"

"Oh," Kate's eyes widened as she looked at Simonetta. "Sort of, my father's Italian."

"So, you speak Italian?"

"Sadly not. My father has always refused to speak of his life in Italy. I'm not sure what happened, only what my mother has told me. He was a prisoner of war in Scotland and they met at the end of the war. They married and he stayed and opened a café in Edinburgh. She mentioned once that his family had all been killed, I think reprisals by the Nazis, and he would never speak of it."

"*Eh*," Simonetta sighed through her teeth, "so many

families lost in this way. Do you know where this happened?"

"No, only that he came from a village or small town somewhere in Tuscany."

"I think maybe you have more than one journey here, but first let us return to the diary. This young man who is missing, what do you know of him? I think he also was a prisoner of war and," she paused looking through the window into the distance, "yes, he escaped. It would have been hard to survive in the woods and hills …."

Kate knew that if she was going to walk away from this woman, now was the time to do it, but something held her there. Was it really that strange? Before she could find an answer, Simonetta continued.

"He had help. *Va bene?*" Simonetta enquired, watching Kate with care from unusually grey eyes.

"Er yes, I was just thinking ..."

"Whether to leave or stay and listen to this crazy woman?" Simonetta smiled. "I mean you no harm."

Again surprised by her acuity, Kate flustered, "I … er …. I'm sorry, but yes I suppose I was and, well …. I know ..."

"Bene, now tell me what you know."

Kate told her what she had learned about Charles Forbes and his incarceration in the camp at Laterina, but she had been unable to find any record of his death.

"*Allora,* if you want to know more I think this is where you should start. I have friends who live in that area who may be able to help you. Would you like me to arrange a meeting?"

"Oh, er …. thank you, if it's not too much trouble." Kate managed to say, unable to pause the speed at which her journey was now moving.

"It is no trouble, in fact, if you like I can take you there as I have not seen them for some time and it would be a pleasure for me. Also it is not an easy place to find without a car. Let me call them and see if they are free. Do you have any plans over the next day or two?"

"No nothing, just the usual tourist stuff."

"*Benissimo*, how can I contact you, you have a mobile?"

Kate gave her the number which Simonetta tapped into her phone, then handed her a business card which simply had her name and contact number.

"Please be free to call me if you need to."

Kate accepted the card and thanked her, beginning to feel she had known her for years, not less than an hour. Simonetta stood up to leave.

"I will call you, probably later today, but now I must go."

They said their goodbyes and Kate remained seated for a few more minutes, bewildered by what had just taken place. She returned Hettie's diary to her bag wondering what kind of box she had opened by bringing it here to Florence. Hoping to regain a sense of normality, she once again became a tourist and perused the map she had bought to find somewhere that had nothing to do with Hettie or her diary.

It was not that she had travelled that much, especially on her own, but when she had, she liked to find the places off the tourist track. It seemed difficult to do at first as at every corner, every turning, there was a statue, a work of art of some description, some architecture that held historical significance.

She wandered down narrow streets, dodging speeding *motorini*, and enjoying the specialist independent shops that were fast becoming a rarity at home. Enchanted by a shop that sold hand made paper and books covered in exquisite designs, she bought a marbled notebook to record her holiday.

As she was leaving the shop her mobile rang and she heard Simonetta's distinctive voice asking if she was free tomorrow. Saying she was, they agreed to meet at Kate's hotel at ten o'clock when Simonetta would take her to meet her friends who lived in the Valdarno, an area about an hour's drive south of the city and, Simonetta assured her, very beautiful.

Kate put away her phone and, feeling suddenly hollow, probably because it was time for lunch, but also due to the morning's unexpected activity, she went into an *osteria* opposite the shop. She ordered *bruschetta* to start, followed by *tagliatelli con tartufo* and found herself wondering what her father would think if he were here. So many dishes on the menu were familiar to her and, she wondered about her father's life in Italy. Why did he not speak of it? How hard had it been for him not to return to the place where he had grown up? So much she had taken for granted about him, his presence, his passion for 'good food', and his silence about his past. She promised herself when she returned she would go to see him and try to talk to him, little knowing how much she would have to say.

2

Simonetta arrived at Kate's hotel on time and they walked the short distance to her car. Kate had slept well and felt more reconciled to the adventure before her.

The sun picked out the red lights in Kate's hair, which was set off by an apple green top against her fair skin. In contrast, Simonetta wore grey linen trousers with a soft pink, short sleeved linen top, casually elegant against her olive skin and the steel grey of her sharply bobbed hair. Each woman beautiful in her own unique way, Kate more oblivious to her beauty than perhaps Simonetta.

Simonetta pointed out familiar and less familiar landmarks as they drove out of the city. Once on the autostrada she continued to comment as they passed towns and valleys lined with sentinels of cypress trees and the architectural umbrella pines. She pointed out the castle at Incisa, the mountains of the Pratomagna which still held a high line of snow, remarked each time they crossed the Arno and commented on anything she thought would be of interest.

They came off the autostrada and as they skirted a large town, Kate was assaulted by a plethora of signs and hoardings, giving directions not only to other places but also to shops and businesses in the locality. Soon they were out of the town and once again crossing the River Arno. After a few more kilometres Simonetta turned off the road and up a dirt track that cut through woodland until they reached an avenue of cypress trees that led to her friends' villa. As she parked the car, a man and a woman appeared from the side of the villa to greet them.

"*Vieni,* come," Simonetta directed Kate towards the couple that she introduced as Umberto and Claudia. Amid a warmth of hugs and kisses they welcomed Kate to their home, complaining that they hardly saw Simonetta these days and were curious as to what had brought her here this time. It was all said with good humour and they were clearly happy to see her.

Inside the villa it was what Kate would have called old-fashioned. Dark furniture that did not look that comfortable, ornate mirrors, family photographs in silver frames, all very formal. Claudia led them through to the back of the villa where a terrace looked out across the valley and the seating looked faded and more comfortable. Kate had not realised they were so high and was amazed by the panoramic view across the valley bordered on each side by distant mountains.

They sat round a table shielded from the heat of the approaching midday sun by a large umbrella pine. Claudia offered fresh, home-made lemonade and insisted on hearing all Simonetta's news and the reason for her visit.

"We do not see her these days without good reason, you know," Umberto smiled at Kate.

"*Allora,* now that's not fair, Umberto, it's not that long." Simonetta said with feigned indignation.

"And Kate," Umberto turned his attention to her, "what brings you here and how have you managed to become mixed up with this strange woman?" He waved his arm in the direction of Simonetta.

"Umberto!" Simonetta looked through raised eyebrows. "Really, I met Kate yesterday, she is here on a quest and I was hoping you may be able to help her."

"A quest you say, now I am intrigued. *Dimme,* tell me."

"I think it best if Kate tells you, Kate?"

"Oh, er ... well, it started when I moved house and I found this diary that had been stuck at the back of the kitchen dresser for years." Kate continued to relate the diary entries, her research and how it had led her to this holiday.

"Kate is also half Italian, her father, he was in a prisoner of war camp in Scotland."

"Ah, like so many." Umberto looked wistfully across the valley.

"I was hoping you might be able to tell Kate something about the camp at Laterina," Simonetta said, a softness entering her voice.

"*Eh*, of course," Umberto snapped back to the present. "What would you like to know? In fact, I can take you there, show you where it was anyway."

"Why don't we all go, *cara*, we could have lunch at that little place that's built into the wall, if it's open. That is, if you'd like to?" Claudia looked from Simonetta to Kate in search of a consensus.

"*Perfetto*, Kate?" Simonetta turned to Kate for agreement.

"Yes, that would be lovely."

"*Va bene*, Umberto, you don't mind to drive, do you?" Claudia asked her husband.

It was only a short drive from the villa to Laterina. Claudia explained as they passed, how the station called Laterina was actually in Mont Alto and that the town of Laterina was a little further on. The camp had been situated below the town on a flat plain between the road and the Arno. Row upon row of single storey buildings ran either side of the road that led to the river. Some were now used by factories and other businesses, some were untouched, left as they were.

"It was not a good place, I believe," said Umberto. "I have an aunt who would tell us stories about it. She said that many of the prisoners escaped and hid in the woods. It was very hard for them as they had little shelter or food and the

The Diarist

Germans were everywhere. She and a friend would sometimes take food to them, it was quite an adventure, I think. They were young girls and maybe not aware of the great risks they took."

Umberto turned off the road and drove through a modern housing estate that climbed up towards the old town.

"We will have a good view from here," he said as he parked the car.

Looking at the terrain Kate imagined what it must have been like for Charles on the run, hiding from the Germans, his life dependent on the generosity of local people. What happened to him? Where did he go?

They walked into the old town, along narrow streets, washing draped along balconies of houses that appeared to grow from the rock from which they were hewn. The restaurant was tucked away in a corner, the entrance through a wrought iron gate that led to a terrace with views out to the river. They peered inside, dark after the bright day outside, and were greeted like long lost family. Umberto and Claudia knew Mario, the owner, their regular custom having developed into a good friendship over the years.

"I think we can find a sheltered table outside then we can enjoy the view," Umberto led the way out to the terrace to a table shaded from the sun.

"So, you don't know what happened to this man in the diary?" asked Claudia once they had ordered and wine was poured.

"No, only that he was reported 'missing in action', but ..." Kate paused and glanced in the direction of Simonetta.

"I believe," said Simonetta, "that he escaped. It was common, especially here."

"*Eh, davvero*, they say about half of them escaped and who can blame them, the conditions were so bad." Umberto shrugged his shoulders.

"I wonder, *caro*," Claudia looked to Umberto, "there are people who remember that time, maybe there is someone who could help?"

"Yes of course, old Enzo might and there's Maria – her sight might not be as good as it was but her mind is probably quicker than mine," he laughed.

"*Allora*, let us make some enquiries, ask around, speak to people and perhaps, Simonetta you could return with Kate when we know more," Claudia said.

"Well ...," "Kate began, embarrassed by the attention her search was creating.

"A good idea, Claudia, I'd be happy to," Simonetta said firmly, casting a smile in Kate's direction.

The waiter arrived with their first course before Kate could object and amid sounds of appreciation Umberto wished everyone, "*buon appetito*." And a few moments of silence followed before the conversation resumed.

After her first glass of wine Kate relaxed and allowed herself to enjoy the company. They spoke in English so she could understand with only the odd lapse into Italian when no other words would do. She learned that Simonetta was a respected academic in Florence, an expert on Florentine history, as was Umberto and their friendship spanned many years. Claudia on the other hand, although well-educated, had devoted her life to Umberto and bringing up their four children who were now all adults with families of their own.

Kate enjoyed the camaraderie, something she realised was lacking in her own life and wondered when and how this had happened. She felt included and the familiar need to hide, to retreat, was no longer there. Uplifted and happy she joined in, occasionally looking at the strange woman she had met only yesterday and already she felt her life changing at a deep subterranean level in a way she was yet unable to explain.

Finally, after coffee and effusive thanks to Mario and his family, they left the *ristorante* and returned to the car. As they drove back to the villa, Umberto and Claudia bemoaned the state of the Italian economy, their hopes for radical change in the government and Simonetta agreed that, if Italy was to survive, it must rid itself of the corruption that had stifled it for decades. Kate thought how similar their complaints were to those in England, so much greed, so little understanding of people's needs.

Within a few minutes they were back at the villa, the sun was hot and everyone mellow after the food and wine. It was siesta time and resisting invitations to stay, Simonetta explained that as much as she would like to spend more time with them, she had to get back to the city. She and Kate said goodbye amid enthusiastic promises to meet again soon.

"Maybe next time you can leave your paradise and come to the city. It is not so bad." said Simonetta as they got into the car.

"*Certo, certo,* we will be in touch very soon, once we have some news." Umberto called as Simonetta started the car.

The return journey passed very quickly for Kate, her mind revisiting the last few hours and wondering, hoping that she might learn more about Charles Forbes and his time in Laterina. Simonetta's voice interrupted her sleepy reverie.

"What will you do now?"

"Erm ... I'm not sure," Kate paused as she considered the question. "Maybe read more of the diary, see what else Hettie did while she was in Florence."

"*Bene,* if you like, I can also make some enquiries about this Charles, what did you say his name was?"

"Forbes," Kate confirmed, "but ...."

"Please, do not worry, it is something I would like to do." Simonetta smiled and pulled up outside Kate's hotel. "I will let you know as soon as I hear from Umberto and now, enjoy Florence, allow it to unfold its beauty."

"Thank you, I'll do my best." Kate waved at Simonetta's

retreating car, turned to enter the hotel and fell into the arms of a man as he caught her from falling in front of one of the ubiquitous *motorini*.

Shocked and confused Kate looked up into a pair of clear blue eyes that crinkled with a hint of amusement.

"You are alright, I hope," he said in accented English, still supporting her as she found her balance.

"Oh .... er .... yes, I, I think so, thank you. I..."

"It is nothing. This your hotel?"

"Yes," Kate tried to extricate herself but he still held her elbow and guided her to the entrance.

"Maybe a cup of tea?" he said and again there was that hint of amusement in his eyes.

"Oh, because I'm English you think we all drink tea?" Kate faltered as her voice came out louder than she had wished. Trying to recover her composure she added, "Of course you're probably right."

Still holding her elbow he guided her to the lounge and ordered a pot of tea for her and a *caffé* for himself.

"If you don't mind I will keep you company while you recover?"

"Er no, but I think I'm alright now."

"You did not hurt yourself I think, maybe your ankle?" he enquired, at the same time looking down at her ankles.

"No, no, no. My ankle is fine, thanks to you." Kate felt the words jumble in her mouth and was surprised when they came out in order. She wondered if she was blushing.

"You are on holiday?"

"Yes, it's my first visit to Florence, it's very beautiful."

"Ah yes, it can be very seductive if you are not careful." he said, his face lighting up with a smile that Kate found herself involuntarily mirroring.

"Hm, maybe I need to be more careful." Kate was unsure why she was once again having a conversation with a total stranger, certainly not something she made a habit of.

"*Eh,*" he shrugged and displayed upraised palms, "the,

er, *motorini* are notorious and your attention, it was somewhere else *no?"*

"Yes, I was just saying goodbye to a friend." Kate said, supposing that Simonetta was now a friend.

"So, you have friends in the city?"

"Yes, I suppose I have, but..."

"It is not my business but I am happy that you are not alone here. A city can be a sad place without friends to share the journey." He drank his coffee and stood to leave. "And now, if you are sure you are recovered, I will leave."

"Yes, thank you, I'm fine now." Kate stood, they shook hands, said goodbye and he turned and left. She watched him disappear through the hotel doors to be devoured by the throngs of tourists in the street outside. She sat for a few more minutes and pondered on the incident, the man and the amused expression in those clear blue eyes, so present one minute and then gone, probably never to be seen again. This holiday was turning out to be stranger than she could ever have imagined.

She felt her energy sink and, suddenly tired, went to her room, fell on to the bed and slept. Woken by the arrival of a text, bleary eyed she reached for her bag. As she made sense of her surroundings, she sat up and found her phone. The text was from Emma, asking how it was going. What could she say? She had not told Emma about the diary so she thought her mother was simply visiting Florence for the usual tourist reasons. Kate tapped out letters to say it was more beautiful than she had imagined, lots of art, sun and wonderful food. She pressed send and leaned back into the pillows. As the phone returned to its clock face she saw that she had slept for almost two hours.

She gathered memories of the day, Simonetta, her friends, the lunch, the man outside the hotel, and tried to orientate herself. Her mouth was dry and her head muzzy, the after effects of lunchtime drinking. She got up from the bed and walked over to the window desperate for fresh air but when she opened it and leaned out the air was warm and filled with noise. She took a bottle of chilled water from the small fridge, rolled it across her forehead before opening it to quench her thirst. Slowly her day fell into place and she returned to herself. Her head began to clear and she picked up her bag and took out Hettie's diary. She turned the pages.

Aunt Issy is so kind and I'm having a marvellous time but I knew I had to talk to her about Charlie, it's just that it hasn't been as easy as I thought it would be. Anyhow, today I did it. Well, I started to and she, being Aunt Issy, was even more marvellous than I had imagined and, before I had finished the first sentence, she said we must look for him together. Tomorrow we're going to the place where he was last heard of. Uncle Vittorio says it was a prisoner of war camp. When he made enquiries after the war this was the last place you were, that you escaped and that was why you were 'missing in action'. Sounds awful. Oh Charlie, I'm so excited, and a little nervous, but I do feel closer to you now that I'm here, in Italy I mean.

Kate moved on to the next entry.

Uncle Vittorio drove us to the camp. The countryside is so beautiful yet for me there was a sadness as I imagined you Charlie, possibly on the run, hiding, cold and hungry. And the camp, so dismal and spartan. Long rows of empty buildings now deserted, still full of silent memories of what had been. Aunt Issy said there must be some records we can see so we went to the local Comune but we were too late, they are only open mornings so we will have to come back.

Kate felt Hettie's sadness as she turned the page.

Another outing with Uncle Vittoria to the villages near Laterina. Where are you Charlie? In each village we go to

The Diarist

the bar and speak with the local men. I notice sometimes they are not so open. Uncle Vittoria tries to tell me a little about what happened here during the war and the rifts it caused within families and friends. He is reluctant to say too much, I think he fears he will upset me and does not want me to know the horrid details.

We have been to three villages this morning and we stopped for lunch at a place called Civitella. It stands high above the surrounding landscape. A walled town, it has a ruined castle that the Germans used as their headquarters but it was later bombed and not much remains. It is a strange place and Uncle Vittorio tells me terrible things happened here. He thinks it unlikely Charlie would have come here. We haven't really found out anything more than he escaped. Oh dear, it's beginning to feel hopeless now. Maybe Ma was right - no, I don't ever want to think that!

Kate closed the diary unable to take in any more. She went to the bathroom and showered to clear the fog that still clung around the edges from her afternoon sleep. Refreshed, she put on linen trousers in a soft coral and a cream cotton jumper, and with a little make-up and her hair pinned up she went down to the restaurant. Even after two years on her own there still remained a sense of something missing as she sat alone. She pushed a stray hair behind her ear as she looked at the menu.

If she could have seen herself she would have seen an attractive, mature woman who appeared younger than her actual years, with a natural elegance and a sharp intelligence in clear, amber eyes. Kate, however, was oblivious to her own beauty, so focussed was she on what was lacking in her life, it clouded any reflection.

Her thoughts drifted to the man who had caught her earlier that afternoon and the frisson she could no longer deny. Maybe there is hope for me after all, or at least for my imagination and she smiled quietly to herself.

3

Kate spent the next day as any tourist, soaking up as much as possible of the beauty that Florence so generously offered. She visited L'Accademia and marvelled at the smooth and perfect marble figure of David, and then the San Lorenzo Duomo where she learned more about the Medici and their knowledge of alchemy in the creating of the old sacristy. She walked the streets admiring the elegant architecture, and rubbed the shining nose of Tacca's *Il Porcellino,* the bronze boar of *Mercato Nuovo*, for luck. By the end of the day she was exhausted from, but content with, her exploring around the city. The holiday was beginning to take effect as Kate gradually relaxed and surrendered to it. She decided not to eat at the hotel and, with a new found confidence, tried a nearby *osteria.* Again, her thoughts turned to her father as she tried to imagine him in Italy and, with a mixture of sadness and affection, she appreciated the richness he had brought to her life.

In the short time she had been there she had already found so much that was familiar and a slow sense of belonging had gradually emerged and embraced her. By the time she returned to the hotel she felt an inner glow, as much to do with the wonderful food and wine as it was to do with a burgeoning happiness that penetrated the seams of her defences. That night she fell asleep with a smile.

She was woken the next morning by the ringing of her

The Diarist

mobile and was greeted by Simonetta's now familiar voice.

"*Buongiorno* Kate. I hope I do not disturb you too early but I have a meeting very soon and I wanted to speak with you first."

"Good morning, erm …." Kate said, trying to sound more awake than she was.

"I have been speaking with Umberto and he has contacted the local Comune. Are you free to meet for a coffee later this morning about eleven?"

"Er, yes, I don't have any plans. Shall I wait here in the lounge for you?"

"*Perfetto,* I shall see you then." Simonetta said and was gone.

Kate looked around the room to get her bearings and when she put down her phone she saw that it was already a quarter to nine. She leapt out of bed, amazed she had slept so long. Showered and dressed she went down to the restaurant for breakfast where she sat at what had become her usual table on the terrace overlooking the river. She loved the view of the Ponte Vecchio and beyond, the bridges leading the eye out of the city towards distant mountains. Kate sighed, wondering how she was going to fit in everything she wanted to do and pursue Hettie's story. She had been unprepared for the strong feelings that were emerging about her father and his roots here in Tuscany. There was now a gap in her own history waiting to be filled with a new knowledge and self identity. She looked towards the mountains, a yearning pulled from deep within and she knew she had to go there.

She checked her phone for the time and there was almost an hour before Simonetta would arrive. She returned to her room and picked up the little marbled notebook she had bought to record her holiday. Sitting at the desk she opened it and wrote the date and Florence on the first inner page. She paused, hesitant about how to start. It had been a long time since she had written anything for pleasure and was surprised by the wall between her and the page. Her thoughts turned to Hettie and she wondered if she had experienced a similar obstacle but dismissed the idea as what she had read of her diary seemed fluid and easy. Where to start?

As she looked out of the window a surge of energy swept through her and her pen touched the page. She wrote without stopping for ten or so minutes, about her experiences and feelings since arriving in Florence and after pausing for breath she continued, musing on Hettie's search for Charles and what might have happened to him. When she had run out of words, she put down her pen and as she read what she had written, a sense of relief and lightness, like a gentle wind, blew through and round her.

"Oh," she said out loud, surprised by the sound of her own voice as it broke into the private world she had occupied. It was almost time to meet Simonetta so she placed the book in the desk drawer, made a last visit to the bathroom, picked up her bag and once again went downstairs.

Shafts of light beamed through the windows into the lounge highlighting motes of dust in a golden mist that settled on every surface. Kate sat in one of two tub chairs at a small, low coffee table near the window. Simonetta arrived on time, effortlessly elegant as always, and greeted Kate with kisses to each cheek before sitting down and ordering *un caffè*. Kate ordered a *cappuccino*, her second that morning, and prayed the caffeine would not have her climbing the walls.

"*Allora,* I have a little bit of news for you," Simonetta said as Kate looked at her expectantly. "It is not much, I'm afraid," she added, "but I think it is hopeful."

There was a pause as the coffee arrived and Kate held her breath in anticipation. As soon as the waiter left, Simonetta continued.

The Diarist

"Umberto called me yesterday evening to tell me that he had been to the *Comune* and had also spoken with Enzo and Maria and he thinks we should meet them. Their memories are distant and not perfect but he believes they may be able to tell us something that will help your search."

"That's wonderful," was all Kate could say as she felt herself pulled back into Hettie's world.

"We should go. If you are free, we could go this afternoon." Simonetta offered.

"Yes, yes of course, but ...."

"*Bene,* that is settled, I can be here at two thirty." Simonetta drank her little cup of coffee and stood to leave. "Now I must go. *Á dopo,* until later."

Kate stood and they once again exchanged kisses, followed by many a reciprocal *ciao* before Kate sat to finish her coffee and absorb this new information and ponder on what it could mean. She checked the time on her mobile and decided to explore the area round the hotel.

Outside the air was warm and filled with the loud hum of cars and *motorini* and the shady street was lined by tall grey buildings with shops and restaurants on the ground floor. Uninspired she kept walking, turning here and there, and with the shops becoming less evident she worried she may be lost until she felt the sun's rays as the street gave way to a piazza and the *Basilica di Santo Spirito.* She remembered reading about it in one of the guide booklets and now wished for more time to explore but it was almost time for lunch and Kate felt she needed more than a snack to sustain her for the afternoon ahead. She liked the relaxed atmosphere, so different to the Florence she had already seen, more quirky, less ostentatious and formal, and promised herself she would return another day. She spotted a nearby *trattoria* and headed in its direction.

"*Signora, signora!*" A voice called, gaining in volume as it became closer and with one more breathless,

"*Signora,*" a hand touched her arm.

Kate stood still unable to believe the call was intended for her and turned to find the same pair of clear blue eyes that had met hers outside the hotel the previous day.

"Forgive me, I did not mean to startle you. You are now fully recovered?" His voice rose in a question.

"Oh ... er ... yes, thank you." Kate answered, gathering herself.

"You are going to eat here?" Again the rising inflection.

Kate thought quickly, and her instinct was to get away.

"No, I ...er have to be somewhere and was thinking I must come back another day." She said thinking that it was not a total lie.

"I am sorry, I do not mean to intrude, but ..."

"No, you're not at all," Kate interrupted.

"*Bene.* Maybe you will allow me to show you a better place to eat another day." He calmly reached into his pocket and took out a card which he handed to her, still maintaining eye contact. "I am Giancarlo. I am a lecturer at the university. I am very respectable if you are worried. I do not make a habit of accosting beautiful women, but you did, well, fall into my arms." he said as his face creased into a broad smile showing even white teeth.

Kate's mind raced with warnings of charming Italian men that should be avoided at all costs but there was an openness in his face that she found hard to resist.

"As I said, I have to be somewhere, but yes, maybe another time. Thank you." she said returning the smile.

"May I call you at the hotel? To make an arrangement?"

"Oh, yes," she said and gave him her name which he tapped into his mobile.

"I will call you. *A presto,* see you soon." And he was gone as quickly as he had appeared.

Flustered and filled with conflicting emotions, Kate retraced her steps back to the hotel. She walked through to the restaurant, to her familiar table on the terrace, now shielded by a large umbrella from the glaring heat of the sun. She ordered a simple lunch of *spaghetti carbonara*, seeking comfort in the rich creamy sauce, and a glass of wine hoping to calm any inner disturbance.

She turned the meeting with the man, Giancarlo, over and over in her mind and wondered what she could have done or said differently. She was unused to male attention, always sheltered by her marriage and then her retreat into widowhood. Distant memories of teenage angst seemed irrelevant and outdated now leaving her awash in unfamiliar, yet recognisable, emotions.

She picked at a piece of bread, dipping it in a small saucer of olive oil, in an attempt to quell a growing turbulence in her solar plexus. The waiter placed the pasta in front of her, she accepted his offer of parmesan and thanked him before slowly twirling the ribbons of *spaghetti* on her fork. The flavours brought her taste buds to life in appreciation of the subtle blend of herbs, cream and cheese and assisted by a sip of wine she was momentarily distracted from her concerns.

However, his blue eyes and open smile danced in and out of her thoughts while she ate, despite efforts to dismiss it all as ridiculous nonsense. She was a grown woman, she told herself, not a lovestruck young schoolgirl. Why was this stranger having such an affect on her? Stupid, stupid, stupid, she chided.

By the time she drained a cup of decaffeinated coffee, the combination of food and wine had had the desired effect and a soporific sense of peace displaced previous feelings of agitation.

"*Buona sera,* Kate," Simonetta joined Kate where they had sat a few hours earlier. "Is all well with you? You ..."

"No, no, I'm fine. Probably the glass of wine with lunch has made me sleepy." Kate replied hoping to avoid Simonetta's acute perception.

"*Va bene,*" Simonetta shrugged, not wishing to press her but knew that something had happened between their meetings. "Shall we go?"

The journey took a little over an hour during which time they talked about the places that Kate might still want to visit. Simonetta avoided anything personal and waxed lyrical about the many treasures of Florence and beyond.

"It is a great shame you are here for such a short time. Maybe you will return so you can enjoy more."

"I know, there's so much and ….. maybe yes, maybe I'll have to come back. I, er...," she paused, not sure how much to reveal, "I didn't expect it to have such an effect on me."

"*Eh,* it is part of who you are, *no?*" Simonetta kept her eyes on the road but Kate felt she was looking directly at her.

"Yes, I suppose it is." She left it there as they approached Umberto and Claudia's villa.

Alerted by the sound of scrunching gravel, Umberto and Claudia were already in the courtyard to greet them. And after an effusive welcome, Simonetta and Kate followed them through to the garden where Claudia had prepared an umbrella shaded table with a jug of lemonade and biscuits.

They chatted about the weather, the journey and how good it was to see each other again after such a short time.

"*Allora,* Umberto," Simonetta said, "what is the news you have?"

"*Eh,* as I told you on the phone, we went to the *Comune*, and the Signora there was very helpful. You know they have the records of everyone who was held at the camp, but she was unable to give us any new information I am sorry to say. She could only confirm that your man had escaped as so many did. She was very kind and gave us some books but they are in Italian so I don't know how helpful they will be to you Kate."

"And Enzo?" Simonetta prompted. "You mentioned you had spoken with him....."

The Diarist

"*Si, si,* he is very keen to meet you, Kate." Umberto cast a smile in her direction. "He was a child at the time so I don't know how much he will be able to tell you, but you never know, there may be something that will be of use."

"And Maria?" Simonetta asked.

"*Eh, si,* Maria. She is a similar age to Enzo, so was also only a child then but, unlike Enzo, she is prone to exaggeration, if you know what I mean, and will sometimes say what she thinks you want to hear. Please do not misunderstand me, she does it from a good heart but it does not always work out for the best. *Pah,*" he shrugged with upraised palms, "there it is."

"As Umberto says," Claudia turned toward Kate, "she does not mean any harm but you have to, how do you say in English, take it with a pinch of salt?"

"Yes, do you say the same thing in Italian?" Kate asked.

"It's similar," Claudia replied. "We say '*con un pizzico di sale!*'

"So," Umberto cut in, "we can go to see Enzo and then Maria, although I expect that Maria will have heard of our visit and will turn up at Enzo's anyway."

Kate was thoughtful and felt a little uneasy.

"You are worried?" Simonetta asked her.

"Er, not really. I'm just not sure I know what to ask them, that's all."

"Oh, don't worry," Umberto laughed, "there will be no stopping them once they start, though I think you will have to sieve through what they say for what is relevant. Come, if you are ready, we can go."

They soon arrived in a nearby village and Umberto pulled up outside a small *casetta*. As he turned off the engine, a short man with a shock of white hair stood in the front doorway leaning on a stick. As Umberto climbed out of the car, Enzo waved his stick in the air, shouting, "*Salve!*"

The rest of the company left the car and followed

Umberto's lead. Enzo greeted them with a smile that creased his weathered face and shone through dark brown eyes that twinkled with mischief. Umberto made the introductions and they each shook hands with him exchanging the usual salutations before being shown through to a small room, overfilled with large furniture in a dark wood that created an unexpected sombre atmosphere. Ornaments and family photographs covered every surface, a reservoir of memories over generations.

They sat in upright chairs, each with a small round table to one side. Enzo opened a cabinet and produced five small glasses.

"A small *vin santo?*" he winked and was met with a chorus of, *"grazie."*

He passed round glasses filled with the amber liquid and sat down before raising his glass in a toast to everyone's good health.

"Allora, how can I help you, Umberto? You said something about the war and the camp at Laterina?"

"Si, Kate, *la signora Inglese,* she is trying to find out what happened to someone who was in the camp. We have been to the *Comune* and although *la Signora* was very helpful, we hoped you might be able to tell us something."

"Eh, I can try but my memory is not what it was, it was so long ago and ...." his voice trailed off as his eyes looked into the distance in search of something long forgotten.

Umberto related Kate's, or rather Hettie's, story to Enzo, who listened intently, occasionally scratching his head and rubbing his chin.

"Hm," he murmured. "You know, many of the prisoners escaped. It was a big problem for those in charge. They would hide in the woods, in the hills, we used to take food to them. Mind, we had to be careful. I remember hearing my parents say how they wanted to help the men but at the same time they feared any reprisals if anyone was caught. I was only a child and in a way it was all an adventure, I had no understanding of the consequences."

"Do you know what happened to any of the prisoners that escaped, Enzo?" Simonetta asked.

"Well, I believe most of them made their way north but some stayed. They disappeared into the villages, found families that would hide them and then, after the war, became part of life here."

"Do you remember any names Enzo?" Claudia asked. "Or perhaps you might have overheard things, you know how children are. Anything at all, any little thing could help."

"*Eh*, it was so long ago," he said, scratching his chin and leaning his head to one side, hoping for a memory to find its way. When nothing surfaced, he moved his hand to support his face, now etched with a deep frown. "I don't know, maybe Maria, mmm, maybe, maybe she will remember."

As he finished speaking the doorbell rang followed by a shrill, "*Permesso, permesso?*"

"*Eh, eccola,* here she is," his face lit into a beaming smile, "*prego, prego.*"

A small woman entered the room. Dressed in black, with dark hair and eyes, she acknowledged each introduction with a sharp nod. Intense and self-contained there was nothing superfluous about her. Umberto retold the reason for their visit as Maria listened and nodded.

"*Eh,* and you think we can remember, we were only children, we hardly knew what was happening. Enzo, you remember, we were always in trouble for going where we shouldn't or talking to the wrong person. *Eh,* we didn't understand, you remember, *no?*" Maria hardly paused to take a breath before continuing. "Enzo, remember that time when we got lost in the woods, or at least they thought we were lost and ..."

"*Si, si, si,* we weren't really lost but ....."

And everyone listened while Enzo and Maria, searched

their memories, each encouraging the other's reminiscences, already forgetting the purpose of the meeting.

Kate struggled to grasp the meaning of the quickly spoken Italian, seizing at familiar words yet unable to give them a context. Watching the exchange between Enzo and Maria, her thoughts once again turned to her father. He was a few years older than them but would have grown up in the same world. Eventually Enzo broke the spell.

"*Allora,* Maria, *aspetta un po',* we are forgetting our guests." Enzo turned towards Umberto, "Forgive us, these memories have become precious, like little treasures, but this is not what you want to know ..."

"Don't worry, Enzo, it is a pleasure to hear your stories, they may all too soon be forgotten," Umberto said with a tinge of sadness.

"So, this man you are looking for, you think he is still here?" Maria demanded.

"*Eh,* nobody knows, Maria. We don't know if he survived the war let alone if he is still alive." Claudia answered. "We hoped that you or someone might remember something that could help us."

Simonetta reached her hand to touch Kate's arm and reassured her she would translate anything she did not understand but so far nothing had been said beyond general reminiscing. Kate smiled and nodded in thanks. Looking around the room at the people who had become involved in her search, she wondered how one little book had made this possible. Since finding the diary she had stepped outside her life into another world and here she was again, almost a stranger to herself. How had this happened?

"*Bene,* let's see what we can do, eh Enzo?" Maria gave Enzo a determined look. "We can talk to Giovanni and, oh, what is his name? Luca, that's it." Turning to Simonetta, she added, "They are a little older so you never know ..... *Allora,* I must go. Enzo, *a domani e piacere a tutti."* She waved an arm around the room and left.

The Diarist

The party stood and thanked Enzo for his hospitality and Umberto asked him to call if he remembered anything at all. They each shook hands and said their goodbyes and walked out into the warm air of early evening.

"Simonetta, Kate, why don't you stay and eat with us?" Claudia suggested as they returned to the car.

"Well," Simonetta looked at Kate, "is that alright with you?"

Unable to think clearly, Kate nodded and managed a, "yes, thank you."

"*Bene,* as long as you don't mind eating a little early. We do not follow the Italian tradition, it is too unkind on the digestion." Claudia smiled as she got into the car next to Umberto.

Simonetta and Kate nodded in approval.

After his guests had left, Enzo sat outside for a few minutes mulling over the conversations that had taken place in his living room. He hadn't travelled that far back in his past for a long time. These days his reminiscences dwelt on memories of his late wife. Even though it was now six years since her passing, he still missed her and expected her to be there, only to be faced with a pained emptiness.

Feeling restless, he got up and walked along the road to the bar where he was greeted enthusiastically by his friends, a group of men of a similar age who had been frequenting the bar for as long as they could remember and had known each other most of their lives. They were the only customers that evening in what was a male stronghold where they could pass hours discussing the two great Italian passions, politics and football.

This evening was no different and Enzo joined them as they complained about the lack of leadership in the government and despaired at the state of the economy. Enzo, however, had his mind elsewhere and was not his usual vocal self.

"*Eh,* Enzo, what's wrong?" Asked a man with a deeply lined face gained from years working outside in the sun.

"Oh, nothing Ludo, just I had some visitors today asking about the war and the camp down at Laterina and I suppose it got me thinking, that's all. They were trying to trace someone who had disappeared there."

A handful of faces turned towards him and as memories stirred, stories tumbled out in a competition of who remembered the most. One or two of the men were a few years older and although too young to be involved in any fighting, were old enough to be aware of the darker side of war.

Meanwhile, not far away, Kate was enjoying an evening with her new friends, oblivious to the emotions her recent visit had disturbed elsewhere.

"*Allora,* Kate, how many days before you return to England?" asked Claudia as she passed round small cups of coffee.

"I leave Sunday morning."

"Oh, so soon," Umberto said between sips of coffee, "it seems you have only just arrived ."

"I know, it's gone so quickly, I can hardly believe it."

"You must come back again soon and of course, you are very welcome to stay with us if you wish," Claudia enthused.

Si, si, Kate, you are welcome anytime," Umberto confirmed his wife's invitation.

"Well, thank you, that's very kind of you ...."

And, don't be English about it, Kate," Simonetta interrupted. "They mean it so please, when you do return, which I'm sure you will, please let my friends entertain you."

Kate smiled, she was getting used to Simonetta's occasional brusque way with words and said, "Yes, of course I will and I'll try not to be English about it."

"Good, that's settled then." Simonetta said looking

pleased with herself.

"What plans do you have for the rest of your visit?" Claudia asked. " I hope we will be able to see you before you leave?"

"Unfortunately we are away this weekend but, c*ara,*" Umberto said turning to Claudia, "don't we have to go into Florence tomorrow, maybe we could meet for lunch or an early supper? And you also Simonetta if you're free?"

"*Eh,* I have a meeting tomorrow so the evening would be better if that is alright with you Kate?" Simonetta asked.

"Yes, that's fine with me, I have no definite plans."

"Bene, shall we say six o'clock at your hotel, Kate?" Umberto took charge of the arrangements. "We can have an *aperitivo* and then find somewhere for supper."

"Perfetto," Simonetta confirmed and looking at Kate said, "I think it is time to go."

"Oh Simonetta, so soon, must you?" Claudia frowned.

"Claudia, *cara,* as much as I would love to stay and enjoy more of your company I have to prepare for this meeting tomorrow and," she paused, "I will see you tomorrow evening."

Umberto and Claudia walked their guests to the car where they exchanged hugs and kisses and several "*a domani."*

As they drove back Kate reflected on the day and thanked Simonetta for a wonderful afternoon and evening. Simonetta waved her hand in dismissal saying it was nothing.

"It is a shame your visit is so short but I think you will come back soon, *no?*"

Kate looked at Simonetta and wondered if this was an innocent question or a premonition on her part, but before she could say anything Simonetta continued.

"They say, once you have visited Florence, you will always come back." Keeping her eyes on the road she added, "You will know when the time is right."

"I certainly hope so," Kate laughed hoping to make light of it. "I mean, I'd love to visit Florence again."

Simonetta held her counsel and concentrated on driving. She did not want to push Kate. She knew from experience how people could put up resistance to what they didn't understand. She also knew this was an important journey for Kate and her role was merely to guide and assist when and where necessary.

They arrived at the hotel and said goodnight. Kate's mind was full of questions yet when her head touched the pillow she fell immediately into a deep sleep.

The Diarist

4

Friday arrived late for Kate. Surprised she had slept so long she decided to take the day quietly. She picked up her journal and took it down to the terrace restaurant where she ordered coffee and a pastry. She looked out across the river trying to recall the sequence of events since the last entry. It seemed like forever yet it was not long at all. She found that once she started the words flowed and in the writing she was able to integrate the whirlwind of people and places. She paused and mused on how the holiday had turned out to be far removed from anything she might have imagined.

Her mind wandered from the words filling her journal and the soporific view along the Arno that periodically distracted her as she realised the morning had already passed. She put down her pen and ordered a light lunch.

After eating she went for a short walk along the narrow shadowed streets in the vicinity of the hotel before returning to her room. Unsure how to fill the short time remaining, she showered and dressed ready for the evening. Her mind was still caught in the words and images of the last few days and she found it hard to settle.

She was beginning to feel anxious about the evening but could find no reason for it. She was meeting with people she already knew, so why the butterflies. She put the final touches to the little make-up she wore, changed her top, twice, before deciding on the first one and feeling more tense by the minute.

There was still twenty minutes before she had to meet them and Kate decided a glass of wine beforehand might calm this irrational anxiety. She went down to the terrace where she would be able to see them arrive and ordered a small glass of V*ernaccia di San Gimignano*, a wine she recognised as liking when visiting Umberto and Claudia.

The early evening air still held its warmth and as she sipped the wine and watched the changing light on the river, she allowed herself to relax.

Umberto and Claudia were the first to arrive and greeted her with their usual enthusiasm.

"Simonetta will not be long and is bringing a friend, I hope you don't mind. She thinks he may be able to help with your search." Claudia said.

"Yes, he is a colleague at the university and his family live not far from us." Umberto added. "First, let us order. What are you drinking, Kate?"

She told him and he suggested they order more of the same.

Kate tried to shake herself from her solitude and engage more fully with what promised to be a sociable evening.

Umberto ordered a bottle of the wine and as their glasses were being filled Kate could see Simonetta through a group of tourists that had gathered at the entrance of the hotel. As she approached Kate felt her anxiety return as she saw the silver haired man who accompanied her.

Amid the usual greetings Simonetta introduced her friend to Kate but before she could finish the man interrupted her and taking Kate's hand said, "Ah, *la signora,* you are now fully recovered, I hope."

"Oh, you already know each other?" asked an astonished Simonetta.

"*La signora, eh, mi dispiace,*" he corrected himself, "I'm sorry, Kate and I met when she nearly collided with one

The Diarist

of our ubiquitous *motorini*. You hurt your ankle I think?"

"Oh, not really. Thankfully you caught me before I fell." Kate felt herself flush and hoped it did not show.

Umberto and Claudia exchanged raised eyebrows and Simonetta watched Kate with interest. Kate wanted to excuse herself and run as far away as possible from the situation and the rapidly surfacing feelings that were threatening her breath.

"Well, I'm glad you were not hurt," Simonetta smiled and placed her hand over Kate's. As she did so, Kate's anxiety dissolved. Confused, she turned to Simonetta who merely smiled and added, "it would have been a shame to spoil your holiday."

Kate returned the smile in an attempt at normality and was saved from any further comments by the waiter arriving to ask if they would like anything else.

As he left Simonetta picked up the conversation.

"I have known Giancarlo for several years, Kate, and until today did not know his family live close to the place where the person you are looking for disappeared. I thought he might be able to help you in some small way. You never know," she said shrugging her shoulders.

"I am happy to help if I can, of course. You must tell me more about this person. Simonetta has told me a little, about a diary and that he was a prisoner of war at Laterina. Can you tell me a bit more."

Kate steeled herself as he focussed his attention on her.

"Well, the diary is written by his sister who came to Florence in 1952. She stayed with an aunt and they managed to trace him to the camp at Laterina but she didn't have much success after that and she stops writing after a while. Thanks to Umberto and Claudia we managed to confirm that he was at the camp at Laterina and that he escaped, but that's as far as we've got."

"I see. Hmm," he frowned as he considered the matter for a moment. "Would you be free tomorrow? I would like to invite you to my parent's home. I go most weekends and they may have some ideas about what happened to this young man. You never know with something like this, someone knows someone who knows someone and .... then, *presto*, there is your answer."

"*Perfetto!*" Simonetta exclaimed. "Kate, you have time? I mean, you do not leave until Sunday, do you?"

"Er no, if you are sure?"

"*Certo, certo,* it would be a pleasure, Kate."

"Thank you, if you think it will help ...."

"I hope so but no promises," he gave a lop-sided smile. "I can pick you up about ten thirty if that is ok with you?"

"*Bene,* that is settled then," Simonetta clapped her hands. "Where are we eating?"

There was a discussion in rapid Italian and it was Umberto who turned to Kate and said, "If you do not mind, Kate, I think we would like to eat here. It is so beautiful with the view of the river and I'm sure the food is excellent."

Kate shook her head, "I don't mind at all, Umberto."

"*Bene,*" he said and called a waiter to arrange a table.

"If you will excuse me, I am not able to join you for supper." Giancarlo stood and turning to Kate offered his hand. "It has been a pleasure to meet you properly, Kate, and I look forward to seeing you again tomorrow."

"Yes, thank you," she replied and as she accepted his hand he covered it with his other hand before letting it go and turning to the others to exchange the usual goodbyes.

Kate watched him walk away bewildered by what had just taken place, and wondered whether if, in fact, anything had. Whilst the evening was enjoyable and her friends delightful and entertaining, her attention was divided between them and the man who had again unexpectedly appeared. What she found more disconcerting were the disturbing feelings he had awakened and it was these that would consume her thoughts later when she was alone.

The Diarist

    Simonetta observed the change in Kate since her friend's departure and again held her counsel despite 'seeing' what she would call 'possible futures'. It was for Kate to find her own way without any prodding from her.

    After a wonderful meal that Umberto assured Kate was some of the best food available in Florence, he insisted on paying. Claudia repeated, more than once, her and Umberto's offer to stay with them should she return and Simonetta, who Kate thought was somewhat subdued, said she would call her.

    After many hugs and promises to stay in touch, they said goodnight. Kate went to her room, tired after the spirited conversation of the evening and the thoughts that now rushed to fill her mind.

What is wrong with me? It must be my imagination. I mean, nothing happened, he was just being polite so why...? why did I feel so ...... so what ..... awkward, no, it was more than that. Yes, he is very attractive and I could be flattered if I was sure I wasn't imagining it.... but why would he be interested in me? Hmm, is it so long since a man showed any interest in me other than John?

    Memories of John flooded in, his smile, his eyes, his charm as she remembered the love and affection they had shared. Tears rolled down her cheeks in acknowledgement of not only the loss of a loving husband but also in recognition of the defences she had constructed since his death that were now being threatened by another man.

    Looking in the bathroom mirror she dried her eyes. She was different. So much had happened over the last few months and the realisation dawned on her that it was time to let go of the past and step into this new life that welcomed her or stay as she was and live a half-life.

    Maybe it was loyalty to John that held her, yet she knew that he would have wanted her to be happy and she could no longer hide behind his memory. She went to bed apprehensive of what the future held. How much easier it would be, she thought, if we could know beforehand ...... a silly thought ..... and she drifted into a dream-filled sleep, all to be forgotten and lost to her on waking.

Giancarlo arrived to collect her as agreed. Kate tried to appear calmer than she felt. She had spent the earlier part of the morning trying on the few items of clothing she had brought with her in all their combinations before settling on a simple linen dress in a soft coral colour that complemented the amber of her eyes.

They exchanged greetings and he led her to the car. She noted his manners, stepping back to allow her through the door first, walking between her and the road and opening the car door for her. She liked this and how it made her feel.

They took what had become a familiar route out of the city and along the *autostrada*,. Conversation was polite, relaxed and not intrusive. Slowly Kate relinquished her guard as Giancarlo told her more about his family, their history and who she would be meeting at lunch. Encouraged by his openness she shared a little about her own and by the time they reached their destination she felt less anxious and was looking forward to the lunchtime gathering.

They drove along a dirt track edged by woods on either side that opened to reveal an aged and substantial villa that Giancarlo told her was known as the *Leopoldina* style and typically Tuscan.

As they parked the car and approached the villa they were met and greeted with enthusiasm by Giancarlo's parents who led them up a flight of steps to the living quarters. Like most Tuscan villas the ground floor was used for storage of such things as olive oil wine, tools etc., and life took place on the upper floors.

They entered a large living room where Kate was introduced to Giancarlo's aunt and uncle, Maria and Giovanni. A younger man came in from another room that

The Diarist

Kate thought must be the kitchen given the wonderful aromas of garlic and herbs that emanated from there. Extending his hand he said that he was Leo, Giancarlo's brother. He was followed by his wife who introduced herself as Sofia. She had an engaging smile and Kate took an immediate liking to her.

Lunch was served outside where a long table was set to accommodate the whole family. Several courses and a few glasses of wine later Kate had learned their history and answered their many questions about her life in England and why she was there, in Italy. They were fascinated by her story of Hettie's diary and offered many suggestions as to what may have happened to Charles after escaping from the camp.

"Many escaped on the marches from the camp to Montevarchi and others found ways out of the camp and along the river. I believe some joined the partisans in the hills and others were taken in by local families until it became too dangerous." Giovanni offered.

"I heard some made it up to Civitella, but then there was that awful massacre ….." Maria's voice trailed off.

"Of course," said Giancarlo. "That could be a good place to start. It's not far and worth visiting for the views alone. That is if you like to Kate?"

"Er yes, but …."

"*Eh,* no buts, I am happy to take you. It is not far and it would be a shame for you not to go there before you leave."

Kate thought she caught unspoken words pass between Giovanni and Maria but was quickly swept along in new conversations before she could dwell on it.

By the time the coffee arrived, Kate was not only full from the meal but also the many possibilities she could pursue if she had not been leaving the next day. The sun, the wine, the company were all seductive and she was sad to say goodbye to it all.

5

The car snaked up the steep hillside to the walled hilltop village where they parked on the edge of the piazza which was home to an *osteria* and *macelleria*. A cobbled street to the right led them higher still and Kate followed it upwards to a larger *piazza*. Here she found the church at one end and further along what was once the water cistern for the village. It was octagonal in shape with five steps at its base and Giancarlo explained that it dated back to the 18th century.

"Once it was the only water supply for the village and essential for its survival. When the water ran out they had to fetch water from below, carrying it up to their homes. It is hard to imagine now that we are so used to having constant water, *no*?"

"Oh, how awful, do you think that happened often?" Kate asked as she tried to imagine carrying water up the winding road they had climbed in the car.

"I don't know. They would have been dependent on there being enough rain to sustain them, so a long hot summer would not have been welcome."

"Mmm," was all she could say as she thought of the hardship and endurance.

"Come, see the view," he said leading the way along a path to the right where, beyond a low wall, the forest descended to the valley below. From their high eyrie the view stretched for miles above the wooded valley to mountains in the far distance.

The Diarist

"It's breathtaking," Kate said as she looked down along and beyond the valley.

As they turned round Kate noticed a plaque on the wall and stopped to read it. It was written, in capital letters, first in Italian and then in English.

From the Testimony of a Survivor
English Inquiry Commission
15 November 1944 (Reference W0204/1 1479)

"While we were in the square, we were frisked by the German soldiers who took our wallets and our watches and put them in their pockets. A German screamed in Italian 'Cinque! (Five).' So five Italians were led towards the backyard of the school.
Then a German soldier came ahead with a gun and aimed it to the back of the back of the man's neck who was on the right side of the row, Don Alcide Lazzeri, then he pressed the trigger. So the soldier passed along the line, behind the Italians from left to right.
In the square we were grouped in five and led towards the backyard of the school. So the same German soldier raised up his revolver. I saw Tiezzi Daniele, who was one of the five in the row, throw himself to the left and run. I was the second from the left. My turn had arrived. I saw him aiming the revolver to my head. I put my hands on both sides of my face, and I turned towards my left. Immediately I felt a piercing pain on both my hands, my face, my mouth and my throat, and realising I was still alive, I slid down to the ground and lay there pretending to be dead."

Bartolucci Gino

Kate stood still, silent for a moment before looking up to where Giancarlo stood to one side waiting for her to finish reading. "Is this what your aunt was talking about, the massacre here?"

"*Si, si.*" he replied.

She looked over the wall at the wooded descent sensing the partisans hiding, the Germans commanding possession of the village. Giancarlo moved to stand next to her.

"*Si,* a tragedy. Reprisals by the Germans. It was war. The partisans killed a German and later, in retaliation, the Germans killed some partisans. They told the village there would be no reprisals. However, after a couple of weeks they came to the village and shot … well, most of the village was wiped out. Not just here, so many places..."

Stunned, Kate's thoughts turned to her father and his family. Myriad questions filled her mind. If they had come from this area had they been among those killed. Was this why he refused to talk about his Italian roots and early life? How hard it must have been for him to be safe elsewhere unable to do anything.

Giancarlo's voice tugged her back to the present. "You are alright?" he asked. "Come, sit down." He put his hand under her elbow and guided her to a nearby wall where they sat without speaking for a moment or two.

Kate struggled to find and articulate the right words. Eventually she managed to say, "I think so, it's a bit of a shock. A lot to take in. My, er ….."

He frowned. "What do you mean, Kate?"

"I, er ….," she hesitated.

"It's ok, please take your time," he reassured her.

"Well, oh dear, where to start," she said lifting her eyes skyward in search of inspiration.

"At the beginning, maybe?" he smiled and Kate felt herself relax under his gentle gaze.

"I, erm...., as I said my father is Italian. He was a prisoner of war in Scotland where he met my mother. When the war was over they married and he stayed. He's always refused to talk about Italy and his life here. All he would say was that he had no family, that they were all killed in the war, and that was it." She turned to look at Giancarlo. "You

The Diarist

see, I think, no I'm sure, this is where his family came from and he believed they were all killed while he was in Scotland."

"I see."

"I can't explain it but I'm sure that's right." She said with conviction.

"*Va bene,*" he said, his voice quiet and even. "If you wish, we could make enquiries, see if there are any records of your family. Who knows, perhaps there is someone who remembers them. It's possible."

"Really? Do you think there might be?" As the idea began to settle Kate felt her heart swell and tears threaten her eyes. The words 'your family' resounded in her head as she struggled to take it all in.

Giancarlo sat patiently and watched conflicting emotions flit across her face. He wanted to take her hand, comfort and reassure her but restrained from doing something that could be misunderstood. He saw a beauty in her vulnerability that stirred emotions he thought were buried and long forgotten and realised were a pleasant surprise.

"*Certo*, but today the *Comune* is closed, so …."

Disappointment eclipsed the fragile hope that Kate held.

"*Allora*, we can look in the *Sala della Memoria,* maybe we can find a clue there."

Kate followed him past the water cistern and along a loggia that ran the length of several buildings. Housed in one of these was the *Sala della Memoria.* The walls of the room were covered in photographs showing the devastation caused by the bombing, newspaper cuttings of the village's liberation and the names and photos of many of the people killed on that fateful day.

Giancarlo watched from a respectful distance as she focussed on a cabinet displaying the named photos. Her hand went to cover her mouth as she caught her breath and let out a partially swallowed, "oh."

There it was, Bernini. Her family name. She held the edge of the cabinet for support and Giancarlo moved to her side.

"What is it, Kate?"

Taking a deep breath she straightened to her full height, and gathering strength said, "There," she said pointing to one of the photos, "that's my family name..... Bernini. And," she paused, "his face, he.... he's so like my father, it could so easily be him when he was younger."

"Ah, so this is not the person you have been looking for ......"

"No, no, not at all," she said suddenly animated. "You know, it's strange but in some way I knew. Remember, I said something earlier about this place and my family?"

"*Si, si.*"

"I mean, how could I ..... know?"

""*Eh*, I don't think that is so unusual. I think there are times when we all have a, *come si dice,* how do you say?" he paused as he searched for the word, "a gut feeling, is that how you say?"

"Yes, it is but ...," Kate smiled, "but I'm not sure what to do now."

"Well, if there is nothing more you wish to see here, let's find a place where we can sit and explore the options, *si?*"

"Ok," she agreed, wondering what on earth her options could be since she was leaving the next day.

They walked past the ruins of the castle and followed the road down in a circle returning to where they had parked the car. Giancarlo explained that the castle, which the Germans had commandeered as their head quarters, had been bombed by the allies and never rebuilt. As they turned the corner the view from the other side stretched across a plain towards Arezzo and more distant mountains. There was so much beauty in the landscape that Kate thought she would burst.

The Diarist

She was still struggling with the discovery in the *Sala della Memoria* and what she should do about it when they reached the car. She did not have enough information to take to her father and what would she tell him? She was leaving the next day and there wasn't time to find out more. That is if she wanted to know more. Suddenly the impact of such knowledge dawned on her and she was not sure whether she wanted the responsibility at all.

Giancarlo's voice cut across her thoughts.

"Let's sit awhile," he said indicating to some tables and chairs on the edge of the piazza.

Kate accepted his invitation. A waiter crossed the square to where they were sitting and Giancarlo ordered *un caffè* and Kate ordered the same.

"It is a shame that you are leaving tomorrow. Are you not able to prolong your stay?"

"I'd love to but I do have to get back." Kate replied and instantly wondered what it was she had to get back to. She looked out across the panoramic view trying to find space in the thoughts that were now crowding in.

"Maybe you can make another visit. If you like I can make enquiries for you, see if anyone remembers your family."

There it was again, the words 'your family'. Kate turned towards him, "Thank you, but I don't want to put you to any trouble and ….. well ….. I'm not sure what to do really. I mean, it's all so unexpected and ….."

"*Lo so*, I know," he placed his hand over hers where it rested on the table, squeezed it gently before letting it go. "I think perhaps you will need time to get used to the idea a little first, *no?*"

Kate managed a faint smile, disturbed by the moment of intimacy. "Yes, I'm sure you're right."

"Please let me speak with my family. They will be doubly happy to have a second mystery to solve."

"Thank you. Yes, there's no rush is there?"

"Kate, may I say, this has been secret for many years so I think it can wait a little longer while we find out more."

"Yes, of course, and ... erm ..... if you would speak with your family that would be wonderful." Her smile grew as she relaxed a little.

"*Allora,* we must keep in touch, email, phone and, I sometimes have to come to London ..... maybe we could meet?"

"Er yes, of course." she stumbled over the words as she took out pen and paper to write down her details.

"Thank you. I will email you as soon as I have any news for you." He placed the piece of paper in his wallet before adding. "You have my card I think. Please if you should need anything, or just to talk, you will call me, please?"

It was Kate's turn to thank him and she hoped she wasn't blushing as she tried to stem rising emotions. She looked away to the far mountains in search of calm.

"Yes, thank you," she eventually replied.

"*Niente*, I am happy to help in any way I can," he said, following her gaze and wondering how he could be of help both practically and emotionally. He turned to look at her and admired her delicate profile. She turned towards him, aware of his attention and of the silent words that passed between them as they each spoke at the same time.

"I was ...."

"I, er ......"

"I'm sorry ....."

"No, forgive me, please go first."

"Oh, I was just thinking how lovely it is here and how sad I'll be to leave."

"Yes, it is a shame."

"So much has happened and I don't know ...... and today, well ... it changes everything. I started out coming for a holiday and to explore a bit of Hettie's diary while I was here, and it's all turned out rather differently, I mean, I've

The Diarist

had a wonderful time ...... it's all just, unexpected."

Giancarlo watched and listened as she spoke before saying in a quiet voice, "I think you should be gentle with yourself and allow these changes to slowly immerse themselves in your life. Be open to them and what they have to offer. As I said I am happy to help in any way I can."

Kate looked at her hand that rested on the table where he had touched it a few moments ago. Now his words touched her with an unexpected tenderness.

"I'll do my best. I just need time to get used to it all."

"Of course. If you are ready, we can go. It has been a tiring day for you, *no*?"

"Yes, I suppose it has." Kate was reluctant to bring the day to an end but logic reminded her that she still had to pack and be ready to leave the next morning. She pushed the chair away from the table and stood as Giancarlo left a note and some coins on the table to cover the cost of their drinks before walking over to the car.

"You are ready to say goodbye to this place until next time?" he smiled as he put the key into the ignition.

Yes, I am," she said returning his smile.

"*Bene*, I hope it is soon," he ventured.

Unsure how to take it Kate looked ahead and still smiling said, "Mmm, me too."

On the return journey to Florence Giancarlo shared his knowledge of the area in anecdotes from his childhood and his family. Kate talked of her visit to Enzo who, of course, Giancarlo had known most of his life. There were comfortable silences and Kate thought how pleasant it was to feel so relaxed in his company.

It was early evening by the time they arrived at her hotel. Kate felt her nerves tighten as the end of her holiday drew closer. Giancarlo walked round to open the car door for her and guided her to the pavement. As she stood to face him she wondered how to say goodbye. She envied his calm composure and hoped the tension she felt did not show.

"*Allora*, thank you Kate, I have enjoyed today very much."

"Oh thank you Giancarlo, for a wonderful lunch, your family and ... everything. I .....er....."

"Please, there is no need. Here we say *a presto*, until next time, so *a presto!* I will be in touch as soon as I have more news for you."

Kate smiled as she inwardly struggled under his clear blue gaze. She gave a short nod, "*A presto*. And thank you."

He gently took hold of her shoulders and kissed her on each cheek before saying, "*Buon viaggio*, Kate." He then turned, got into the car and gave a big smile before driving off.

Kate stood for a few minutes watching his car merge into the Florentine traffic. She still felt his presence as she turned to enter the hotel and go to her room. As she opened the door she heard her mobile announce a text had arrived. She fell into the chair suddenly tired. It was from Simonetta asking her to call.

She waited a couple of minutes as she tried to gather her energy.

"*Pronto*," the familiar voice answered.

"Hello, it's Kate."

"*Eh*, Kate. Thank you for calling me. Can we meet this evening? I would like to see you before you leave. I can come to the hotel in one hour?"

Kate breathed deeply.

"Yes, of course. See you then."

Even though she was not hungry Kate went down to the terrace. She needed to do something until Simonetta arrived and eating seemed the best thing. She knew this was not a time to be alone with her thoughts. There were far too many of them demanding her attention.

She ordered a simple risotto and a glass of wine and wished for more time in the hotel, in Florence, to spend with

Giancarlo and to find out more about her family. She ate slowly, not really hungry but in need of sustenance, her thoughts overflowing with the day's events.

Simonetta was punctual as usual and ordered a glass of wine.

"*Allora,* so tell me about your day."

Kate wondered where to start and when she did it all became quite simple as she recounted the conversations with Giancarlo and his family and the visit to Civitella.

Simonetta listened intently, giving an occasional nod, '*eh*' and intake of breath. When Kate had finished she gave a sigh and sat back in her chair. She felt empty and exposed, and imagined Simonetta was assessing the changes in her since the previous evening, as if her very thoughts were on show.

"*Eh,*" Simonetta finally spoke, "you have had quite a day. You must be exhausted."

"Mmm, I suppose I am, a bit."

"Oh Kate, always the understatement." Simonetta gave a warm smile. "What do you think you will do now?"

"I don't know," she said giving a small shrug of her shoulders. "I mean, I don't really know anything for sure so ..."

"True. It is a shame you have to leave so soon. You will come back?"

"Er yes, I think I will have to but ….."

"Remember, you have an open invitation to stay with Umberto and Claudia and they are not far from Civitella and I'm sure Giancarlo will help."

"Yes, he said he will speak to his family, see if they know anything or have any ideas. He also said something about the *Comune*."

"Of course, they may have records ….. it may be some of your family still live there."

Kate sat up and leaned towards the table. "Do you think that could be possible? My father always insisted he had no family, that they were killed."

"I know, but he was not here, so it is possible."

Kate felt something shift within her, a change of gear as a surge of energy confirmed she would be returning and soon.

"Will you say anything to your father?"

It was the one question Kate had been avoiding asking herself and now she was faced with it she knew the answer.

"Not yet. I think it would be better to wait until I have more information. It will be a shock and he is in his nineties...."

"I think you are wise to keep it to yourself for a while," Simonetta said, nodding her head in agreement.

"It's strange, part of my reason for coming here was to follow Hettie's diary and see if she ever found her brother. I suppose I could have read the diary before I left and I would have known that she didn't but it seemed more interesting to follow it day by day .... and now ...."

"And now you have found something you were not looking for but more meaningful to you, *no*?" Simonetta raised a perfectly arched eyebrow.

"Yes, but ....."

"Sometimes things are not as we expect, things change and life takes us in a different direction. We can either try to hold on to our expectations and struggle or we can go where life takes us. I know which I prefer." Simonetta said with a slight shrug of her shoulders.

"You mean I should forget about Hettie and her brother?"

"I'm not saying that you should forget about them, just don't hang on too tightly when you are being led somewhere else."

"Hm, I see what you mean."

"Kate, you are tired, a lot has happened today. Please take your time with it and when you get home, you will contact me if you need anything?"

The Diarist

"Thank you. And thank you for all you have done ..."

"*Niente*, I am happy to help and it is meant to be so."

Kate was too tired to ask more questions. She felt her presence in Italy fading and her home calling her.

Simonetta stood, ready to leave.

"Remember Kate, you have friends here and we all hope to see you soon. *A presto.*"

They exchanged hugs and kisses after which Simonetta turned and left. Kate watched her go until she turned into the street. She sat down to gather her thoughts before taking the lift to her room.

Once inside the emptiness returned and she felt bereft as she packed her suitcase ready for her departure the next morning.

ENGLAND

1

It took Kate a while to settle. Emma had met her at the airport and although they chatted amiably on the journey home Kate revealed little of what had happened on her holiday. Once inside the cottage, Emma had made tea and told Kate that she had done some shopping and already prepared supper for her.

"I thought you might be tired and it would be the last thing you'd want to think about, shopping I mean."

"Thanks Em, that's wonderful. I really appreciate it."

Once she had finished her tea Emma said she had to get back and would call her in the morning.

Kate ignored the pile of post demanding her attention and wandered round the cottage before taking her case upstairs. When she opened it memories of the last week spilled out as she sorted her clothes into the washing basket and the wardrobe. Each item held a memory of a different day, in particular the pale coral dress she had worn on her visit to Civitella with Giancarlo. Was it really only yesterday? She wrapped herself in a reverie of an open cobalt sky, the warmth of the sun's rays on her skin, the pleasure of good food and mostly, a pair of clear blue eyes.

She looked around her bedroom, left the rest of the unpacking and went downstairs. It now seemed unreal especially in the greyness of the day that had greeted her at

The Diarist

the airport. Caught between the two she wanted to hold on to her sense of the last week but could feel it slipping away minute by minute.

She sighed as she sat down at the kitchen table and, looking at the post, decided it could wait until the morning. This is where the adventure had started she thought and little had she known then where it would take her. And now? Now she would have the supper that Emma had so kindly left for her and everything else could wait. Tomorrow was another day. She was just not yet ready to let go of Italy and slip back into village life. She had not been prepared for the profound effect of the place and the sense of belonging she had felt or the change that accompanied it.

Whilst her home was familiar, she was almost a stranger there. Had she changed so much? She decided to have a shower, wash away the journey and have an early night.

When she woke the next day she could see the sun's rays forcing their way through the gaps where she had failed to close the curtains the previous night. She looked at the bedside clock in disbelief. It was later than she thought and she did a mental check of where she was and what day it was before slowly leaving the bed and heading for the bathroom.

Washed and dressed, she went down to the kitchen to see what she could find for breakfast. Dear Emma, she thought, there was fresh fruit, and a choice of bread or croissants to go with butter and jam. She put a croissant in the Aga to warm and the coffee pot on the top to percolate.

When it was ready she sat down at the table. Her mind wandered to the view of the Arno she had enjoyed for the last week, the ever changing light on the water and the colourful *Ponte Vecchio*. As she finished her second cup of coffee she dragged her thoughts back to her kitchen and decided to deal with the mound of post at the other end of the table.

A large brown envelope caught her attention and she opened it, curious until she saw the name of her solicitor on the post mark. She had forgotten where she had left her life before going to Florence and now she saw the long awaited deeds to the cottage emerge. She pushed her breakfast things to one side and spread the contents out on the table in front of her. The letter apologised for the delay and hoped she would find what she was looking for. So do I, she thought. Energised by the idea of new information she looked at the first document which was an Epitome of Title that listed the conveyances, searches and miscellaneous papers dating back two or three hundred years.

It showed that the cottage had remained in the same family for many years and was only registered prior to the penultimate sale. Kate opened and released the conveyances from their folds and ribbons, fascinated as the history of the cottage unfolded before her eyes. She was uprooted from the past by the immediate call of the telephone ringing. Startled, she jumped up from her chair banging her leg against the corner of the table as she rushed to answer it.

"Hi mum, how are you this morning? You landed yet?"

"Oh Ems, hi," she said, still distracted. "Er, yes I think so. I was just looking at the deeds to the cottage, they're ...er... very interesting."

"That's great, mum."

Kate could tell she was not that interested and was being polite but nevertheless she appreciated the call.

"Oh and thanks for the shopping. It was very thoughtful."

"That's ok, I know what it's like when you've just got back. It's the last thing you want to think about. Catch up soon then?"

"Yes, that'd be good."

"Great, I'll call. Maybe the weekend?"

Kate agreed and they said their goodbyes.

The Diarist

Her daughter's call brought her back to the present. She picked up the phone to call Annie and let her know she was back and an intermittent beep told her she had a message. When she tapped in the number to access it she heard that she had three messages.

The first was from Bernard asking her to call him. The second was from Betty hoping she'd had a good time and asking her to call. The last one was from Annie inviting her for coffee/lunch/tea/wine whenever she was ready. Kate smiled, it was good to hear Annie, her enthusiasm was contagious and she called her straight back.

"Hi Kate, you're back. Did you have a wonderful time? I can't wait to hear all about it. How about coffee?" The words tumbled from Annie in quick succession before Kate could even say hello.

"Ok, yours or mine?"

"Mine ok? I'm just about to brew some so will add an extra spoon."

"Great, see you in a few minutes."

Kate looked at the table, left the documents where they were and removed her breakfast things to the sink, satisfied she had created some order.

Annie opened the door and greeted Kate with a beaming smile, clearly happy to see her. Kate followed her through to the kitchen where Annie poured two coffees and led the way through to the conservatory.

"Well, tell me all about it," she demanded, as she sat on the edge of her seat unable to contain her excitement.

Kate relaxed back into her chair, wondering where to begin and how much to tell. She could not remember how much she had told Annie before she left so kept it vague and described some of the places she had visited.

"And ...... did you find out anything about this Charles?" Annie asked, eyes wide in expectation.

Kate, remembering how much she had revealed to

Annie before she left, was able to answer honestly.

"Well, yes and no. I met a couple who lived near the camp in Laterina and they took me there. Apparently he escaped from the camp but the trail stops there."

Annie slouched into her chair, clearly disappointed.

"They did say they would speak to some of the local people and see if they can get any more information but I think it is unlikely....."

"Oh," Annie frowned, "what a shame." Then immediately sitting up said. "But I saw Bernard the other day and he's very keen to see you when you get back. Maybe he's found something, though he was keeping it to himself."

"Yes, he rang and left me a message. I wonder what that's about. I'll call him when I go back."

"Ooo, let's hope he's found something," Annie said eagerly.

"Hm, we'll see." Kate was not sure if she could take in any more information especially if it meant some action may be required of her.

"Ok, ok," Annie raised her hands in surrender. "I know, you've only just got back, but you will let me know if I can do anything, won't you."

"Of course," Kate reassured her. "Now, what have I missed here, and how's Ben? Still working hard?"

"Ben's fine, thanks. He's off on some assignment and back on Thursday so why don't you come and have supper? What is it today, Monday? Come tonight if you like and we can catch up on the gossip then."

Kate quickly weighed up the options of having to shop against having supper cooked for her and decided the shopping could wait.

"That would be great, Annie, that way I can forget about shopping for another day. Thanks, what time?"

"Say about seven?"

"Perfect. I'll go and call Bernard and see what's going on there, then I'd better finish unpacking."

The Diarist

"Welcome home," Annie said giving her a big grin and a hug. "It's good to have you back."

"Thanks Annie." Kate turned to go towards her cottage as a little bit more of Italy slipped further away.

Back in the cottage she called Bernard. There was no reply so she left a message to say she had called. Next she phoned Betty who also was not at home and she left a similar message. What was going on, she thought.

Since she couldn't speak to anyone she went upstairs to finish unpacking. She tried to ignore being drawn in to the memories that each piece of clothing held and sorted them into hand and machine washing. She was about to sit on the bed and give in to reminiscing when the phone rang.

"Hello?" Kate said.

"Kate, it's me, Bernard. I'm so glad you're back. I wonder would you be able to come over this afternoon?"

"Yes, of course Bernard. Can you give me a clue?"

"Er no, I think it can wait until I see you. Shall we say about three o'clock?"

"Yes, ok. I'll see you then."

What on earth was he being so secretive about Kate wondered as she realised the morning had already disappeared. She first loaded the washing machine then looked in the fridge to see what she could find for lunch. Again she thanked Emma as she found a choice of cheeses and some vine tomatoes. There was bread which she could toast and rub with garlic, drizzle with olive oil and arrange the cheese and tomatoes on top. She then put the whole thing in the Aga to melt the cheese, content that would keep her going until supper. What she had not bargained for was Bernard's idea of afternoon tea.

By the time Kate left her cottage to go to Bernard's she walked with a lighter step and growing curiosity. She had dealt with her post and overcome her resistance to turning on her computer. She checked her emails and once she had deleted the ones asking her to sign petitions or donate money there were not that many and she dealt with them with ease.

It was a beautiful afternoon, a cloudless sky and late spring flowers brought a smile to her face. It wasn't so bad, her life here, she thought, as she walked up the path to Bernard's front door.

He was already opening the door before she could raise her hand to knock.

"Ah Kate, welcome back. It's good to see you, come in."

"Thank you," Kate said as she followed him through the narrow hall to the living room where he indicated for her to sit in one of the armchairs on either side of the fireplace.

"Now, before you tell me all about your holiday Kate, what tea would you like, Earl Grey or Builders?"

"Oh, Earl Grey would be lovely, thank you Bernard."

"Right I won't be a minute, the kettle's just boiled. Just make yourself at home," he said and disappeared into the kitchen.

Kate leaned back in the chair and watched the sun's rays light up motes of dust in a slice of gold between the two chairs. Bernard returned with a tray filled with tea things and a plate overflowing with cakes. There were slices of ginger cake, shortbread and scones.

"Now, what would you like? Please help yourself, Betty has been busy making and I can't eat it all."

Kate looked at the cakes and wondered how she could help him out without adding too many inches to a waistline that she was certain had expanded over the last week. She took a slice of ginger cake and Bernard poured the tea into pretty floral china cups.

"So tell me, how did it go?" he said as he sat down.

"Bernard, it was wonderful in so many ways. It really is very beautiful there and ....."

"And did you manage to find out about our friend

The Diarist

Charles?"

"Sadly, not much more than we already knew. I met some lovely people who took me to the place where the camp had been and they are also seeing if they can find out more about him. All we discovered was that he escaped from the camp but no more."

"Hm, I see," Bernard took a mouthful of cake and looked thoughtful.

Kate wanted to tell Bernard about her visit to Civitella but didn't think she could do so without telling him about her own discovery there and she was not ready to share that with anyone, not yet.

"Well Kate, I've been doing a little bit of research of my own, I hope you don't mind but I can't help myself once that curiosity bug has bitten as it were...."

"Of course not Bernard," she reassured him as she wondered what he could have been up to. "Did you find anything?"

"Er, it was Betty actually. She's a bit of a one when she gets the bit between her teeth and you certainly gave her the bit asking about the history of the cottage."

"I see," Kate smiled to herself wondering whether either of them needed any encouragement. "But, it was Betty who suggested I speak to you, I didn't think she knew anything about the cottage."

"Ah well, be that as it may, just the thought of something interesting whet her appetite and she started to make enquiries of her own. I mean, she didn't mean any harm, she just wanted to help."

"It's alright Bernard, I really don't mind," Kate said leaning forward, "but did she find anything?"

"As long as you're sure, Kate," he said looking a little sheepish. "I wouldn't want you to think we were poking our noses in where we weren't wanted."

"Please Bernard, what did you find out?" Kate pleaded, thinking it was becoming like pulling teeth.

"Ah yes, of course. Sorry Kate," he sighed as he leaned back in the chair. "Well, the long and the short of it is that Hettie had a son and he doesn't live a million miles from here."

"Oh .... I mean, how did you......?"

"Find out?" Bernard asked.

"Well yes ...."

"Hm, that's where Betty comes in." Bernard took a slurp of tea before continuing. "Remember before you left we'd been looking for any records relating to Charles?"

"Yes, that's when we found out that he'd been in the camp at Laterina and ...."

"Not long after you'd gone I met Betty in the village and she asked if I'd been able to help you. Anyways, I told her that we'd had a little bit of luck but not much. So, next thing I know she's on the phone telling me about this son. She'd been doing a bit of research herself and was very cagey about it. She still won't tell me how she found out, maybe she'll tell you more."

"Er, if she won't tell you Bernard, I don't see her telling me. I mean, she hardly knows me."

"Well nevertheless, as I said he doesn't live that far from here and," Bernard slurped his tea again, "and ...."

"And?" Kate prompted.

"We .... er .... well we went to see."

"Went to see what?" Kate's thoughts returned to pulling teeth.

"Where he lived."

"Oh," Kate tried to refrain from laughing as she imagined him and Betty going on their expedition. "Did you see him?"

"No," he frowned. "We didn't mean to intrude, just have a look, that was all."

"I see."

"It was a cottage, bit like yours."

"Like so many round here, I suppose." Kate said not

The Diarist

wanting to imbue it with more meaning than it deserved.

"Hm, yes I suppose."

"So what will you do now?" she asked.

"Oh, it's not what I'll do, my dear. We thought you might want to write to him. Here, this is his address," and he handed Kate a slip of paper.

"Ah, thank you Bernard." Kate looked at the address. "What do you think I should say?"

Oh, I don't know, hadn't really thought about it. Betty did get the telephone number ……" he ventured, "but I told her I thought you would prefer to write."

"I see," Kate said not sure what to do with this new information. She could not now tell Bernard about the diary as it would be clear she had been keeping it from him. That would have been an obvious reason to contact this man; maybe when she took a closer look at the deeds she might find something she could use. She was still amused by the idea of Bernard and Betty sleuthing in her absence when Bernard stood to offer her more cake.

"Oh no thank you, I really couldn't."

"I know what you mean dear, can I give you some to take home, I don't know what I'll do with it otherwise."

"Ok, if you're sure."

"Oh I'm sure alright, I'll just get something to put it in."

He came back with some kitchen foil and wrapped a piece of the ginger cake, then a couple of scones followed by some shortbread.

"You can have a tea party," he laughed.

"Thank you …"

He sat down again. "Now, you're not cross with us are you, I mean doing this while you were away."

"Of course not Bernard, and I'll have a think about what to write to him. There's no name on the address, do you have it?

"Oh," Bernard said feeling foolish, "didn't I put it down. Now what was it? Oh dear, I'll have to ask Betty and let you know. I'm sorry."

"Don't be sorry, it's wonderful that you did this much."

"Oh good, do you think so? We only wanted to help."

"I know. I just have to think about what to do now."

"Of course you do. I'm sure Betty will want to see you. She would have come today but she had to be somewhere."

"Never mind, another time." She said thinking it was time to leave. She sat forward on the edge of her seat. "Thank you so much for the tea Bernard and for all you've done …."

"Oh there's no need Kate, I've enjoyed it – makes life more interesting,"

Well, I must go, I still have …"

"Of course, of course, you've only just got back and … well, I'll let you know the name as soon as I have it."

"Thank you, don't worry I'll see myself out."

Kate walked quickly back to the cottage. She wanted to have a closer look at the deeds. Was there a clue there? And what should she do about it if there was?

Back in her kitchen she looked again at the Epitome of Title and the names of the various owners of the cottage. It wasn't much help. There was Jonathan Smalley, the owner before her, then before him a Pamela Routledge. who must have been the owner when it was holiday lets. Before her, it seemed to have been in the same family for years and their name was Danby, not Forbes, unless of course Hettie's sister had married into that family. She thought that Betty, or was it Bernard, had said that she lived here alone.

Another dead end, she thought. First the diary goes nowhere, then Charles disappears without a trace, and now this. Let alone the other discovery of finding possible evidence of her father's family, who may or may not all be dead.

Not one to give in easily, Kate opened out the conveyances and went through them one by one. She looked

The Diarist

at the most recent ones, comparing dates and names with what she had already been told. She concluded that at the time Hettie's sister lived there it was owned by an Edward Danby. What was Hettie's sister name? Had she been married to Edward Danby or had she rented from him. She pushed the papers away from her, her mind busy with unanswered questions.

Her thoughts then turned to her father and what she should tell him, if anything. She knew she ought to call her parents but would she be able to do that and not tell them about her visit to Civitella? She played various potential conversations in her mind and decided it was probably best to wait a few more days as long as familial guilt did not take over. Maybe she would hear from Giancarlo.

Her thoughts followed another tack and her body told her how much she hoped to hear from him. Nervous butterflies filled her abdomen as she imagined answering his call, hearing his voice. She tried to push her feelings aside, unwanted and embarrassing. For god's sake, I'm a grown woman not a lovesick teenager, she berated herself again, surprised by the intensity of her emotions.

She revisited each moment since they met when she fell into his arms outside her hotel, to saying goodbye at the same place. Feelings, long dismissed were surfacing when a loud ring called her from her reverie and she realised the phone was ringing.

"Hello?"

"Hey sis?" and she immediately warmed to the soft Scottish burr of her brother's voice.

"Hi, how are you?"

"Good thanks, but that's not why I'm calling Kate ….."

Immediately wary at the use of her name she demanded he tell her.

"Why, what is it? Is it ….."

"It's *babbo*. He's alright, there's no need to worry or anything. I just thought you should know ……"

"What, what happened?" she cut in.

"He had a fall. Nothing serious. He cracked a small bone in his hand and has a few bruises, mainly to his pride. You know how he is, still thinks he's thirty."

"I'll check flights. I can be there tomorrow and ..."

"No, no, he doesn't want a fuss. He's fine and already enjoying the attention he's getting. I just wanted to let you know, that's all."

"Ok, thanks," she said reluctant to give in to his 'big brother knows best' and knowing at the same time it was futile to pursue the matter.

"So how's the new home? Why the move?"

"It's great, I love it. What about you? Still building your empire?"

"Not sure I'd call it an empire sis, but yes the restaurant's doing well and we open the deli next week."

Kate smiled at the way he always said 'we', still including his father even though the latter had retired several years ago. Or maybe he would never let go. The cafe he started that later became a restaurant had been his whole life and even though her brother had taken over the reins, she could not imagine her father giving up completely.

"That's great, congratulations."

"Thanks sis, and look don't worry, all's fine," he said hoping to reassure her.

"Ok. Bye for now."

"Bye."

Once she got over her irritation at the big brother in charge of little sister, she picked up the phone again this time to call her parents. Odd she thought that she had been thinking about whether to call them only a short time earlier. Her mother answered.

"Hello?" she said with a slight huskiness that Kate always attributed to her French ancestry. Even at almost ninety it was unmistakeable.

The Diarist

"Hi *maman*, Luc just rang, told me about *babbo* ...."

"Och, he is a naughty boy. There was no need to worry you ...."

"What do mean, *maman*? How is he?"

"Well, apart from tying him to his chair to keep him from carrying on as normal ...." She could almost see her mother rolling her eyes. "He's fine Kate, You really do not need to worry. And please, don't do anything silly like coming all this way when there's no need. We'd love to see you, of course, but wait awhile, come when your father's less .... erm," she paused while she searched for the best word to describe him.

"Irascible?" Kate offered.

"Indeed!"

"Ok but ....."

"No buts darling, now tell me about your little cottage."

Kate regaled her mother with details of each room of her new home, the village and the new friends she had made in the short time she had been there. She wanted to tell her about the diary and her holiday but did not feel ready and was saved from having to when she heard her father's accented voice demanding to know who was on the phone.

"I'll pass you over darling ...…." and was cut off before she could say anything further.

"*Eh*, so you heard. Didn't take long then. Luc was it?"

"Yes, *babbo*. How are you?"

"It was nothing. I'm fine. I just tripped and, well, it's just a few bruises .... I don't know what all the fuss is about. What about you, *amore*, I hear you moved?"

"Yes," Kate replied suddenly feeling ten years old. "I bought a little cottage. The old house was too big for me on my own and this is just perfect. I ….."

"*Eh*, I suppose. What about Emma and David? They well?"

"Yes *babbo*. I saw Emma yesterday. She's working hard as always but is happy. As for David I rarely hear these days so hope no news is good news. I get the odd text but that's about it."

"Humph, well give them our love won't you? Maybe see you at Christmas."

"*Babbo* that's months away!"

"I know, I know..... but it seems to be the only time these days that the whole family gets together." He gave a short laugh followed by an, "ouch."

"*Babbo*...."

"*Eh*, forgot I mustn't laugh, especially at my own jokes, so stop fussing. It's good to talk to you but I can hear your mother setting the table ...."

"Ok, it's good to talk to you and take good care of ...."

"Of your mother, of course I will. Stop worrying about me *amore*, I'm fine. *Ciao, ciao.*"

"*Ciao babbo.*" and Kate was left holding the phone listening to the dialling tone. She looked at her watch and wondered where the afternoon had gone; it was almost time to go next door to Annie's.

Relieved that her father was alright she quickly folded the conveyances and tidied the table. Her parents seemed to lead charmed lives in that they were both relatively healthy and active considering their great ages. Maybe that was the secret, they had always both had varied interests and were busy doing something or other. Maybe she was being over protective and should tell them about her holiday and its revelations.

She went to the bathroom and tidied herself before returning to the kitchen where she picked up a bottle of Chianti she had bought at the airport as a thank you for Annie along with a big chunk of *parmesan* cheese. She knew she had probably paid over the odds for the wine but with the new regulations on liquids in hand luggage she'd had no option. She had not wanted to risk putting it in her case and she knew how Annie appreciated wine and hoped she would also like the cheese.

The Diarist

"Ooooo, thank you so much, Kate," Annie cooed when Kate handed over the gifts. "I've already opened a bottle of *Rioja*, do you mind if we keep this for another time?"

"Of course not, and it's for you to enjoy whenever you want."

"Oh no, it wouldn't be the same. I mean, you and Italy go together, so next time," she said with a conspiratorial grin. "Now come and sit down, the food is almost ready and I can't wait to hear more ….."

They went through to the kitchen and Kate sat down at the table while Annie checked the oven and put some vegetables on to steam.

"Well?" she demanded.

"Well, I'm not sure there's much more to tell except .. "

"Yes," Annie prompted.

"I went to see Bernard this afternoon and he and Betty have apparently been carrying out there own investigations and found out that Hettie had a son. Seems he doesn't live that far from here. Can you believe they even went to the village to see his house, I mean … "

"Ooo, how exciting," enthused Annie. "Trust those two to get up to something. Bit of a dark horse, that Bernard I reckon."

Annie got up, opened the oven and took out a dish which she placed on the table on a trivet in front of Kate.

"It smells wonderful, Annie," Kate said breathing in the heady herby aroma that rose from a piece of salmon on a bed of leeks surrounded by thickly sliced potatoes.

"Hope you don't mind red wine," Annie asked. "I can open some white though if you prefer."

"No, no, I'd much prefer red, thanks."

Annie checked the vegetables and emptied them into a bowl and put them on the table next to the fish.

"Please, help yourself," she said sweeping her arm across the table before sitting down and pouring them each a glass of wine.

Once they had divided the food between their plates Annie raised her glass and Kate reciprocated as they toasted each other with a happy *salute*.

"Oh, the deeds arrived. They don't reveal much either. There are no Forbes there. It looks like a family called Danby owned it before the people who did the holiday lets. There's nothing about Hettie's sister so I thought maybe she rented it from the Danby people."

"Or maybe she was married to one of them?" Annie suggested.

"Yes, I did wonder but I don't know how we'll ever know."

"Maybe Bernard and Betty will come up with something."

"Mmm, I don't know Annie, it's already gone further than I anticipated. I mean, I was only curious about who had lived in the cottage before and, well ..."

"I know, but it is kind of fascinating once you start isn't it and I imagine Bernard and Betty are enjoying it. Nothing like a bit of mystery and all that."

"I know but I don't want to intrude in other people's lives, they might not want to know ...."

"What, you mean rake up the past and ...."

"Well yes, I suppose so." Kate took a sip of wine and, waving her fork that held a piece of salmon and leek, said, "Annie this is really good, you must give me the recipe."

"Oh, well there isn't one really, I sort of made it up. I just put it all in a dish with some olive oil and herbs and put it in the oven."

They discussed making up recipes from whatever was available which led on to Italian food and Kate's holiday. Annie made lots of appreciative sounds as Kate described the food, shops and places she had visited in her much too short a stay. She kept it impersonal and avoided any mention of the diary or her own family and after a couple of hours decided it was time to say goodnight which she did amid

The Diarist

promises to cook the next time.

As she settled on the sofa with a herbal tea and the local paper Kate's mood became reflective. She turned the pages without absorbing anything she read, her mind filled with what-ifs from the earlier phone conversations with her brother and parents.

Relieved that her father was his usual cantankerous self she could not help think about what could have happened and pondered on the fragility of life.

She put down the paper, folded it and allowed her thoughts to meander. What if it had been serious and she had not told him about going to Civitella. Anyway what could she have said, apart from having seen a photograph of someone who looked like him with the same family name and that she now knew about the massacre.

She ran her fingers through her hair and looked round the room. The question that now occupied her mind was whether she should return to Italy in search of more answers, if in fact there were any. Eventually she surrendered to the frustration of not knowing and went to bed.

2

Another day arrived, grey and wet. Kate had not slept well and her feet and heart felt heavy as she made her way to the kitchen. As she looked out of the window on to the garden she could almost hear her mother's voice talking about all the grateful gardeners who would not have to water their gardens and she managed a weak smile.

Determined not to be overwhelmed by recent events she sat at the kitchen table with her morning mug of coffee and started on a shopping list.

The phone rang before she had finished writing the first two items.

"Hello."

"Hello dear, it's Betty. You got my message?"

"Yes, thank you Betty. What can I ....."

"Good. I wonder dear if you'd like to pop round for a coffee, that's if you're not busy?"

"Well, I was just going ....."

"It shouldn't take too long and ..."

"Is it about the cottage Betty? I hear you and Bernard have been up to ...."

"What do you mean dear?"

"Well, I saw Bernard yesterday and he told me that ...."

"Oh, I see. So you know ...."

"About you and Bernard ......?"

"What?"

The Diarist

"The research you and Bernard did, Betty and ..."

"Oh that. Yes well, I don't know if it's of any use but he may be able to tell you something."

"I'll see, maybe I'll write to him, and thanks Betty."

"Oh it's nothing dear, I quite enjoyed it. How was your holiday?"

"It was lovely, thanks."

"Well, I'd better get on. See you soon dear. Bye for now."

"Bye, Betty."

Kate put down the phone and returned to her shopping list hoping the mundane would keep her occupied and avoid the pressing melancholy.

She was just about to leave, car keys in hand, when the phone rang again. She looked at it, then at the door and decided in favour of the door which she opened as the phone stopped ringing and went to the answering service.

As she drove to the supermarket she heard her mobile indicate she had received a text. She tutted at the intrusion, aware of contradictory feelings pulling her towards the new life she was creating and at the same time, wanting to retreat to the known and familiar.

She arrived at the supermarket and parked the car. She pulled out her mobile to find the text was from Emma asking how she was. She sent a quick reply confirming all was fine and maybe they could have supper soon then focussed on doing her shopping and getting home in as short a time as possible.

It turned out not to be that simple. As she was heading towards the checkout she heard someone calling her name and she turned to see Betty heading straight towards her.

"I thought it was you, though it's not always easy to tell from behind. Anyways, I'm glad it was." she smiled enthusiastically, clearly pleased to see her.

"Er yes, I know what you mean …." Kate said trying to

stir some enthusiasm of her own.

"Awful isn't it when you get back from a lovely holiday and have to get on with things just as you did before you went away. Always takes me a few days to get back to normal, whatever that may be."

"I think you're right Betty. Maybe a little bit of me is still there, not quite ready to come home."

They said their goodbyes and promised to meet again soon. Kate, now smiling, carried on to the checkout.

So was that it? As soon as Betty had said the words a weight lifted that she had not realised she was carrying. Now free of her melancholy and instilled with a fresh sense of purpose, she wanted to get home.

By the time she reached the cottage the sun was high in a soft blue sky and all evidence of the early grey dampness had disappeared. Kate put the shopping away and opened her laptop to check her emails. Her breath caught in her throat when she saw Umberto's name.

She scanned it quickly then re-read it so she could take in the details. He had spoken with Enzo again who had been talking to some of the families he knew. Though no-one could say they remembered Charles, they did remember some of the English men who escaped from the camp. Enzo thought it might be a good idea for Kate to speak to them herself and bring a photo if she had one.

He finished by reminding her of his and Claudia's offer of hospitality when she did visit.

She fell back against the chair and, staring at the screen, her mind raced through various possibilities. There was no reason why she could not go back, but a photo? She could write to the son unearthed by Bernard and Betty; would he have one tucked away in a family album somewhere? Then there was Giancarlo. Yes, then there was Giancarlo. Her mind slowed as she contemplated whether seeing him again was a good idea or not, or whether it was even a possibility.

The Diarist

She pushed the chair back and walked over to the fridge in search of food. She took out a bag of salad, mozarella and a tomato, toasted a slice of bread, arranged it all on the top, added some torn up basil leaves and drizzled olive oil to finish. Anything to distract her from thoughts of Giancarlo. She had been taught from an early age that food was the answer to almost everything.

It was later that afternoon when going to make a call that she heard the beep indicating a message. It was then she remembered the phone ringing as she left the cottage that morning. She waited and listened.

"*Ciao* Kate, it's Giancarlo. I hope all is well with you. I will call again, *Ciao, ciao.*"

Oh no, why didn't I answer it. If I hadn't been feeling so sorry for myself ...... but maybe it's a good thing I didn't speak to him then. He did say he'll call again. She replayed the message wanting to listen again to his soft accented voice.

A knock at the door ended her reverie and, shaking her head, she walked to the door and opened it to a resolute looking Bernard.

"I hope I'm not disturbing you Kate. I mean, please say if I am, but I was passing and ...."

"That's alright, Bernard. Come in, come in," she said leading the way down the hall and into the kitchen. "Cup of tea? I'll put the kettle on."

"Er yes, thanks," he replied with a slight hesitation. "If you're sure ..."

"Of course, Bernard. Please, sit down."

She brought a teapot down from the dresser and two cups and saucers.

"Biscuits, cake?"

"Oh no thank you, Kate. I think I may have overdone the cake recently," he said patting his stomach.

She made the tea and joined Bernard at the table.

"Now, what can I do for you, Bernard?"

"Well, I got to thinking see, after your visit yesterday, and …."

"And …..?" Kate was getting used to encouraging him.

"I er, was wondering if you were going to write that letter?" Bernard coughed. "I got his name from Betty. It's George Danby."

"Thanks Bernard. Yes, I think I will, in fact I was about to ….."

"Good, I don't know why Kate, but it somehow seems important."

"Oh, well in that case ….. what do you think I should say?" Kate asked. Although she knew what she would write she was interested in Bernard's thoughts as he did not know about the diary. She was beginning to wish she had not been so secretive about it now.

"I'm not sure Kate. Shame you can't find something that might belong to his family then you could ….."

Kate did not hear the rest of the sentence. Was Bernard psychic or something?

Before she could think of what to say next there was another knock at the door. When she opened it she was greeted by a smiling Annie.

"Hi Kate, I hope I'm not disturbing you but have you got a minute?"

"Of course, come in. Come and join us, Bernard's in the kitchen." Again Kate led the way to the kitchen wondering how many more people were going to knock at the door.

"Hello Bernard, how are you?" asked Annie.

"Tea?" Kate asked looking at Annie.

"Ooo, yes please, but please don't let me interrupt, I can come back another time."

No, no, it's fine," Kate reassured her. "Would you like a biscuit, some cake?"

"I won't thanks," and Annie sat at the table next to Bernard. Kate poured her some tea and sat opposite them.

The Diarist

"I was just saying ..... sorry Annie, has Kate told you about ...?"

"Oh about your little discovery?" Annie gave him a knowing smile.

"Hm," he gave a slight cough to hide a shade of embarrassment. "Er, what do you think? I was just saying ..."

"Bernard was saying that he thought I ought to write to this son, though I'm not sure what I would say." Kate looked from one to the other.

"I see," said Annie, looking thoughtful and unusually quiet. "I mean, what reason could you have for contacting him?"

"Er, I don't know," Kate said, again wishing she had not been so secretive about the diary. "Something to do with the cottage? But then I'd have to explain how I knew about him." Kate sank back into her chair.

"Look, don't give up, I'm sure we can think of something." Annie said in her usual optimistic way. "Is there any mention in the deeds?"

"I don't think so but I could take a closer look," Kate replied with little enthusiasm as she began to feel defeated by her inability to reveal the truth.

"Hm," Bernard began but was cut short by yet another knock at the door.

"Who on earth can that be?" Kate asked and looking from Annie to Bernard, she got up and went to the door where she found Betty with her hand raised about to knock for a second time.

"Oh, I'm sorry dear, I wasn't sure if you were in and I hope you don't mind me just popping round but ...."

"No, not at all, Betty, come in and join the party," Kate invited her in the direction of the kitchen as she wondered what was going on. It seemed that the quiet life she had envisaged had taken a different turn since her return from Italy.

In the kitchen they all greeted each other with polite

surprise.

"I'm sorry Kate, I didn't mean to interrupt anything, I'll er …," and she turned towards the door.

"You're not, Betty, please sit down. Can I get you a cup of tea?" Kate asked thinking she looked like a cornered bird.

"Well if you're sure, that would be lovely, thank you," and smiling, she relaxed and sat down.

It was Bernard who led the way as he explained what they had been talking about.

"So, you see, we were wondering what reason Kate could give for writing to this ….. er …. , son you uncovered."

"Ah, yes well …."

"Can you tell us how you came to find him?" Annie asked as Kate put a cup of tea on the table in front of Betty and sat down.

"Oh," Betty looked down at the table with pursed lips. "It's a bit awkward ….. like I don't want to get anyone into trouble …," she said as she looked from one to the other round the table.

"Now come on, Betty, it can't be that bad," Bernard encouraged.

Kate began to feel she was becoming part of a conspiracy without her consent, and yet one in which she had played a crucial part in creating.

"Betty, whatever you tell us, you know it will stay in this room," she said hoping to reassure her.

"Of course, you mustn't worry," Annie confirmed.

Bernard reached out and patted her hand. "It's alright, whatever it is you can tell us."

"Well, it's nothing really, just that," she looked across the table at Bernard before continuing. "You know I've got a cousin who works at the council, well we were talking and the conversation got round to the cottage and its history. He suggested taking a look at some of the registry records and ….. well, it costs money and so he said he'd see what he

The Diarist

could do. I just don't want to get him into trouble, that's all."

"Don't worry Betty, we won't say a word. But I don't see how that helps us with this letter," Kate said, wishing she had never mentioned anything about wanting to know more about the cottage in the first place.

"Yes, what you need is to find something that belongs to the family so you can then return it to him then that would explain why and how you had to find him." Annie suggested.

"Well, there isn't, so .... ," Bernard began then turned to Kate, "but maybe .... have you made a thorough search of the cottage?"

"Er, I think so," Kate said as a plan began to form in her mind. "I can look around again though in case I've missed anything, if you like?"

They all nodded in agreement that would be a good idea and there was a sigh as they each relaxed back into their chairs.

They finished their tea and after a discussion about various village related items they said their goodbyes. Annie was the last to leave.

"I'd be happy to help you look if that wasn't too intrusive?" Annie suggested.

"Thanks Annie, that would be great. I think I've had it for today but if you're free tomorrow why not come over for coffee and we can make a start?"

"Ok, about 10.30?".

"Perfect, see you then."

Kate closed the door and returned to the now empty kitchen and collapsed onto one of the chairs. What, why and how questions rushed through her mind. Somehow she was going to have to hide the diary so Annie could find it or, would it be better to own up to having already found it. Subterfuge was not part of her nature but ...... what would Annie say if she knew Kate had known about the diary all along? Better this way. She had not intended to be dishonest and she had certainly not expected Bernard and Betty to get so involved. It really was getting out of hand. And she thought she had moved here for a quiet life!

The sound of the phone ringing made her jump and she reached behind her to the dresser, where this had all started, to answer it.

"Hello?"

"*Ciao,* Kate, it's Giancarlo. How are you?"

"Er, c*iao,* yes I'm well thank you. And you?"

"*Bene, grazie*" and after an awkward silence he continued. "I may have some news for you about your family."

"Oh," Kate gasped as the words 'your family' echoed round her head still not familiar with the term in an Italian setting. She sat forward with her elbows on the table, one hand holding the phone and the other supporting her head.

"*Si,* my uncle, not Giovanni, another one, he is one of those men who knows everyone and everything, always at the *circolo,* erm, a kind of club, *come si dice,* social club I think you say. *Eh,* my father was telling him about your visit and he said he would see what he could find out. The next day he called to say that he had spoken to a friend who recognised your family name and was making more enquiries."

Kate tried to form words but her mouth would not co-operate.

"Kate, you are there?"

"Er, yes .... I , er ....."

"Forgive me, you were not expecting this. I should not have been so enthusiastic in ....."

"No, no, it's fine .... thank you," she managed to say as she sat up and looked out on to the garden in search of an anchor. What to do, what to say? She heard his voice, soft and deep, ameliorating, but not the words.

"I'm sorry, could you say that again?"

The Diarist

He repeated his apologies and asked whether she had heard from Simonetta.

"No, I haven't but I did receive an email from Umberto. He asked if I had a photo of Charles as he thought it would be a good idea to bring it with me on my next visit."

"You are planning another visit?" Giancarlo asked, hopeful of an affirmative response.

"Oh, I don't know, I've only just got back and ...."

"We would be very happy to see you again, and maybe this time you will find what you are looking for."

"Er, thank you Giancarlo," she said unsure of the meaning of his words. "I mean I'd love to visit again but......"

"But? Life is too short for buts, *cara*."

Did he just call her *cara?* Maybe it was a term he often used with friends though she always understood it to be a term of affection. It was like swimming underwater and trying to find the surface.

"Of course, but ...."

"Another but?" he said teasing her.

"Ok, ok," she capitulated as she imagined the clarity of his blue eyes looking at her. "I'll think about it."

"*Bene,*. You have my phone number if I can be of help."

"Yes, and thank you, and your uncle. Everyone has been so kind and helpful."

"*Niente,* it's nothing. If I hear more I can let you know."

Was that a twist of language or deliberately ambiguous, she wondered.

"That would be great," she said aware of a hollowness to her words.

"*Ciao,* for now."

"*Ciao,*" she said as she listened to the call end and revert to the dialling tone.

She leaned back in her chair exhausted by the day's events but smiled as she mused on the call.

3

Annie arrived eager to get on with the search. Kate had returned the diary to the back of the dresser drawer and then decided against it. After wandering around the cottage she had finally opened up the loft. It had been insulated and partially boarded and she climbed up to take a look round. She put on the light and was disappointed by the emptiness. Not the best hiding place, she thought and, after a last look she turned off the light, climbed down and returned to the kitchen. She stuffed the diary behind the drawer where she had originally found it and hoped it was not going to be a waste of time. Again, she wondered if it would not be easier to just own up to having already found it.

"Coffee?" Kate asked.

"Thanks, I've not long had one. Shall we make a start and then have coffee?" Annie said full of enthusiasm.

"Ok. Start downstairs? Why don't I take the living room and you take the kitchen?" Kate suggested.

"Sure," and Annie was off already looking in corners as Kate went through to the living room and hoped Annie would not take too long finding it. She looked around the room and could bear it no longer. She strode through to the kitchen where Annie was moving towards the dresser. Kate paused as she reassured herself she was about to do the right thing.

"Annie, look, let's have that coffee now, I need to tell you something. Come and sit down," she said and went to boil the kettle.

"What is it, Kate? You look serious. Is something wrong?" Annie frowned as she sat down.

"Sort of, but not really. Let me make the coffee," she said putting coffee into a cafetière and pouring on the hot water. She carried it over to the table with a jug of milk and two mugs before sitting down opposite Annie who was watching her intently.

"Kate?"

"I have a confession to make," Kate began. "I don't know why I didn't say anything at the time but I didn't and now it's just getting out of hand. You see, I didn't think it mattered and I didn't expect so many people to get involved."

"Kate, I'm intrigued, what is it you've not told me?"

"Not long after I moved in," Kate began and, taking a deep breath, went on to tell Annie about finding the diary. "I don't like deception and as I said …."

"Oh Kate, don't worry about it. I'm not and I don't think Bernard will think any less of you, he'll most likely be even more intrigued. And, now you have a reason to write that letter, so it's all prefect."

"In a way, that's what worries me, Annie. It's all happening so quickly and I suppose that's why I didn't say something in the first place. I mean, I wasn't sure what to do with it and I had no idea it would get this complicated or go this far."

"Can I see it?" Annie ventured.

"Yes of course," Kate replied and got up and went to the dresser. She opened the cupboard, bent down and reached up inside to remove the diary from the back of the drawer. She stood up and handed it to Annie.

"So this was written by the mother of the man that Betty was talking about?" Annie asked as she leafed through the diary.

"So it would seem."

"And you took this to Italy?"

"Yes, I suppose I thought I could follow in her footsteps, see if I could find out more about Charles, you know, what happened to him, and …. ."

"And? Did you …...?"

"Not really, only what I told you, that he escaped from the camp but after that, nothing so far. Also you'll see Hettie stops writing about him after a while and then stops altogether so …."

"Oh yes," Annie said as she skimmed through Hettie's entries. "She writes more about her stay there and then stops. I wonder what happened?"

"Mmm, me too."

"Will you tell Bernard?"

"Yes, I'll have to. I'm sorry to have let it go this far. I mean I didn't imagine it would become important."

"Oh dear Kate, welcome to village life," Annie grinned. "The slightest sign of intrigue and, well …... you can see what happens."

"I didn't think of that. Where I lived before people tended to keep to themselves and …."

"Don't worry, they don't mean any harm, especially Bernard, he's a real sweetie with a heart of gold under that gruff exterior."

Kate sighed with relief, not just at having eased herself free of concealing the diary but also having her assessment of Bernard confirmed. She hoped he would be as understanding as Annie. She would call him and arrange to see him later, take the diary and apologise for keeping it from him.

It was mid afternoon when Kate walked with determination to Bernard's cottage. She had spent the time since Annie left convincing herself that she had done nothing wrong, Bernard would see that and understand her reluctance to tell anyone about it. After all it was her concern. She had called him asking if she could pop in that afternoon. She walked up the lavender edged path and knocked on the front door.

"Ah Kate," Bernard croaked as he straightened up from the flower bed where he had been working at the side of the cottage. "Come in, come in."

Kate followed him as he led the way in along the hall to the sitting room.

"Make yourself at home dear, I'll just put the kettle on."

"Oh, don't go to any trouble ….."

"No trouble at all, you just sit down, it won't take a minute."

While she waited Kate silently rehearsed what she intended to say until Bernard returned with what was becoming his usual tray of tea and cakes.

"So to what do I owe the pleasure, has something happened?" he asked as he poured the tea and offered cake which Kate politely refused.

"Not exactly," Kate said and waited for Bernard to sit in the chair opposite. "I have a confession to make."

"Oh dear, that sounds serious, what have you done my dear?"

"Well, it's not so much what I've done it's more what I didn't do, or what I didn't tell you."

"Now I am intrigued ..."

"Remember, when I first came to see you asking about the history of the cottage, well ……." Kate began and went on to tell Bernard about finding the diary and the whys and wherefores of not mentioning it until now. "You see, I never thought it would become this complicated and ..."

"That's wonderful Kate, now you have a valid reason to contact Hettie's son." Bernard sat up straight suddenly animated. "No need to worry your head about it. There was no reason you should have said anything and, as you say, you weren't to know how it would turn out."

"Oh ...." Kate began but Bernard was quick to reassure her before she could go any further.

"Look, let's forget all about it and get on with the matter in hand. Now did you bring it with you?" said Bernard in a matter of fact way.

"Er yes, here ....." Kate replied, taking the diary from her bag and passing it to him. "It doesn't really tell us much more than we already know, unless something happened and Hettie didn't write about it."

"Oh but, I don't think that matters now, who knows what we might find out when it's returned," he said as he skimmed through the pages. "Have you decided whether you will write or phone?"

"No, not yet. I'd like to phone and get it out of the way but I think it would be better to write first and I can give him my phone number and email so he can reply."

"Good idea. Now, have you drafted the letter?" Bernard asked eager to get on with it.

"I'll do it when I get back. I probably won't make today's post but I'll make sure it goes by the first one tomorrow morning."

"Good, so he should get it the day after that. Let's hope he contacts you quickly. Maybe he'll have photos, you know a family album or something," Bernard rubbed his hands together. "More tea?"

"No, thank you Bernard. I ought to be getting back really. I just wanted to explain and ...."

"Not another word about it, my dear," Bernard said handing her the diary and patting her knee. "Just let me know as soon as you hear anything."

They both stood, Kate insisting she could see herself out and reassuring Bernard that she would keep him up to date.

It did not take Kate long to write a short letter to George Danby explaining how she had bought the cottage, found the

The Diarist

diary at the back of the dresser and made enquiries to find any remaining family members. She hoped he was one of them and gave her phone number and email address for him to contact her.

When she had finished she printed it, signed it, and put it in an envelope before realising she needed a stamp. Looking at the clock, she picked up her bag and sprinted to the post office hoping to get there before it closed.

"If you're quick, dear, you'll just catch the post. It's a late one today," the woman behind the counter advised her. Kate thanked her, turned and quickly left the shop. She was heading for the post box a few feet away when the red Royal Mail van pulled up alongside it. She dropped the letter in the box with a prayer before retracing her steps at a slower pace to the cottage.

Kate had no sooner put the kettle on when there was a knock at the door. Exhausted by the thought of more visitors, she sighed as she walked down the hall and opened the front door to find Annie eager to know how her afternoon had gone.

"Sorry, sorry, I know ….. but I just couldn't wait and ..." Annie babbled.

"It's ok Annie, come in," Kate invited. "I was just putting the kettle on but maybe a glass of wine would be a better idea?"

"Oh I don't want to ….."

"You're not, Annie," Kate pre-empted. "It's good to see you. Red ok?"

"Yes, thanks. Did you see Bernard? And ..."

Kate recounted every detail of the afternoon as Annie sat in rapt silence absorbing every word.

"Wow, well done you," she beamed. "So, now we just have to wait and see if this man contacts you?"

"Yes, I suppose so," Kate leaned back and took a slurp of wine. "Let's hope it's sooner rather than later."

Annie raised her glass. "Yes, let's drink to that," and they clinked glasses.

"When's Ben back?"

"Oh, the day after tomorrow, I think."

"In that case would you like to stay and have supper? Nothing fancy, just some pasta and salad." Kate offered. Annie was good company and would deter her from dwelling on things too much. "But no talk about diaries."

"Thanks Kate, that would be great. I just need to finish something at home. Can I bring anything?"

"Just yourself," Kate smiled.

"Ok, about half an hour?"

"Perfect."

4

A couple of days passed without incident and Kate was able to catch up on the laundry, the garden, which was becoming a riot of overcrowded colour, and generally enjoying being in the cottage.

She tried not to think about the diary, the letter and the call from Giancarlo. Especially the call from Giancarlo. It was hard not to imagine his playful smile, those clear blue eyes, his rich accented voice, which then led her into the memories of the time spent with him. She frequently pulled herself back to the chore at hand, cursing her meandering mind.

After lunch she checked her emails and there it was. George Danby. She clicked on it and began to read ….. *thank you for contacting ...... would be very interested in seeing the diary ..... happy to come to the cottage ..... passing by Monday morning if convenient .... understand if short notice ....*

Kate's heart beat faster as she pressed reply. She confirmed she would be at home and looked forward to meeting him. She refrained from writing more despite the stream of questions that wanted to teem on to the page. She pressed send and, leaning back, stared at the screen.

Eventually she tore herself away and returned to her gardening. Unable to contain her thoughts and anticipation any longer she rang Annie in the hope that Ben had not yet arrived home.

"Ooo yes, come over, I'll put the kettle on," Annie enthused when she told her about the email. Kate momentarily pondered on how lucky she was to have Annie as a neighbour as she locked up and walked from her cottage to Annie's next door.

"Come in, come in. I thought we could sit in the garden since it's so lovely. Would you prefer tea or I've some home made lemonade, not by me though." Annie's words flowed like a burbling brook as she led the way through to the garden.

"Lemonade would be lovely, thanks." As she sat down and Annie went inside to fetch the drinks, Kate appreciated the beauty of the day that she had so far ignored. Annie returned with a tray filled with a jug of lemonade, glasses and biscuits.

"Lemon shortbread," she announced, "and no, I didn't make them either."

"Ben back yet?" Kate asked.

"No, he says tomorrow evening. But enough, tell me about the email." Annie demanded sitting on the edge of her seat.

"Well, there's not much to say really, just that he's going to call in Monday morning."

"Oh, that's wonderful," Annie said clapping her hands together.

"Hm, I don't know," Kate said as the excitement left her. "I mean, he may not know anything or even want to talk about it."

"But he answered your letter so quickly so he must be interested, don't you think?"

"I suppose."

They spent the next hour happily chatting. By the time she returned to her cottage Kate felt more settled and a little embarrassed by her initial excitement. After all, it was only an email and she did not want to get caught up in a non existent drama.

As she waited for him to arrive Kate took one last look at the diary that had been so instrumental in the recent changes taking place in her life. In the short time since opening it she had been to Italy, made new friends, there and in the village, and become embroiled in the intriguing life of a stranger. She was reading the last entry and wondering why Hettie had stopped writing when there came the anticipated knock at the door.

Kate felt her adrenaline rise as she walked along the hall to open the door. When she did she was faced with a man of a similar age, a little taller than her, dark hair touched with grey and warm brown eyes edged with thick dark lashes that any woman would envy.

"Good morning, I'm George Danby and you must be Kate. I'm pleased to meet you," he said as he offered to shake hands.

Kate's hand met his briefly.

"Yes, thank you for coming, please come in," she said somewhat flustered as she led the way through to the kitchen. "Please sit down. Can I get you something? Tea, coffee?"

"Coffee would be welcome," he said, his voice warm and mellow.

Kate made coffee which she put on the table with two mugs and a jug of milk.

"You said in your letter that you have something that may have belonged to my mother? A diary?"

"Yes," Kate said and went on to explain how she had come to find it.

"I see. May I take a look?"

"Of course," and Kate took the diary from the dresser and handed it to him. A polite tension hung in the air between them.

He paged through it, nodding here and there and as he

looked up towards Kate, the tension dissolved as he said, "Yes, this is my mother's. I wondered what had happened. You see, we, "he paused to correct himself. "I have a diary for the latter part of that year and I couldn't understand why she had not made entries for the first part as she was an avid journal writer."

"Then you must have it," Kate said, sad to relinquish it. "I do have some questions though if you have time?"

"Of course," he smiled as he closed the book. "What would you like to know?"

"Well, Hettie, your mother, went to Italy to find her brother, do you know if she did, find him?"

"Ah, sadly not, but maybe you would like to read the other diary for that year. It might answer some of the questions you have. I'm working on a project not far from here and could drop it off tomorrow."

"Oh, well thank you. Yes, I'd love to read it." Kate hesitated before asking her next question. "Is she ….."

"Still alive?" he finished her question. "Yes and no," he said looking down at the diary before raising his eyes to meet Kate's. "She is …. her body is alive for all intents and purposes, but alas her mind is not."

"I'm sorry …."

"Please, there is no need. She's very frail now, a shadow really, so I'm afraid her diaries will have to speak for her."

"You have more?"

"Oh yes, years of them. Mainly her thoughts, often not interesting. The Italian ones are probably the best ones. Look, why don't you come over for lunch tomorrow and you can go through them. I don't live far from here and …." he searched for words to avoid any embarrassment. "I can assure you I'm quite safe if you are worried …."

""Not at all," Kate gave him a reassuring smile that belied the feelings she was hiding below the surface. "I feel I sort of know your mother and …."

"Here's my address," he said taking a business card

The Diarist

from his wallet. "Shall we say about 12.30, we can eat and you'll have the afternoon to read to your heart's content."

"Thank you, that's very generous."

"Not really, it's nice that someone is showing an interest. She really was a remarkable woman," he said, again his eyes fell to the diary as he asked, "may I?"

"Yes, of course." Kate confirmed, not knowing what else to say. She had a strong sense of Hettie's presence that she put down to the intensity of their conversation about her.

"I had better go. Thank you for the coffee and," he paused as he stood, his head tilted slightly, "and thank you for this." He held up the diary. "I'll see you tomorrow then."

Kate walked with him to the door where he again offered his hand. Kate shook it as they said goodbye and she watched him walk away along the path to his car parked outside on the road.

Turning, she leaned her back against the door. Mixed feelings flooded through her as she peeled herself from the door and went to the kitchen. She looked at the emptied coffee pot and mugs on the table and the space where the diary had been. She was lost in the silence until it was suddenly broken by a knock at the front door. Annie, she thought.

"I'm sorry, I just couldn't wait. I heard the car door and saw him drive off. He looked very nice. What was he like, what did he say?" Annie released a torrent of questions as Kate invited her in.

It seemed strange sitting at the table where she had only a few minutes earlier been talking to him.

"Er, well he didn't actually say very much." Kate began. "Only that it was his mother's diary and that he had a lot more. Seems she was a prolific diarist."

"So he took it and that's it?" Annie probed.

"No, no, he …. er, invited me to lunch tomorrow so I can see the other diaries. I think …….."

"What at his house?"

"Yes," Kate said with a frown. "It seems there are two diaries for that year. Maybe she lost one."

"Kate," Annie squinted her eyes at her, "you're going to the house of a man you hardly know?"

"What do you mean, Annie?" Kate's frown deepened. "I don't think he's a mass murderer, and it's only lunch."

"Hm, I suppose. Just be careful."

"Oh dear Annie," Kate chortled. "I'm sure I'll be fine. He seemed very nice and had impeccable manners."

"Ok, just saying. You're probably right. You will let me know as soon as you get back won't you?"

"Of course, but won't Ben be back by then?"

"Nooo," Annie sighed, "he's going to be at least another day."

Kate suddenly felt anxious for her friend. She couldn't quite put her finger on it, just a passing flutter, then it was gone.

"Have you told Bernard?" Annie asked.

"No, not yet. I think I'll wait until after my visit tomorrow." Kate replied, thinking she'd had enough of being caught in Hettie's world for one day.

Annie got up to go. "I'll see you tomorrow then." She let herself out and when she heard the front door close, Kate walked through to the garden and her weeding. Something normal to escape the whirlwind of thoughts racing round her head.

Was she being foolish? Was Annie right? How, why had it all become so complicated? Simonetta, Umberto, Claudia, Giancarlo and now …... George? All in the last two weeks. She sat back on the grass, trowel in one hand, weeds in the other and wiped her damp forehead with the back of her wrist. No wonder she was exhausted, she had done more in the last two weeks than she had probably done in the last two years.

She eased herself off the ground, went inside for a glass of water and came out again to sit at the table and admire her handiwork. A sense of calm pervaded her as she observed, at last, some evidence of the garden taking shape. She had always loved gardening, even as a child when her father allowed her a small patch of her own to plant as she wished. The memory caught images of him kneeling beside her and teaching her the importance of keeping it weed free. It also brought her back to her present dilemma of whether to return to Italy or if she should leave well alone.

She sat up and in that moment knew she had to go back. The sense of belonging she had experienced there was now so strong she was unable to ignore it. She smiled as the knowing grew and that it was the right thing to do.

First, she decided, she would wait until she had seen George again and hear what he had to say. That way she may have more information about Charles. Yes, she thought, that's what she would do and, filled with a new sense of purpose, set off to tackle more weeds.

5

Kate pulled up outside the house. She had imagined she would be nervous and was surprised that was not the case. Calm and assured, she rang the bell. As the door opened she felt a little surge of excitement and took a deep breath to contain it.

"Kate, please come in. How are you?" George greeted her and led her through to a conservatory that overlooked a cottage garden. There was a patio edged with herbs close to the house and a suffusion of flowers overflowed from the borders that edged the lawn.

"Please sit down, lunch will not be long. Can I get you something to drink?" he offered.

"Thank you, a soft drink please as I'm driving." Kate replied.

"Some elderflower cordial?"

"Lovely, thank you." Kate replied and turned towards an old, rose coloured sofa and two armchairs that looked as if they had been relegated from the house when newer ones arrived, or maybe they were merely faded by the sun. Kate sat down in one of the armchairs. The sun had not yet reached the conservatory and it was still cool enough to be comfortable. Kate noticed the pine table at the far end set for two. All quite civilised she thought.

George returned with two glasses of elderflower cordial then immediately excused himself to finish preparing lunch.

The Diarist

Kate enjoyed the view of the garden and searched for ideas for her own. She liked the softness of the taller flowers falling over shorter ones in waves of colour.

Very soon George returned with an oblong plate which he placed on the table.

"When you're ready." he said.

Kate stood and walked over to the table where she saw, to her pleasure, that he had prepared a plate of *antipasti*. There were sun dried tomatoes, artichoke hearts, olives, *salami* and *prosciutto* and a basket of warm bread.

"I thought you might appreciate a little bit of Italy since it is part of your reason for being here." he said as they sat facing each other.

"It looks good, thank you, but ...."

"Please do not say anything about going to any trouble. I love food and I enjoy cooking. Please help yourself," he said waving an arm across the table. "And perhaps a small glass of wine with your meal?"

"Ok, but only a small one, thank you."

They chatted about the garden, then generally about Italy and Kate's recent trip as they ate their way through the *antipasti* which was followed by a wild mushroom risotto and salad. As they came to the end of their meal, George went to make coffee. When he returned he suggested they move to the sofa and chairs and he put the small cups of coffee down on a low glass table.

"I've found the other diary for that year and a few more if you'd like to read them. I'd be happy for you to take them with you so you can take your time."

"Oh, thank you, are you sure, that's very generous. I'll take great care of them of course."

"It's strange after all these years that they have come to life again. My mother loved Italy. It is where she, well," he waved a hand dismissively, "you will discover more as you read them. I don't want to spoil the enjoyment for you."

"Oh you won't," Kate said eager to know more.

"Maybe," he said looking thoughtful. "First, tell me about you and Italy."

"Well, my father is Italian and," Kate began and went on to tell her father's story and how Hettie's diary had led her not only to Florence but also to the village where she thought her father had grown up.

George listened attentively and when she had finished she was surprised she had told him so much. She stared into the empty coffee cup still in her hand and wondered if she had said too much.

"I see," he said in a quiet voice. "It must be difficult for you, the not knowing."

"Er, yes," she said suddenly feeling exposed. She put the little cup down on the table. "I mean, I don't really know anything for sure and even if I did I don't know ….. "

"Whether to say anything to your father?"

"Yes, exactly. He's in his nineties ….. I don't know what the shock might do and …."

"If it's any help, and of course it's none of my business, but I have found it is best not to have secrets." He looked directly into her eyes and Kate knew he was right.

"I'll try to remember." she looked down at her watch and wondered if this would be a good time to leave despite a burning curiosity to know more.

"You have to go?" he asked.

"I ought to,"she said, embarrassed by his acuity.

"Let me know when you have finished with the diaries and I can collect them."

"Of course, and thank you for a wonderful lunch." she said and, not wanting the conversation to become stilted, she stood and picked up her bag and the diaries.

George led the way to the front door where they said goodbye and he thanked her for coming.

Kate pulled over into a lay-by not far from the village. She had managed to walk calmly to the car and drive off but now, she needed to stop and take stock. What was going on? What had happened to her? It was all going well until, until what? She could almost feel herself blushing at the thought of having said too much, being too open. She hardly knew him and she had told him things she had not told her friends or family. In fact, she had told Emma, her own daughter, hardly anything.

She looked at the diaries spread out on the passenger seat. Opening one had set all sorts in motion, what stories or secrets might the others hold and what had George meant when he said it was best not to have secrets.

She started the car and drove home. Once there she took the diaries into the garden, put them on the table and began reading. She wanted to be outside where there was still a clear sky, more space for her thoughts.

The diaries were in order of the years 1952 to 1956. She chose the one for 1952, the partner to the one that had set her off on this venture. It picked up not where Hettie had left off but in September.

I was not going to write again, or so I thought. I suppose I did not want to admit failure. I went to Florence in the hope of finding Charlie. Oh, dear Charlie, what happened to you? Anyway when I couldn't find you, I sort of gave up and didn't want to write about it. I did write for a little while about Aunt Issy and the wonderful places she and Uncle Vittorio took me but my purpose faded and when I came home in July, the heat, it was so hot, intolerable really, and I left my diary. Or at least I think I did as I didn't have it on my return.

Anyway I am going to Florence again next week so maybe I shall find it. Ma was not surprised when I returned empty-handed as it were, but at least she managed to refrain from saying 'I told you so'. I do wonder if it has more to do with her disapproval of Aunt Issy than it has to do with me. Needless to say she's not happy about me going again.

However, I have to go.

Kate read on and after a few entries in much the same vein, scanned forward to the entries written once Hettie was in Florence again. Even here Hettie's writing was about the places they went, a little about the people they met or who visited her aunt's villa but nothing more personal until ….

He has promised to meet me tomorrow in the Piazza della Signoria. I can hardly wait. I have not said anything yet to Aunt Issy. I think I will say nothing for now, only that I wish to visit the Uffizi again and I know she will not want to do that. And it may not be a lie as we may do just that.

Kate leafed over to the next day ….

He was there waiting for me by the statue of David. He is so handsome. His eyes are so warm, the colour of chestnuts and edged with long dark lashes that match his almost black hair that falls over one eye and refuses to stay back as he brushes it away with his hand or a toss of his head. I like that he is not too tall and he has such style no matter what the occasion. Thankfully he speaks good English although I would not care if he spoke none at all. I am able to understand some Italian now but not confident enough to speak much at all.

We went to the Uffizi so I will not have to lie to Aunt Issy and then we walked along the river to a small bar where he ordered prosecco to celebrate our first date. I think I'm in love!

Kate looked up from the diary. So Hettie found romance and eager to find out more turned the page to the next entry.

It is difficult to get away again for a day or two as Aunt Issy has so many things organised that I'm not able to

The Diarist

extricate myself easily. I do not think I should tell her anything yet. She will want to start organising that as well and as much as I love her I couldn't bear it. I need a distraction, a reason to go out on my own so she won't become suspicious.

I shall tell her I have decided to have Italian lessons and that I have met someone who has agreed to teach me. It would not be a total lie. Now I have a plan.

The next few pages were blank and Kate took the opportunity to pause and reflect on her earlier meeting with George. Her embarrassment had mellowed and aware of how little he had divulged about himself, reading the diaries began to feel like an intrusion into his privacy.

A large grey cloud passed obscuring the sun and Kate gathered her things from the table and went inside, amazed how quickly the afternoon had passed. There had been no sight or sound of Annie and she thought that Ben must be home by now otherwise she would certainly have been knocking at the door to ask about her lunch with George. She could have done with her company. She had a need to share her thoughts but there was only Annie who knew about it and she was not ready to share it with anyone else just yet.

She had not long concluded the thought when there was a knock at the front door. She got up slowly, half wanting to ignore it. She opened the door and a shadow of Annie stood there, pale-faced, red-eyed and sniffling.

"Annie, what is the matter, come in," she said and ushered her into the kitchen.

"I'm sorry Kate, I didn't know …."

"Look, sit down, I'll put the kettle on or would you like something stronger?"

"Thanks, think I'd better stick to tea though," Annie said forcing a half smile.

Kate made the tea and sat at the table with Annie. "Now, what's happened?"

"Oh Kate, I feel so foolish. I mean, it's probably nothing but I can't help thinking ….. and I've got myself all worked up and …."

"It's ok, take a deep breath and tell me from the beginning." Kate breathed deeply by way of encouragement.

"It …. oh dear," Annie sniffed then took a tissue from her sleeve and blew her nose. "It was this morning, I was getting everything ready for Ben coming home and he rang, not to say that he was on his way but to say that he wasn't coming home."

"What do you mean, not coming home?"

"That's it, that's what he said. So I asked him the same thing. Oh Kate, it was so unexpected." she said between more sniffs. "He said he needed some space, some time away. So I asked if there was someone else, you know, that was the first thing in my mind but he said no, it was nothing like that. He just said it wasn't me, it was him and he just needed some time to sort himself out. Oh Kate, I don't know what to do …"

Kate looked at her friend wondering how she could best help her and reached out and put her hand over Annie's arm.

"Is that all he said? Did he say where he's going or anything?"

"Er yes. A friend has said he can use his place while he's away and ….. oh, I can't bear it if he leaves."

"Oh Annie, I'm so sorry but it doesn't sound as if that's what he's saying …."

" I don't know Kate, I don't know anything anymore. I thought everything was good between us, I mean it was. I don't understand what's happened to change that …."

"Did he say anything else, like how long or anything like that?"

"No, not really. He just said he needed time and he had the opportunity and …. oh ….." Annie's brow creased in a deep frown. "He did say that he's not going anywhere, that it's not the end, but ……. oh, I don't know Kate, I can't help

The Diarist

thinking and ...."

Kate squeezed Annie's arm. "There you are. I know, it's so easy to imagine the worst but that's not it, is it? Look why don't you stay and have some supper then we could find a film to watch or something. How does that sound?"

"That would be lovely, thank you. As long as it's no ..."

"Stop right there," Kate said holding up her hand. "Now let me see what's in the fridge."

Annie blew her nose again as Kate went to examine the contents of the fridge. An aubergine, peppers, salad, there was always salad. She decided to roast the vegetables with some shallots and garlic cloves, make a fresh tomato sauce and serve it all with some pasta. It would take about an hour so she took out some olives in oil and garlic, and cut up some bread to keep Annie occupied in the meantime.

By the time Kate served two bowls of steaming pasta and freshly grated cheese and opened a bottle of wine, Annie was calmer and asking about her lunch with George.

"I'm sorry Kate, I've been so self absorbed with my own drama that I haven't asked how your lunch was."

"Don't worry, Annie. I don't know what to say really. It was pleasant enough. I don't know why but I told him about my trip to Italy and, oddly enough, he told me very little about himself. He did, however, give me some of Hettie's diaries to read and it seems she fell in love while she was in Florence."

"Do you think that's why she stopped looking for Charlie?"

"Mmm, I suppose it could be or maybe she just came to a dead end. Anyway, I've only read a little bit so far. Strange, it seems a bit intrusive now .... I don't know why."

"Maybe because the diaries have a home and are part of someone else's history?" Annie suggested. She looked a lot better, Kate thought, the colour had returned to her cheeks though that could be the wine and her eyes had lost the red puffiness.

"Maybe."

"So how did you leave it with him?"

"Oh, I'll let him know when I've read the diaries and he'll pick them up."

"And?" Annie said giving Kate an old-fashioned look.

"And nothing," Kate said indignantly. "Don't go fishing where there aren't any fish!"

"Ok, ok. He just sounded rather nice, that's all and...."

"And nothing. That's enough."

By the end of the evening as they said goodnight, Kate thought Annie was brighter if not her usual effervescent self.

After loading the dishwasher Kate curled up on the sofa with the diaries and continued reading.

So he has to speak to me in Italian then I can convince Aunt Issy that I am learning something. We went to the Boboli Gardens today. He is so charming and attentive I feel as if my heart might burst. He wants to take me to Rome but I don't know how I can get away. I need a plan. The thing is I am old enough to do as I please but Aunt Issy thinks I'm her responsibility and I don't want to upset her, or Uncle Vittorio, they've been so good to me. Maybe there's a trip to Rome I can say I am joining, something to do with learning Italian. I'll test the water at dinner, gradually introduce the idea.

Kate read on as Hettie, over the next few days, persuaded her aunt and uncle of the importance of her going to Rome to improve her Italian. Surprisingly, they were encouraging and thought it was a good idea that she was meeting people her own age. By the time Kate's eyes began to droop, Hettie was packing her suitcase ready for her clandestine trip.

Surrendering to the late hour, Kate went to bed hoping that whatever was going on with Annie and Ben was no more than a blip that would right itself.

6

Kate had not slept well. Thoughts of Annie and Hettie and the fragility and complexity of relationships whirled round as she tossed and turned in search of a quiet oasis. How lucky she had been with John. They had had their differences, naturally, but never anything they had not been able to resolve. Their love for each other somehow overrode any need to be right.

Unable to sleep, Kate had got up to make a hot drink and take the diaries to bed. She was disappointed that the entries were not more exciting. She had imagined Hettie as a passionate and independent young woman but this did not come across in the later entries.

She read on hoping for more than descriptions of visits to the usual tourist sites of Rome. Hettie wrote little about the man she seemed so enamoured by save for descriptions of the places he took her and the odd word here and there about his charm and attentiveness.

Kate put the books on her bedside table and within a few minutes found the elusive sleep she had been hoping for.

As she sipped her first coffee of the morning, and despite the urge to give in to a lack of energy, she decided to call Bernard and bring him up to date on the recent developments.

"A happy ending, then. That's nice," he said when they

once again sat in the two armchairs facing each other in his living room, drinking tea.

"Well so far, it would seem so. There are a few more entries I've yet to read. I just thought you'd like to know what had happened so far."

"Thank you Kate, I appreciate that. So, what else did this George have to say?"

"Like I said, not much really. I get the impression that he thinks the diaries will speak for him. We'll have to wait and see what the rest of them hold."

"When will you read them?"

"Oh, probably later or tomorrow. I don't want them to take over my life, if you know what I mean?" Kate imagined that Bernard would have stopped everything and read them from cover to cover in one sitting.

"Yes of course, you're right Kate. Very sensible."

"Well," Kate began, not sure whether she appreciated him referring to her as sensible, she hoped it was not to be equated with boring or maybe it was just her tiredness. "You'll be the first to know Bernard if I unearth any treasures."

They both laughed and, as usual, Bernard tried to persuade her to have some cake and this time she gave in to a piece of lemon drizzle cake.

"Lovely cake Bernard, one of Betty's?"

"Can't keep up with her you know," he said rolling his eyes. "So will you see this George again?"

"Yes, he said when I've finished with the diaries he'll come to collect them. Seems he's working on a project nearby."

"Oh yes, what is it he does?"

"You know I don't know, he didn't say." Kate said and remembered the business card George had given her but not the details.

"Sounds like he didn't say much," Bernard said with a snort.

The Diarist

"No I suppose he didn't but then I didn't ask."

"S'pose we'll just have to see what else these little books reveal then."

Kate finished her cake and stood to leave. She promised to call Bernard if the diaries divulged any more and, after thanking him, said goodbye and began her walk back to the cottage.

It was a beautiful morning, the sun was already high, and Kate decided to take the long route home by walking round the village. As she passed the village stores she met Annie as she was leaving the shop.

"Oh, hi Kate," Annie said looking a little sheepish. "Run out of milk," she added holding up the carton of milk she had just bought. "Must dash."

She rushed off down the road before Kate could say anything and, somewhat perplexed, she continued on her walk. No doubt Annie would explain when she was ready.

Back in her kitchen she looked at the diaries now in a small pile on the table. She was not sure if she could read any more right now, it was beginning to feel like mental indigestion.

There were so many other things she was trying to make sense of and whilst this was an interesting distraction she felt pursued by it. Over the last two years, as she became accustomed to being on her own, her days had lacked any spark of interest and a blanket of apathy had enveloped her. It was shortly before finding the cottage that she had started to pick up the threads of her life again. That all seemed so far removed from what was happening now.

With a sigh she opened the fridge in search of something for lunch. There was a bowl of pasta left over from last night's supper, that would do. As she reheated it she thought of Annie and wondered what could have happened between then and her running off this morning.

Half an hour later, mug of tea in hand, she wandered

aimlessly round the garden. There was a small wood and iron bench in the shade of the cottage and she sat there hoping for inspiration. As she sipped her tea her thoughts slowed. She remembered how her garden had always worked its magic. It was a place where, over the years, she had found solace, peace and inspiration and this garden was no different.

She closed her eyes and a wave of appreciation flowed through her as she let go of the need to control the recent changes that she now realised had obscured her sense of belonging. A belonging to herself, her home, her family. She sat for a while enjoying the silence, punctuated by occasional birdsong and the humming of a nearby bee.

By the time she went inside again she was able to sit down at the table, open the diaries from a different, and calmer perspective. She opened the one she had been reading at the bookmarked page and continued to read.

The first few entries continued to describe Hettie's dates with Giorgio. Ah, now he had a name. Hettie was besotted but then there was an abrupt change in the tone.

Why why why? How could I have been so foolish? How could I have got it so wrong? It seems he doesn't love me at all and I feel like a stupid lovesick cow. How could he, how could he deceive me like that? Oh God, I feel so foolish. I can't stay here and yet I can't bear the thought of going home to lick my wounds. He didn't even have the courtesy to tell me, he sent a note, a note! Gone, gone to America. I just do not understand.

Oh, so not such a happy ending then, Kate thought as she turned the page to the next entry.

I have told Aunt Issy that it is time for me to go home and have booked my train ticket for the day after tomorrow. She was very sweet in that she did not ask any questions, only saying I must do whatever is right for me. I'm not sure I know what is right for me anymore. In fact, I'm not sure I know myself at all!

There were more soul searching entries in the same vein before and after Hettie's journey back to London. Determined not to expose the pain she felt in her heart, she launched herself back into the social life she had left behind. She must have been an attractive woman, Kate noted, as she read about the round of futile dates amid the pining for what could have been. Kate read on.

I am thinking of getting a job, I have to do something. Ma, of course, thinks I am mad and should be looking for a husband. Why on earth would I want to do that, especially after that last fiasco, not that Ma knows anything about it. She keeps arranging dinners where these single men arrive alone and are usually seated next to me. It's all so embarrassing. The only man I've been able to have a decent conversation with is Charlie's dear friend Edward. I have known him forever and after Charlie, well, we always stayed in touch and he listens. Maybe that's why I told him. First about Charlie and then, a little bit about Giorgio. It's good to have someone to talk to, someone I can trust.

Kate turned the page.

I think I must have eaten something last night that upset me. God I feel awful. Another boring dinner with another boring young man selected by mother. Has she nothing better to do, I'm no longer eighteen and am quite capable of finding a man should I ever decide to do so ever again! Don't think I will. I had lunch with Edward and he said that his mother is exactly the same, always inviting available young women in the hope he will settle down with one of them. I think they live in another world and do not want to move with the times. Maybe I'll take a job as an artist's model that would show them.

Kate laughed as she turned to the next entry.

Another day of this awful sickness. Maybe it is some kind of stomach thing though I don't know anyone else who has it. It's a month now since I left Florence and not a word from Giorgio. Not that I thought there would be and if there was I'm sure Aunt Issy would have passed it on. I no longer want to die I think I now want to kill him. How could he? Edward thinks it better this way. Imagine, he said, if you found out later what a cad he is. I suppose he's right but it doesn't make me feel any less cross! I do hope I feel better tomorrow.

There was a knock at the door and Kate closed the diary and went to answer it, slightly annoyed at being disturbed. She opened the door to Annie who stood there holding a bunch of flowers.

"Annie," Kate smiled, "come in."

"No, I won't thanks. I just wanted to apologise for rushing off earlier," she said as she handed Kate the flowers. "I will explain but not right now if you don't mind. I'll call as soon as I …. er, well … soon."

"Of course, Annie. Look, if there's anything I can do?"

"No, no, it's fine. Thanks. I'll call," she forced a smile, turned and left.

Kate watched her walk down the path before closing the door. What was that all about? What is going on with everyone? Always more questions.

Back in the kitchen she returned to the diaries. She turned to the bookmarked page. There were two or three blank pages followed by a few short entries.

Oh dear, this is not what I expected. Wrong, wrong,

wrong! What will I do? How could I not have noticed! It was so embarrassing, fainting in the haberdashery department in Marshall and Snelgrove, of all places. Ma came to fetch me and called the doctor who said he was certain I was pregnant. A baby, I'm going to have a baby. Oh God, what am I going to do?

Ah, so that was it, Kate thought. Could that be baby George, and if so his father must be the Italian man Hettie was seeing in Florence. She read on to the next entry.

Ma has suggested I go to one of those beastly mother and baby homes and give my baby away. At least she has managed not to say I told you so, but I can't bear her organising my life and the future of my baby like that. I don't know what to do. I think I could manage with the little income I have but it would be, oh it doesn't bear thinking about.

Poor Hettie, Kate thought as she turned the page. It would have been so different then.

I've been talking to Edward, he's so kind and understanding. He was so sweet when I told him what happened in Florence. At least I have one person I can talk to who does not judge me. Oh dear, I still don't know what to do. One minute I don't want this to be happening and another I just go all soppy at the thought of it all. I feel like a rubber band being stretched to its limits.

There were a few more blank pages before Hettie continued.

How things can change. Edward has been an absolute darling. I know he's always had a sort of soft spot for me but this, it just came out of the blue. We were having lunch in that nice little restaurant in Chelsea and he said he had the perfect solution and then proposed! I know he had a sort of crush on me when we were younger but this! He said to think about it before I answered. I'm thinking, and thinking that it might, just might work. I'll see him tomorrow.

I said yes! It will have to be before Christmas of course and that does not leave much time. I told Ma and she just shrugged and sighed and then asked if I'd had any thoughts of a venue. I suppose I can't blame her, it's not really what she would have wanted. I am beginning to feel a bit excited about it now and happy, yes happy. I think it will work out just fine.

Kate closed the diary and thought about Hettie's words. She noted that she never mentioned her father and wondered what had happened to him. Had he also been killed in the war? How awful for Hettie's mother if that was the case, losing a husband and a son. She understood very well the pain of losing a husband but could not contemplate the despair of losing a son.

She shook her head and stood, answering a need to move. She looked at the clock and, surprised to see it was after seven, decided on a quick supper and some mindless television.

However, the diaries called her and unable to resist she continued to read. Again the entries were short and covered the preparations for the wedding, followed by the Christmas and New Year celebrations. Kate would have liked more detail say, of Hettie's thoughts and feelings and wondered why she bothered keeping so many diaries if they only touched the surface of her life.

She selected the next diary and read on into the following year to find Hettie happily reconciled to her life with Edward and her flourishing pregnancy. Then came an appropriately early birth, followed by details of the baby's first few months of life. All seemed well and Kate opened the next diary which was written in much the same vein.

Kate scanned the pages until the word Italy jumped out of the page and she paused to read more slowly.

Aunt Issy has invited us to stay with her and Uncle Vittorio. Edward has not been to Florence and I wonder how I will feel going back there. I am happy with my life here and absolutely in love with little George. Ma of course will not join us. I don't know why she hates Italy so or maybe it's just the travelling, anyway she's quite adamant. Nevertheless it will be strange to go back.

Kate flicked forward to see if the diary revealed anything of interest but, as before, Hettie's writing was limited to describing the beauty of the places she visited and odd references to little George and anything else was left to the imagination. Kate did enjoy reading the accounts of Florence, she could see the places in her mind's eye, some more familiar than others. She tried to suppress a growing longing to return to the city that had touched her so deeply and now called her back.

7

Kate was in an industrious mood, determined to get on with things. First, she emailed George saying she had read the diaries and was happy for him to collect them. Then she went through the post she had put to one side and methodically made two piles, one she binned, and the other she went through, dealt with and filed where necessary until the kitchen table was clear.

She looked at the sparse contents of the fridge and sat down to make a shopping list when her mobile rang. She answered it without looking to see who it was and was surprised to hear Simonetta's voice.

"*Buongiorno*, Kate. You are well?"

"Er, yes thank you, how are you?" It all felt a bit stilted.

"*Bene, bene, grazie. Allora,* we have been talking, that is Umberto, Giancarlo and myself. They have made more enquiries on your behalf and it may be time for you to visit again."

"Oh," Kate said, unsure how to respond then remembered the email from Umberto. "I did have an email from Umberto but I haven't really had much chance to think about it."

"Kate, I think you will find the time is right. Please give it some thought. Of course, you can stay with Umberto and Claudia. We would all like to see you again, so please do not be English about it."

The Diarist

Kate sensed Simonetta's smile as she said this.

"Er, yes I will, of course."

"*Bene.* Let Umberto know and one of us will pick you up from the airport."

"Yes, thank you." Kate said, again at a loss as to what else to say.

"*Ciao, a presto.*" Simonetta said and disconnected the call.

Kate looked at her phone as she tried to make sense of the call. She knew Simonetta could be abrupt and some things got lost in translation but she struggled to understand why it was suddenly so important for her to go now.

She opened her laptop, thinking there could be no harm in looking at flights, and found that George had replied to her email. He suggested calling in later that afternoon or tomorrow morning. Kate sent a quick reply suggesting four o'clock that afternoon, hoping that would be convenient. At least that would be one thing out of the way.

While she was looking at flights George replied confirming he would see her at four. She picked up her shopping list and decided now was probably the best time to do it.

As she walked down the path towards the gate she saw Annie who stopped and waved.

"You going out?" Annie called.

"Yes, just to the supermarket. You ok?"

"Er, yes thanks." Annie attempted a smile.

Kate thought she looked pale again and certainly not her usual effervescent self.

"Look I've got to rush as I've got someone coming round this afternoon, maybe we can catch up this evening? A glass of wine about seven?"

"Oh, I'm not sure if I can, ok if I let you know later?"

"Of course, just give me a call." Kate said as she got in the car. She looked in the rear view mirror and watched Annie return to her cottage. A frown of concern creased

Kate's forehead as she drove off.

Kate managed to get through the afternoon without interruption or incident. She had put the diaries on the kitchen table ready for George to take away, unsure whether she was happy to see them go or not.

He arrived shortly after four and was politely apologetic for his tardiness. Kate made tea and offered biscuits, suddenly eager to see the diaries go.

"So you now know my story." George said once the usual pleasantries were out of the way.

"Yes, I suppose I do." Kate replied, uncertain how she should respond to having such intimate knowledge of someone she had only just met. "Have you always known?"

"No, I haven't. It was only when my mother went into the home and I was going through her things that I discovered the diaries and, as you can see, the truth."

"It must have been a shock to find out you're half Italian when you have spent your life believing you're English."

"Indeed, but it did answer a few nagging questions."

Kate thought he seemed relaxed to be sharing what she deemed to be such personal information.

"I see."

"Sadly, I have not been able to speak to my mother about it and my aunt is no longer with us, so all I have are the diaries and they don't reveal a great deal."

"No, I suppose they don't." Kate said looking into her empty teacup. "More tea?"

"Thank you." He moved his cup towards her. "Will you be going back to Florence?"

"Er, I don't know. I mean I've thought about it but that's as far as I've got." she said, disconcerted by the change of subject.

"I just wondered if you were going to follow up any leads on Charles?"

"Well, I haven't found much to go on really," she

The Diarist

replied, then remembering Umberto's email asked, "I don't suppose you have a photo of him do you?"

"Oh, I'm sure there's one somewhere in one of the albums. I'll fish one out for you if that would help."

"I think it might, though I'm not promising anything."

"I'll have a look when I get home and let you know." he said, running his fingers through his hair. "I wonder ... would you like to have dinner tomorrow evening? If there is a photo I could bring it with me and ..."

"Er, thank you but ...."

"Please, I would like to talk more but I have to be back soon for a meeting. I could pick you up around seven?" He suggested, tilting his head to one side.

"Very well," Kate acquiesced. She smiled and, not wanting to seem ungracious, added, "thank you."

He stood, picking up the diaries.

"I wonder what my mother would say if she knew the effect her little diaries had ...." he left the sentence unfinished as he walked to front door.

They said their goodbyes and Kate watched him walk to his car, thoughtful of what he had said about the effect of the diaries.

She returned to the kitchen and cleared the table before sitting down to call Annie.

"Hi Annie, it's Kate. I was wondering if you'd like to come over a bit earlier. I'm free now if you are."

"Oh, I don't know, Kate. I'm not really good company and ....."

"Or I can come to you, if you prefer." Kate said ignoring Annie's resistance.

"Erm ..... ok, if you don't mind. Can you give me ten minutes?"

"Of course, see you then."

Ten minutes later Kate knocked on Annie's door, frozen pizza and bottle of wine in hand.

"Hi, come in," Annie said.

Kate followed her through to the kitchen and handed over the bottle of wine and pizza.

"Thanks, but you didn't need to ….."

"It's fine and I did. I wasn't sure if you needed feeding; now where's the corkscrew?"

"Oh, it's ...er … here," Annie said handing it to Kate. "I'll get some glasses."

Kate recognised the shock she sensed in Annie's demeanour, the hollow emptiness and exhaustion. She bristled slightly at the memory and wondered how she could best support her friend. Probably giving her the opportunity to talk about it would be a start.

"Here," Annie said returning with two glasses that she put on the table.

Kate poured some wine into each glass and handing one to Annie, raised hers in a toast.

"To better times?"

"Yes, to better times," Annie mirrored but less enthusiastically. "Let's go and sit through here where it's more comfortable."

Annie curled up in a corner of the sofa and Kate sank into one of two large armchairs.

"So …. want to talk about it?" Kate asked in a quiet voice.

"I, er, don't know if I can," Annie said and fished up her sleeve for a tissue that she sniffed into.

Kate waited.

"Well, there's not really much to tell. Like I said Ben said he needed space and ..." she paused and sniffed again. "It was just so sudden, y'know, so unexpected. I had no idea."

"What did he say?" Kate encouraged her to continue.

"Not much more than that at first." Annie took a slurp of wine. "I asked if there was someone else and he said no of course not, he just needed some time." She paused and looked into her glass. "Anyway, he called again. It was just before I saw you at the shop. I couldn't stop as it was all going round in my head and ..."

"There's no need to explain." Kate said gently. "Go on."

"Oh yes, he rang again and said he was sorry and that the last thing he wanted to do was upset me. Bit late by then. I'm still not sure I understand but I think something must have happened while he was away filming. He just said that he got to thinking about things, about us, about life, where we're going, that kind of stuff and needed time to work things out for himself. So," Annie let out the breath she had been holding. "he's looking after a friend's house while he's away. It's in Suffolk somewhere. For six weeks. Says, it's not me, it's him. Still loves me. Just needs time." Annie looked at Kate, wide eyed before lifting and finishing her glass of wine.

"I see." Before Kate could formulate what to say Annie continued.

"Said he'll still pay for things as normal, that I shouldn't worry about money. I don't know, Kate. Don't know what to do, don't know what I can do. I just don't understand how ... how he could suddenly... I mean he must have known, y'know, been thinking about it .... why didn't he say something?"

"Maybe, maybe he couldn't. Look, let's put the pizza in the oven. When did you last eat?"

"Oh er ... yes, you're right, I should eat. Come on, I'll see if I can find some salad, if not there might be some in the garden. Thanks Kate, it's good to be able to talk."

And talk they did as they shared the pizza and more wine. After they exhausted the subject of Ben they turned to Kate, Hettie's diaries and George, Kate overcame her natural reluctance and told Annie about George's visit and his invitation to dinner.

"Well, he's looks very nice, you could do a lot worse,"

Annie teased.

"Annie!" Kate feigned shock and was happy to see her friend emerging from her cave a little. "I'm not looking for anything like that at the moment. Really."

"Well, I'm just saying," Annie said with a shrug."I shall look forward to hearing all about it. I wonder where he'll take you?"

"Stop it, Annie." Kate smiled, knowing her friend was not serious. "I think I'd better go, but if you need anything you'll let me know won't you?"

"Of course, and thank you but I feel a lot better now, and do let me know how you get on."

"Yes, yes, yes ….. goodnight Annie." Kate said over her shoulder as she walked down the path.

The Diarist

8

The next day seven o'clock arrived quicker than Kate would have wished. She had lost count of the number of times she had changed clothes and had just finished tidying them away when she heard a knock at the door. She had decided on linen trousers in a soft teal colour, a cream linen, collarless blouse and a short, cotton cardigan that matched the trousers. She wore her hair loose and added a deep coral pendant that contrasted against the cream of her blouse. She hoped she had found the right balance of not too smart or casual.

She opened the door to find George holding a bunch of pink roses which she accepted turning to hide any blushes as she said she would put them in water.

As they walked to his car a few minutes later she noticed that he also appeared to have struck the balance between smart and casual. In dark grey trousers and an open necked soft white linen shirt she thought he looked very stylish.

After a short drive George pulled into the car park of an old pub that looked as if it had been serving the village for centuries. Soft sandstone walls and mullioned windows climbed by yellow roses gave it a timeless charm. Inside however, it was light, open and modern. George led Kate through to the restaurant which was smart and elegantly furnished. They were greeted and shown to a table by the window overlooking a well stocked garden, partly laid to lawn between wide borders and rose arbours that led to a lily filled pond. It appeared to be private and George explained that it was only for the use of guests. Over the years it had transformed from the village pub to a now well known restaurant with rooms, although the original bars had been retained and were still frequented by the locals.

A waiter brought menus and asked if they wished to order drinks first. George ordered two glasses of prosecco after confirming Kate's agreement. She fiddled with the corner of the large damask napkin as George reassured her as to the quality of the food. A waiter brought their wine, olives and bread, and another took their food order.

Kate wished she could feel as relaxed as George appeared. Words, beginnings of sentences crossed her mind but she failed to utter them. He smiled and asked her to remind him how long she had lived in the cottage.

"Ah, so you have not had much time to explore." he said, hoping to put her at ease.

"No, not really," Kate relaxed a little as she breathed out. "It wasn't long before I went to Italy and now, well I've only been back a few days and ..."

"And you haven't had chance to find your place here?"

"Er, yes something like that I suppose," she said surprised by his perspicacity.

Well, if I can be of help. I have been around this area most of my life. You said you lived in Bath?"

"Yes, for many years."

"What made you move here, if you don't mind me asking?"

"No, not at all," Kate replied feeling herself relax a little more as the conversation progressed and probably helped by the wine. "After my husband died I found the house too big for me on my own and then I saw a photo of the cottage, and I er ... I suppose, I sort of fell in love with it."

"I'm sorry, I did not mean to ...."

"It's fine, you didn't...."

The Diarist

"Children?"

"Yes, my daughter lives in Bristol and my son is teaching in the Far East. You?"

"I have a daughter. She's married and lives in London."

Their first course arrived and they continued telling each other about their children and how they wished they saw more of them. He spoke briefly of his marriage and subsequent divorce when his wife met someone else.

Kate took the opportunity to look at him more closely as they spoke. His face had a symmetry that she found appealing and she wondered why she had not noticed it before.

He told her he was an architect and working on an eco-housing project not far from the village. They exchanged thoughts on ecology and environmental issues. Kate wished she could do more, be more conscious in her choices and she experienced a twinge of envy that he was involved in such innovative work.

By the time the waiter brought their coffees Kate was still no wiser as to why he had asked her out. As the end of the evening drew closer she felt an uncertainty and tension creep back. She did not want to misread his intentions and make a fool of herself nor was she sure she was ready for anything more.

It turned out that she had no reason to worry as his behaviour was impeccable and Kate was left feeling embarrassed by her own thoughts. When he walked her to her front door, he merely said how much he had enjoyed the evening and hoped they could do it again sometime soon.

It was just as he was leaving that he remembered the photos he had brought with him.

"I'm sorry I meant to give them to you earlier," he said as he took two photos from his wallet. "One is Charlie in his uniform and the other is my mother and him before the war. They were just children but I thought you might like to see it."

"Thank you, would you mind if I made copies?" she said her mind racing forwards towards Italy.

"Of course not, I hope they are of some help."

"Yes, thank you. And for a lovely evening."

"It was a pleasure, Kate. I'll be in touch."

He turned and left. Kate went inside holding the photos, thoughts whirling of the evening, of him and the possibility of returning to Florence.

The next morning Annie, who seemed more her usual self and eager to hear about Kate's evening, was sitting at her kitchen table while Kate made coffee and warmed croissants.

"So," Annie encouraged, "how did it go?"

"It was a lovely evening, Annie. We went to that place, oh what do they call it ….. I don't remember the name but he said it's a restaurant with rooms."

"Did he indeed!"

"Yes, he did," Kate said ignoring her. "It was very nice, the food was great and he was good company. He also brought a couple of photos, one of Charles in his uniform and one of Hettie and him before the war. I said I'd take copies and return them to him."

"So you're going to see him again?"

"Well, yes I suppose I am." Kate put the coffee and croissants on the table. "Help yourself."

"Thanks," Annie said and poured coffee into a mug and, helping herself to a croissant, added, "we can dunk them French style."

Kate smiled, happy that her friend was more cheerful.

"You can or would you like butter and jam?"

"Ooo, no thanks, this is fine – they're fattening enough on their own."

"I don't think you need to worry, Annie." Kate said raising an eyebrow in the direction of Annie's petite gamine figure.

"Well, you know what I mean, can't be too careful and

The Diarist

all that." Annie shrugged her shoulders. "So, is that it then, a lovely evening?"

"There's not much more to say. He's an architect, divorced and has a daughter who's married and lives in London. He's good company and …."

"And?" Annie egged her on.

"Oh stop it, Annie. And nothing." Kate said with good humour. "Here, have a look at the photos." She reached for them from the dresser and passed them to Annie.

Annie giggled at the dated images.

"Do you think the one of Charles will be of any help? Will you go back to Florence?"

"I don't know," Kate sighed. "It's not really anything to do with me. I mean it's not my family. It's just that I did have an email from Umberto asking me if I could take a photo when I next visited."

"Well, there you are then, how can you not?"

"Annie, I've only just got back!"

"So?" It was Annie's turn to raise an eyebrow. "I can keep an eye on things here if that's what you're worried about."

"Oh thanks Annie, but …."

"No buts, if you want to go then you should go."

"Ok, ok, I'll think about it." Kate raised her hands in surrender. "What about you?" she then ventured gently.

"Ah," Annie said leaning back and looking at her hands where they rested on the table in front of her. "I had a text from Ben this morning asking if we could meet, talk. I'm going to see him tomorrow, in London."

"Good, Annie, that's good." Kate said and nodded her head.

"I hope so Kate, I hope so." she said in a quiet voice.

"If I can do anything ….."

"Thanks."

After Annie had gone Kate opened her laptop and, once

again, looked at flights to Pisa. Maybe she would go for just a few days, a long weekend. She made notes of dates, times and prices from Bristol and also from Gatwick after discovering she could fly direct to an airport just outside Florence.

Next she took a deep breath and emailed Umberto saying that she now had a photo and asking when would be a convenient time to visit. Determined to keep going she opened her bag and took out Giancarlo's card and sent a brief email explaining that she had written to Umberto and hoped to visit again soon.

As she pressed 'send' she let out a long held breath and prayed she was doing the right thing. Before she could think more about it the phone rang.

"Hi mum."

"Ems," Kate said with a big grin at the sound of her daughter's voice. "How are you?"

"I'm good, how are you? I'm sorry I haven't been in touch but you know how it is....."

"Oh, don't be, I'm sorry I ….."

"No worries mum. What have you been up to?"

"Oh, this and that," Kate said, realising there was so much she had not shared with her daughter.

"Well, I just wanted to let you know that I'm going on holiday. I'm going out to Bali and thought I could meet up with David on the way. I know it's all a bit last minute and ..."

"That's great, Ems," Kate said, sincerely happy she was doing something other than work. "Be sure to give him a big hug from me."

"I will, mum. And thanks."

"What for?"

"Oh just being my mum." Emma said affectionately. "Look how about lunch before I go? That little place we used to go to near Milsom Street?"

"Er, the Italian?"

The Diarist

"Yes, then you can tell me all about your holiday."
"Ok let me know which day's best for you."
"I'll text you later. Love you."
"Love you too."

Before she had time to think which day would be best for her an email arrived from Umberto. It said how happy he and Claudia were that she would be returning and she should book the best flight for her as between them they would be able to pick her up from the airport.

Kate felt she had just stumbled on to a new roller coaster and went in search of food, her usual comforter, and in any event it was time for lunch. A small bowl of *spaghetti peperoncino* and salad gave her chance to calm and order her thoughts.

She picked up the piece of paper where she had written the flight details and added a few more things to do. First, she would call Bernard, tell him of her meeting with George and her possible trip to Florence. Next, she would book her flights, or should she wait until she had heard from Giancarlo or at least spoken with Emma, and what about George.

As the thoughts spilled out she became aware that it was her decision when she should go. Her imagined dependency on anyone else was a delaying tactic, a way of putting off taking responsibility for herself, a habit formed in all her years married to John and now no longer available to her.

Chastened by the thought, she looked again at the dates and prices of flights. Thursday, she decided, was the best day. Eager now to get it done she entered her details to fly from Bristol and return the following Monday. Feeling more confident each time she pressed 'enter', she decided to drive herself to the airport and booked parking to coincide with her flights.

She had no sooner finished than there was a knock at

the door. Bernard she thought and was still surprised to see him standing there when she opened the door.

"Hello Kate, I hope you don't mind but I was hoping you might be able to help me out with some of this cake," he said handing her a square plastic box.

"You'd better come in Bernard, I'll put the kettle on."

"Er, I don't want you to go to any trouble now …."

"It's no trouble. In any case I was about to ring you. Come in."

Bernard followed her to the kitchen and sat down at the table.

"You sure I'm not disturbing you?" he said looking at the laptop and paper strewn across the table.

"Not at all. Now, builder's or Earl Grey?"

Kate made the tea, and cut the cake before bringing Bernard up to date with events since she had last seen him.

"So, you're going back then?"

"Yes, in fact you're the first person I've told. I'd just finished booking my flights when you arrived."

"I think that's just great, Kate. I mean it seems a shame not to and you never know what you might learn."

"Nothing too awful I hope, Bernard." She said thinking more of her father than what she might learn, if anything, about Charles.

"I'm sure you'll have a wonderful time," he said, reassuringly patting her hand. "Now, you must let me know if there's anything I can do."

"Thank you," Kate smiled. "I'll only be away four days."

"Well, you only have to ask. When do you go?"

"Thursday," Kate said, hardly believing that she had actually done it. "Back Monday."

After a brief discussion about the garden, Bernard said goodbye and Kate was left alone again. She went back to her laptop and emailed her flight details to Umberto, relieved to be in control of something however tenuous. Within a few

The Diarist

minutes he replied saying that both he and Claudia were able to meet her and he would let Simonetta and Giancarlo know of her arrival.

It was early evening when a text arrived from Emma suggesting lunch on Tuesday. Kate replied confirming she would see her at the restaurant. She wrote it in her diary, feeling the need to start mapping her week. As it would take up most of her day, driving to Bath, lunch and then home again, she would have to be organised if she was going to be ready to leave on Thursday and she started another list.

She was just sitting down to a supper of fennel *frittata* and salad when she heard a car door close followed by the front door opening and closing next door a minute or two later. It must be Annie back from London she thought and hoped her meeting with Ben had gone well. She had just finished the last mouthful of her supper when the phone rang.

"Hello."

"*Ciao,* Kate. It's Giancarlo."

"Oh, hello, how are you?" She said melting a little at the sound of his voice.

"*Bene, bene.* Umberto tells me you will be arriving on Thursday and as I have a meeting in Lucca in the morning I have suggested I could collect you from the airport, if that is alright with you."

"Er, yes," she stumbled over her words. "Of course, thank you, if you're sure it's no trouble."

"It is never a trouble, Kate. I look forward to seeing you again. Until Thursday."

"Ok, I'll see you then."

After they had said goodbye Kate put down the phone and sat very still looking at it. His presence lingered as she replayed his words in her mind. A mixture of excitement, fear and guilt vied for attention. It was settled then, Thursday she would be in Florence once again.

ITALY

1

Thursday arrived in haste and it was a breathless Kate who rushed to the check-in desk to find there was still a queue as she almost collapsed at the end of it. The traffic had been more of a problem than she had anticipated and she then had to locate the correct car park and book in the car as the minutes sped by and her nerves became more jangled. Thankfully the queue moved quickly and she sailed through security to the boarding gate with time to spare.

At last she was able to slow down and gather herself ready for the flight. As she waited she went through a mental checklist confirming that she had turned everything off that needed to be off, packed all that she needed, told Annie to help herself to anything in the fridge, left her a bottle of wine as a token thank you and she now just had to text Emma as promised.

It was hard to believe that it was only the day before yesterday that they had had lunch in Bath. Emma had been in good spirits, excited about her holiday and surprised that Kate was returning to Italy so quickly. Kate tried to remember how much she had told Emma about the first trip, only to realise that she had said nothing about her father's fall. Since it had not been serious she decided it better not to mention it now. They had made various promises about keeping in touch and Kate now fulfilled one of them by sending a text to say she had arrived safely at the airport and was waiting to board the plane.

Then there was Annie who, to Kate's relief, was more her chirpy self since her meeting with Ben. Not that anything had changed, he was not coming home but they had talked and Annie was now able to find a modicum of understanding and patience.

She was just thinking of George, whom she had emailed to say she had copied the photos and would be in touch when she returned, when the boarding gate opened. She stood, picked up her bag, and made sure her passport and boarding pass were ready as she joined the queue.

Soon the plane was in the air. As it rose so did Kate's spirit and she smiled as she watched the ground diminish to an earthy, patchwork quilt below. The sun was bright and she turned her attention away from the window and wondered what the next few days would bring.

About two and a half hours later she had collected her case and was walking out of the departure gate at Pisa when she saw Giancarlo waving to her. She felt her heart skip a beat and straightened to her full diminutive height as she walked towards him.

"*Ciao, ciao,*" he greeted her with a kiss to each cheek. "You had a good flight?"

"Yes, thank you."

"Would you like to eat something before we go?"

No, I'm fine thanks, I had something on the plane."

He led her to the exit and as she walked out into the sun-drenched street, she found the intensity of the heat suffocating and the sun blinding after the air conditioned concourse. Giancarlo watched her pause a moment to adjust.

"It is a little warmer than when you were here last. Come, the car is this way and it has air conditioning."

"Yes, I didn't realise ….."

"It's suddenly hot for the time of year, I hope you'll not find it too uncomfortable. You can understand why everything closes and everyone goes to the sea in August when it is really hot."

Kate absorbed what was becoming a familiar landscape as they drove to Umberto and Claudia's villa. The tall sentinels of cypress trees and the architectural umbrella pines that lined the horizon, edged a valley, protected a villa. The gentle roll of the hills with villas dotted here and there, and bright red poppies that filled the occasional field bordering the road. A chaos of signs indicated shops and businesses as they passed through the towns, and it soon felt as if she had not been away.

They talked about the intervening period briefly and Giancarlo, as before, had anecdotes of places and people he knew along the way. Kate enjoyed listening to his mellow accented voice and by the time they reached the villa she felt more relaxed.

As they drove into the courtyard, Umberto and Claudia were there to greet them, giving Kate a particularly enthusiastic welcome.

"Please, take a few minutes to arrive and join us for coffee on the terrace when you are ready." Claudia suggested as she showed her to her room.

"Thank you, I won't be long." Kate said as she took in the panoramic view. A valley rich in woodland, olive groves, vineyards and statuary cypress trees was edged by distant, mauve mountains on either side. I think I'll enjoy being here, she thought.

Kate unpacked a few things and went downstairs to join the others who were waiting for her on the terrace.

"Ah Kate, perfect timing, the coffee is just ready, and see, I have hot milk for you." Claudia indicated the small jug on the table as Kate sat down. "Are you hungry, can I get you something to eat?"

"No thank you Claudia, I had something on the plane,"

Kate said as she absorbed a new sense of belonging, of being in the right place, happy she had decided to come here.

Claudia poured the coffee into little cups and a slightly larger one for Kate so she could add her milk.

"*Allora,*" Umberto said gathering everyone's attention. "I thought, depending on your schedule Giancarlo, we might have a short siesta and then take Kate for a walk in the woods before supper?"

"Yes, I can do that."

"*Bene,* then tomorrow we can maybe go into Arezzo. I think you will like Arezzo, Kate. We can have lunch and then show you around, if you would like to, of course?"

"Yes, thank you, I'd love to," Kate enthused, excited by the prospect of something new.

"I'm sure you will enjoy it, Kate," Claudia smiled. "It has an interesting history dating back to the Etruscans and if you like the frescoes, there are some wonderful examples by Piero della Francesca in the church."

"It sounds wonderful."

"What about you, Giancarlo, are you able to join us?" invited Claudia.

"I'm busy in the morning but I'd be happy to join you for lunch."

Bene, we can keep in touch by phone and let you know where we are." Claudia smiled, satisfied with the arrangement.

"*Allora,* I'm sure Kate would like some time to rest after her journey, let's have a short siesta and meet again in an hour?" Umberto said, taking charge again. "Giancarlo, make yourself at home, you can use the other guest room if you wish, it will be cooler."

"*Grazie,* I will."

They each went their separate ways and Kate was happy to have some time to herself to process the events of the day. She lay down on the bed but sleep eluded her as she revisited the drive from the airport with Giancarlo who was now joining them for lunch the next day. She remonstrated with herself that she was here to find out more about Charles and her father's family, not being a tourist. But what could one day matter and Umberto and Claudia were only being hospitable. Even so she would have to ensure the days did not slip away too easily.

The hour passed quickly and, after freshening up, Kate joined the others on the terrace which thankfully was shaded from the late afternoon sun.

"It will be cooler in the woods and we don't have to go far, but it will give you a sense of the place, Kate." Umberto said as they set off down a track leading off the courtyard. They passed olive trees on either side and soon entered the cool shade of the wood. Claudia warned that although there were wild boar she did not think they would see one. They also needed to be aware of vipers and, although rarely seen, Umberto led the way hitting the ground with a stick as he walked.

The woodland was dense and the stones and fallen trees covered with grey and yellow lichen. Giancarlo pointed out the different trees, mainly Holm oaks, umbrella pines and other firs. Apart from occasional birdsong and their footsteps it was silent until an insistent 'poo poo poo' caught her attention and Umberto explained it was a crested bird similar to an English jay called a Hoopoe.

They soon completed a full circle and returned to the courtyard.

"Will you stay for supper, Giancarlo." Claudia asked.

"I would love to but I promised to see my parents and also see if they have any news about Kate's family." He turned to Kate. "I hope I will have something to tell you tomorrow."

"Oh, thank you," she said unused to the attention that was now focussed on her.

"Yes, and we also hope to have more information for

you shortly," Umberto enthused. "*Allora*, I think it's Prosecco time, will you have a glass before you go Giancarlo?"

"Thanks but no, it is time I left. I'll see you tomorrow."

2

Kate enjoyed the drive to Arezzo. Long villages edged the road with shops, and bars where men sat outside watching and discussing life. There was no opulence here, merely everyday, rural life. Kate noticed the change in the landscape as they drove across a flat plain of open fields.

Arezzo was different again and, like many a city it was busy, a density of people and traffic. It was set on a hill in contrast to the bowl that held Florence. Many of the streets led uphill to the old town and this was where they headed.

They walked up the Via Corso Italia, lined with its elegant shops and the occasional unusual one, such as one Kate noticed that sold only buttons. Umberto suggested a small *osteria* in one of the side streets which he and Claudia knew well. He made a quick call to Giancarlo to tell him where they were having lunch.

After a brief conversation he turned to Kate and explained that unfortunately Giancarlo would be unable to join them but hoped to call by later. Kate did her best to hide her disappointment and thanked Umberto.

"It is typical Tuscan food, Kate. I hope you like it." Umberto said as they arrived at the entrance.

"Oh, I'm sure I will," she confirmed, thinking it seemed a long time since breakfast.

They were greeted enthusiastically and Umberto agreed to eat outside where the tables were shaded by large umbrellas.

The Diarist

They managed to restrain the affair to three courses during which they discussed where else they might take Kate to experience the real Tuscany.

By the time the coffee arrived Kate was overwhelmed by their kindness and wondered how she would ever be able to repay them.

Over coffee Umberto suggested they take a walk further up the hill where they could enjoy fantastic views over the surrounding countryside before Arezzo opened again for the afternoon.

"You must find our opening hours strange, Kate. In England your shops and businesses stay open all day?" Claudia asked as they prepared to leave the restaurant.

"Yes, a little, though in Florence some of the shops stay open so I didn't notice it too much."

Kate opened her bag to offer her share of the bill and immediately both Umberto and Claudia placed a hand over hers to prevent her going any further.

"There is no need Kate, but thank you for offering. It is all taken care of." Umberto's smile though warm, rebuked any argument.

"Thank you," Kate said meekly and wondered how she was going to deal with future situations. Claudia seemed to sense her concern and as they were leaving explained that as their guest she was not expected to pay for anything; that was the way here and she hoped Kate would allow them their custom. Kate smiled and nodded, unsure how she felt about it.

The afternoon air was hot and as they climbed the hill Kate noticed the specialist food shops and antique shops, all of which were closed until three-thirty or four o'clock. At the top of the hill they turned a couple of corners before reaching the *duomo*, also closed, and eventually came to the gardens on the far side. An avenue of umbrella pines offered shade as they walked through to a low wall beyond which the plain below and around Arezzo stretched for miles.

"It's worth the climb," Kate said having regained her breath. "It's amazing."

"I hoped you would like it," Umberto said. "From here you can see so much more and get an idea of, how do you say, the lie of the land?"

"Yes, it certainly gives it perspective," Kate said as she tried to take it all in.

"If we take our time and walk back slowly we will be in time to show you the frescoes of Piero della Francesca. It is not far from where we had lunch."

As they walked back down to the Via Corso Italia, Claudia explained more about the city. She told how it was famous as a centre for gold dating back to Etruscan times and also for antiques.

"You will see there are many antique shops and on a Sunday once a month there is a big antiques market in the *Piazza Grande* and surrounding streets that attracts buyers from as far as Rome. Sadly you have missed the one this month."

"Do not worry Kate, there are plenty of other things to explore, but here we are, the *Basillica di San Francesco*, or for you, St Francis. Let's go in." Umberto indicated the entrance.

They entered a large open space where the remains of frescoes painted in the Early Renaissance filled the walls. Kate knew the difficulties of the technique and was amazed they had survived this long, as had many others elsewhere such as the ones by Giotto and Cimabue in the *basillica* at Assisi.

Before Kate could object, Umberto had bought tickets for them to see the Legend of the True Cross, thought to have been Piero della Francesca's greatest work inspired by the 'Golden Legends' or 'Lives of the Saints' compiled by Jacobus de Voragine in 1275. Kate accepted the audio guide that took her through the cycle but turned it off preferring to find her own way and reach her own understanding.

It had been a long while since she had taken the time to appreciate art for the pleasure of it and here she was, everywhere she turned there seemed to be another masterpiece and she was loving every minute of it.

On their return journey to the villa Umberto stopped at Enzo's home to show him the photos of Charles that Kate had given to him the previous evening.

"It won't take long," Umberto said as he parked the car. "I'll be right back."

Kate and Claudia waited in the car.

"It is best we wait. If we all go Enzo will feel he must invite us in and it will become an occasion. I think Umberto wants to get home and I imagine you must also be tired."

"A little," Kate said.

"Ah good, here he comes." Claudia waited while he got into the car, then asked, "*Tutto bene?*"

"*Si, si.* He will show it to his friends at the bar and let us know if anyone remembers him. Let's hope so."

They had only just walked into the villa when they heard a car scrunching the gravel in the courtyard.

"Ah, that must be Giancarlo, it seems we only just got back in time." Umberto said and went out to greet him.

Claudia and Kate were sitting on the terrace and the two men came to join them. They exchanged the usual *ciao* and kisses and Kate tried to calm a fluttering in her abdomen.

Umberto recounted their visit to Arezzo and Giancarlo was apologetic and expressed his sadness at not being able to join them.

"You can stay to supper, I hope?" enquired Claudia.

"*Si, si, grazie.* It would be a pleasure." he smiled and, looking at Kate, continued. "It is a shame you are here for such a short time. My parents would like to invite you to lunch tomorrow if you are free, so they can tell you what they have learned about your family."

Kate looked at Umberto and Claudia before answering.

"Yes of course, unless you have plans?"

"Come as well, you know how these family lunches are," Giancarlo waved his arm in invitation, "the more the merrier. Is that how you say in English?"

"Yes, it is." Kate confirmed.

""*Eh*, Giancarlo, we would love to but please check with your mother first." Claudia said raising an eyebrow in his direction.

"*Si, si,* I'll call her now." He took out his mobile and was soon speaking in rapid Italian. "*Eh, va bene, i*t's all organised, tomorrow at twelve."

In less than an hour they were sitting around the kitchen table with steaming bowls of pasta, *spaghetti alle vongole,* warm bread and a colourful salad of leaves and flowers.

"This is wonderful, Claudia, it's one of my favourites, my father also loved it but always complained that he could not get fresh clams for the sauce." Kate said praising her host's culinary skills.

"*Eh,* it is not always easy here. Your father, he teach you about Italian food?" Claudia asked.

"Oh yes, it was his passion. It was the one thing of Italy that he didn't turn his back on. For years he had a café in Edinburgh and as he got older my brother took over and it's now a successful restaurant."

The evening continued with amiable conversation until Giancarlo left. Kate thanked Umberto and Claudia for a wonderful day and retreated to her room to be alone with her thoughts.

The Diarist

3

Saturday arrived with high cobalt skies and brilliant sunshine. Umberto, Claudia and Kate left a few minutes before noon for the short drive to Giancarlo's parents' home where they were given an effusive welcome by each member of the extended family. Giancarlo led them through the villa to the garden where a long table had been set for twelve or so people under a vine shaded pergola. People gathered around the garden, drinks in hand and talking at high volume.

"Prosecco?" Giancarlo asked his friends. "To celebrate your return, Kate."

They all nodded and he disappeared into the kitchen before Kate could respond, and returned a minute later with four glasses which he handed out.

"*Salute,*" he said raising his glass in Kate's direction. "*Allora,* you must meet my uncle, I think he may have some news for you. Come," and he led them in the direction of a silver haired man leaning on a stick and talking to a younger woman, probably about her age, Kate thought.

"Luigi," Giancarlo exclaimed and opened his arms to give the old man a hug. When he stood back he introduced Kate, Umberto and Claudia. "Luigi, this is the young woman I told you about, her family, Bernini, came from near here. You remember?"

Luigi scratched his chin before looking up with a wide

grin, "*Certo, certo*, yes, your father, he think his family were killed in the massacre at Civitella. Hm, maybe, maybe not." He lowered his head, rubbing his chin, lost in thought.

Kate waited patiently, holding her breath.

"Yes, that's it, there was a sister, she was not there that day, she survived. Now very old, older than me," he chuckled, "and I'm ancient."

"Do you know where she lives?" Kate's voice trembled as she spoke and everyone's eyes focussed on Luigi.

"*Eh*, of course, she's still there. A widow now, but the children keep an eye on her, *eh*, and the grandchildren when they visit. You know how it is, the young ones, they want more excitement than what they get here." He chuckled again. "You would like to meet her?"

"Oh yes please," Kate said looking at her friends in turn hardly able to contain her excitement.

"Bene, bene. I shall arrange it."

"Thank you, thank you," Kate gushed barely able to believe what she had just heard. "That would be wonderful."

"Leave it to me," Luigi said and winked at Giancarlo. Giancarlo thanked him and explained that Kate was leaving on Monday. Luigi, to Kate's surprise, took out a mobile phone. Did everyone in Italy have one? He pressed a button and spoke in a heavy dialect that Kate could not understand.

"She will see you this afternoon, after four."

"Oh," was all Kate could say as she felt her legs weaken and, for the second time, Giancarlo saved her from falling.

"I'm, er, sorry. I'm fine thanks," she stumbled over the words as she leaned on Giancarlo's arm to recover herself. At the same moment there was a clapping of hands and Giancarlo's mother called everyone to the table.

Kate had a vague memory of the meal as they followed Luigi's car up to Civitella. A constant flow of food laden dishes had passed along the table, and wine and water glasses were emptied and refilled amid a loud cacophony of conversations vying for attention. She had tried to participate but her mind was elsewhere, occupied by thoughts about the woman she was about to meet who could be her aunt.

Claudia sat next to her in the back of the car enthusing about the lunch and asking Giancarlo if his mother would share some of her recipes. Kate listened and continued to say a few words through the misty veil that surrounded her, aware of attentive looks every now and then from Giancarlo.

They parked their cars and Luigi led the way along the village wall to an old house where washing was draped over a line hung along an upstairs balcony. Cats watched from their corners ready to protect their territory as Luigi rang the doorbell next to an ancient arched wooden door. They all looked up as a voice sounded from above.

"*Si, eh .... arrivo.*"

They waited and the door was opened by a woman a little older than Kate. Black hair, tied back and fastened up with a comb, framed an olive, oval face where friendly dark eyes smiled at the group in the doorway.

"*Eh,* Luigi, *vieni,*"she invited." *Prego, buona sera. Mamma* is expecting you, this way."

They followed her to a room at the back of the house where a diminutive woman sat in an upright chair.

"Luigi, *buona sera,*" she said in a thin voice. "You have brought her?" She added as her dark eyes went immediately to Kate. "Come, come my dear, sit here," she commanded indicating a chair by hers. "Let me take a good look at you."

The younger woman offered seats to the others and opened a dark wooden cabinet from which she took some glasses and a bottle of *vin santo.* She filled small glasses and passed them round. She introduced herself as Rosa and her mother as Adelina.

"This is a special occasion, *eh mamma?*"

Kate looked at them, as they did her, each searching and finding familiarities, the old lady nodding and smiling.

"*Allora,* so you are Enrico's daughter?" she said, a

shaky hand reaching to touch Kate's. "Of course, I see it now. Who would have thought …." She turned to her daughter, her eyes damp.

Kate struggled to compose herself over competing emotions bubbling to the surface.

"*Eh*, after all these years. I thought he was dead you know." Tears now trickled down her deeply lined cheeks. "He is well?" she asked, returning her gaze to Kate, but before she could answer the old lady dissolved in a flood of tears, grasping tightly to Kate's hand. Her daughter rushed to her side offering a tissue to dry her face and handing her a glass of *vin santo*.

"Ecco mamma, take a sip."

"*Bene, bene,* I'm alright." She sniffed. "Now tell me about my brother. I want to hear it all."

Kate took a sip from her glass and told Adelina the little she knew of how her father had been captured and sent to a prisoner of war camp in Scotland and how, after the war, he had stayed and married her mother believing all his family had been killed in the massacre. She went on to explain that it was only when she came to Civitella to do some research into a man who had been a prisoner of war in Laterina that she came across someone with her surname in the *Sala della Memoria*. It was Giancarlo who had then made enquiries and here they were.

Adelina still held on to Kate's hand listening intently to every word, watching her with watery eyes. Kate put down her glass and placed her hand over Adelina's, recognising something of her father in the aged woman's face and mannerisms. They sat like this for what seemed a long time until she heard Rosa asking how long she was staying.

"Oh …. er….. I leave on Monday."

"Did you find the man you were looking for, the one at Laterina?" Adelina asked, letting go of Kate's hand.

"Er, no," Kate replied, the question taking her by surprise. "It seems he escaped and that's as far as we could

The Diarist

trace him."

"Who was he?"

Kate then explained about the diary and how her curiosity had brought her to Florence.

"So this, you, my father, is all so unexpected. And so wonderful," she said with a huge grin. She wanted to hug everyone but felt it might be inappropriate and could be embarrassing for both her and them.

"So cousin," Rosa smiled. "You will tell your father? He has two nephews and three nieces and they also have children. I will find some photos for you to show him."

"Yes, of course I will. I'll call him …..."

"Tell him I never gave up hoping." Adelina said. "I was lucky I was away from the village when the Germans came that day. My brother though, he was among those that were shot. *Eh,* war, it is a cruel thing."

Everyone nodded in agreement. It was Luigi, worried that Adelina was tiring, who suggested it might be time to leave. There were more nods of agreement and Kate promised to call once she had spoken to her father.

They said their goodbyes and, parting company from Luigi, drove first to Giancarlo's where he collected his car and then to the villa in thoughtful silence.

It was already early evening as they sat on the terrace discussing how and when Kate should tell her father that his sister was alive and well. After talking round various options she decided to call her mother and speak to her about it. Claudia showed her to the study where she could have some privacy, saying that she should take as long as she liked.

Kate tapped in the number and waited. Thankfully her mother answered the phone.

"Kate darling, how are you, is everything alright?"

"Yes, I'm fine. I'm in Italy and …."

"In Italy? You haven't had an accident …..?

"No, no, nothing like that. It's …. it's just that I

discovered something quite by accident and, oh dear ......"

"What is it darling? It can't be that bad."

"No, it's not bad, not at all, just a bit of a shock." Kate took a deep breath and told her mother about her visit to Civitella and then later to meet Adelina.

"Oh, I see," said her mother releasing the breath she had been holding.

"Of course Adelina wants to speak to *babbo* but I didn't want to tell him over the phone. I don't know....."

"It's alright Kate, I'll talk to him and then .... then we can go from there. It will be a shock of course .... let's see. Can I call you there?"

"Er yes ...... but I don't have the number. Look, why don't I call you back a bit later once you've had time to speak to him and I can give you the number then."

For Kate the next hour seemed to go on forever as she sat with her friends, there and not there, locked in a world of churning emotions. Claudia gave her their number and she returned to the study to make the second call to her mother. This time it was her father that answered.

"What are you doing there, poking around? What is all this?" he growled. "Why ......"

She could hear her mother's voice in the background trying to placate him.

"I didn't mean to ... I was on holiday and ...."

"But why there? What were you ....."

"*Babbo*, please ...."

"*Babbo,* please nothing. You ....." His voice trailed off, the fight suddenly gone from him. "*Dimme*, tell me, is she well?"

"Yes *babbo,*" Kate gave a deep sigh of relief at her father's lapse into Italian. She went on to tell him about her afternoon with Adelina and her daughter Rosa, and how much they longed to see him, meet him. She heard the warmth return to her father's voice, heard it break at times

The Diarist

with emotion until finally he thanked her before passing the phone to her mother. They agreed that Kate would give Adelina their phone number straight away and speak again in the next day or two.

Exhausted by the intensity of emotions Kate fell back into the chair and breathed deeply for a moment or two. As she turned to get up she saw Giancarlo standing in the doorway.

"You are alright?" he asked.

"Yes, yes. It's just all a bit of a shock I suppose, for everyone."

"How was your father?"

"Well, he was angry at first then he … I don't know, I think he was happy. I said I would give Adelina his number so she can call him."

"If you like, let me. What is the number?"

Relieved not to have to make another call, she scribbled the number for him.

"Why don't you join the others, I'll be there in a minute."

"Thank you," Kate said with a smile and returned to the terrace where the wine was once again flowing and dishes of food covered the table.

"*Vieni, vieni,* come have some food," Claudia said, handing her a glass of wine. "You must be exhausted. How was your father?"

She gave a précis of their conversation and explained that Giancarlo was now calling Adelina with the phone number. At that moment Giancarlo arrived and confirmed that he had spoken to Rosa and could hear Adelina in the background impatiently demanding the number and the phone.

"I think now we can relax, *no*?" Giancarlo said raising his glass in a toast. "To a happy reunion!"

They each raised their glass and repeated his toast in unison amid clinking glasses and big smiles.

Caught between laughter and tears Kate thanked them all for the parts they had played in making it possible and reflected on how it had all started with the diary.

"Yes, we must not forget that," Umberto said. "I'll give Enzo a call, see if he has news."

"Oh *amore,* let's wait until tomorrow, we have enough excitement for one day." Claudia pleaded.

"Yes please, Umberto, I don't think I can take in any more today." Kate added her voice as well.

"Very well then. You are right of course," he said smiling at his wife and casting a wink in Kate and Giancarlo's direction.

They all laughed and spent the next hour in lively conversation though Kate was distracted by thoughts of her father and Adelina. She had decided to call her mother in the morning when Giancarlo announced he must leave and asked if they had plans for the next day, Sunday.

"Since it is Kate's last day maybe we could take her somewhere special and have lunch. What do you think?"

"Oh, I forgot," Umberto began, "Simonetta said something about Sunday and wanting to see Kate. Let me call her ...." He went inside to make the call and returned smiling. "She says she will be here about ten o'clock and we can then go wherever we wish. Any suggestions?"

"Hm, so many places. What about you Kate, anywhere special you would like to go?" Giancarlo asked.

Kate shrugged. "Not really."

"How about we drive into the hills and see where we end up," Claudia suggested. "Remember Umberto, we would often do that on a Sunday and we found places we didn't know existed."

"A good idea, unless of course we hear from Enzo and then we may need to see him."

They all agreed they would wait and see what the morning brought.

4

The next morning arrived with a crash of thunder overhead and torrential rain hammering loudly on the tiled roof. Cracks of lightning flashed over the valley as Kate opened the shutters to see the storm. She showered and dressed resigning herself to not being able to go anywhere until the storm passed.

In the *cucina* Claudia was making coffee and greeted Kate with profuse apologies for the weather and assured her the storm would pass quickly and it would be as if it had never happened.

Kate sat at the table, accepted the coffee and helped herself to a pastry.

"It's very dramatic," she said as she sipped and appreciated the coffee.

"Yes, it is the mountains I think, they add to the drama." Claudia said joining her at the table. "Do not worry, it will not spoil our day."

Within half an hour the sky had cleared to a cloudless blue with the sun high and bright. The landscape, washed clean, sparkled.

"See, it's as if it never happened," Claudia pronounced.

Umberto joined them and poured himself a coffee.

"Simonetta just rang full of apologies. She won't be able to join us for lunch but will come over later."

Kate was not sure if she was disappointed by this. A

part of her felt a sense of relief yet at the same time she would have appreciated her wisdom.

"What a shame, but at least we will now fit in one car with comfort," Claudia said. "Any news from Enzo?"

"No, not yet. I'll give him a call when Giancarlo arrives."

Kate again tried to quell the butterflies that made another unwelcome appearance. And was that a knowing smile from Claudia or did she imagine it. She drank her coffee and hoped she was wrong.

Shortly before Giancarlo's arrival, Umberto called Enzo to see if there had been any developments. After a brief conversation he reported to Kate and Claudia that Enzo had no news but hoped to be seeing someone this afternoon whom he thought may be able to help. Umberto shrugged his shoulders.

"I'm sorry Kate, I had hoped he may have ….."

"It's alright Umberto," Kate said with a smile. "Maybe we'll never know what happened to Charles."

"Oh don't say that," Claudia exclaimed. "You never know, Enzo may still find something. Anyway, let's make the most of the day and go somewhere special. *Eh,* Umberto?"

"*Si, si.* Giancarlo will be here soon and we can go. It's a shame you have to leave tomorrow, so soon." he said tilting his head to one side. "Can you not stay a little longer?"

"Yes Kate, maybe a few more days?" Claudia entreated.

"I wish I could but …."

"Ah, do I hear a but?" Giancarlo joined them.

They all turned round and asked in unison how had they not heard him. He shrugged and gave one of his lop-sided smiles.

"I called when I arrived but there was no reply so I followed the sound of your voices."

"We were just trying to persuade Kate to stay a few

The Diarist

more days," Claudia explained.

"Oh I see," he smiled knowingly at Kate. "Now I understand the 'but'. *Eh,* I agree, but maybe Kate, you have things you need to get back for."

Before Kate could say anything she heard her mobile ring from inside her bag. Thinking it could only be an emergency she delved in her bag to answer it begging "excuse me," to her friends.

"Hello?"

"Hi, it's ...."

"Luc, what's happened, is it *babbo?"* she said interrupting him and thinking the worst as she stood and walked over to the window.

"No, no ..... well yes in a way. What have you been up to? You've certainly set the cat among the pigeons."

"What ...."

"All this business in Italy, what on earth have you been doing? Why didn't you tell me?"

Kate gave a big sigh, suddenly emptied, then took a deep breath before explaining to her brother what had happened during her visit to Civitella and her meeting the previous day with Adelina, their aunt.

"I see, but why didn't you ..."

"Say something? What would I have said? I didn't know anything for certain until yesterday. Look I'll be back tomorrow, can we talk then?"

"Hm, that's why I'm ringing, *babbo* wants to come over. Now."

"What?"

"Yes, now. He's asked me to book a flight for him and *maman,* drive them to the airport. *Maman* says she will call you to organise an hotel. I don't know what to do Kate, he won't listen to reason and *maman* just says he should be able to do what he wants!"

Kate heard the exasperation in Luc's voice and could imagine the strident conversation he must have had with their father.

"Luc, I'm leaving tomorrow …...."

"Well, that's it, he wants you to change your flight and...."

"Look, let me speak to him …...."

"Well, if you think you can talk some sense into him, good luck."

"Luc, you know what he's like, I'll call and let you know how it goes."

"Ok, I'm sorry sis, but with the new deli and everything I'm really stretched and ..."

"This is the last thing you need, I know."

"Well yes, and thanks." he said, sounding calmer now the responsibility had been shared.

Kate turned round to where Umberto, Claudia and Giancarlo were sitting, chatting quietly. Kate explained about her father.

""*Eh*, you must call immediately Kate, please use the phone in the study. And you know you can stay longer if you need to," Claudia said, before adding, "please take as long as you need. I'll make coffee."

After thanking Claudia and taking another deep breath she called her parents. Thankfully her mother answered.

"Oh you know how he is, he won't listen to anyone and he's got the idea in his head to meet his long lost sister now. If he could get on a plane today he would!"

"Oh *maman,* would you like me to talk to him?"

"Och, you can talk to him, whether he'll listen …... what on earth were you thinking Kate? It was all forgotten and now ….."

"I know, I know. It just happened, I didn't mean to …."

"Well, what's done is done. Luc says he'll come over later but …."

"Let me speak to him," Kate said. She could hear her mother calling him as she prayed for the right words to say to him.

"Ah, *amore,* now I want you to stay there and we'll come over so I can see my sister …."

"But *babbo* ….."

"And my nephews and nieces," he said completely ignoring her. Kate breathed slowly and deeply.

"Is it a good idea to rush things *babbo*? Why don't you wait until I get back, I'll come to see you and we can plan it together …."

"You don't understand Kate," he said firmly, "I don't know how long I have and I want to see my sister. Is that too much to ask?"

"No, I suppose not," Kate could find no words or reason to oppose him. "Let me see what I can do. I'm not making any promises but I'll call you back soon."

Kate put the phone down and looked around the room, momentarily wishing she was at home and could get on the next flight to Edinburgh to be with her parents.

She found her friends were now on the terrace and Kate joined them as Claudia poured her a coffee.

"Come, sit down. How did it go?" Claudia patted the seat next to her.

Kate recounted the conversation with her father as they listened intently before all speaking at the same time.

"But of course you can stay and …...."

"But Kate, you must stay on and they can ..."

"Kate you must not worry ..."

It was Umberto who raised his hands, palms outward, commanding silence.

"Kate you know you can stay here and your parents too, we have so much room and it will be a pleasure to be part of this, er … reunion."

"Oh Umberto, I don't know …." Kate tried to object embarrassed not only by their generosity but also having involved them in her family drama.

"Kate," Giancarlo smiled, "you are maybe being a little bit English? It is a pleasure for us all and it will be good for you and your parents to be among friends than a faceless hotel, *no*?"

"Well yes, but ...."

Umberto cut in.

"No buts," he smiled. "*Allora,* go call them and make the arrangements and we will make sure we can meet them at the airport, *va bene*?"

Kate wasn't sure who was more stubborn, Umberto or her father as she thanked them all and returned to the study to call her father.

The second call was easier as she told her father that they could stay with her friends and they would be there to meet them at the airport. All he needed to do was book the flights and let her know when they would be arriving.

"*Grazie amore,* thank you." Kate heard the emotion in his voice and felt tears prick behind her eyes as they said goodbye. She then sent a text to Luc. She hoped he would understand how important this was for their father and organise the flights without too much drama. She understood her brother's concerns, her parents were elderly and even though they were relatively healthy *babbo* had recently had a fall. At the same time she had some understanding of her father's need to see the family he had not known existed. She did not want to be the one who opposed him only to later live with regrets.

Returning to the terrace and still lost in these thoughts, she explained her parents would let her know later when they had booked their flights.

"In that case, I think we should make the most of today. What do you think?" Umberto said looking at each in turn.

"I don't know, *caro,* maybe Kate would rather be here. Kate?" Claudia said as she gently laid her hand on her husband's arm then looked at Kate.

"Oh, I er ...."

"Perhaps it is better to do something than to sit and dwell on what might be?" Giancarlo said. "What if we go for a short drive and then find somewhere for lunch. There is still so much that Kate has not seen and it is always good to have lunch with friends. What do you think, Kate?"

"Er ... yes," Kate struggled under his direct gaze and looking round to the others added, "sounds perfect."

"*Bene, andiamo!*" Umberto exclaimed, keen to get started.

They set off in Umberto's car and for Kate it became a magical mystery tour as they headed towards the Chianti hills. At Ginacarlo's suggestion, their first stop was Cennina, a short drive to Ambra then uphill to the tiny hamlet where small houses were built around the medieval castle ruins that looked down the valley below known as the Valdarno, stretching along the river to Florence.

As they walked up from parking the car to the remains of the castle, Kate marvelled at the stunning views and Umberto and Giancarlo talked of its history. Dating back to the 12th century, and situated at a strategic point between Florence, Siena and Arezzo, it had been destroyed and rebuilt many times. The ruins now housed occasional evening concerts and Kate could imagine how atmospheric that must be.

Houses were built around and below it, many using stones from the ruin. The ones by the castle, their stonework mostly hidden by climbing roses and ivy, appeared to merge with it and Kate absorbed its peace and beauty.

After walking round the castle's perimeter they went a little way along the road in the other direction to admire another spectacular view, this time over the Valdambra, a heavily wooded descent to the River Ambra.

Back in the car Kate and Claudia exchanged effusive comments on the beauty and dominion of the place while

Umberto and Giancarlo debated which direction to take and the best place to stop for lunch.

"The problem is Kate, there are so many places we would like to show you it is hard to choose one. Anyway, we will show you some of what Tuscany is famous for, Chianti. Let's head into the hills and find somewhere for a late lunch." Umberto said, taking charge of the day's itinerary.

After a short time they turned away from the main road and Kate settled back to enjoy the drive through stunning scenery as hairpin bends led them higher to views of rolling hills clothed with row upon row of vines, and tall, elegant cypress trees led the way to magnificent villas. No wonder people fell in love with this place, she thought.

Every now and again someone would point out a famous vineyard or place of interest and inform Kate of its history.

"*Allora,* let's stop here and see if we can find somewhere for lunch." Umberto announced as he pulled into a parking space that had just become vacant. "This is Radda in Chianti, Kate. *Andiamo.*"

They got out of the car and Kate saw how lucky they were to find a parking space as other cars arrived and queued in search of one. They walked round the corner to the bottom of the main street that was lined with stalls as it wound its way uphill.

"*Eh,* it is the *degustazione,*" Giancarlo gave a frown as he remembered the English, ".... the er, winetasting."

They looked at each other and then up the stall lined street. Umberto began to walk in the direction of a nearby restaurant where he had spotted an empty table outside, shaded by a large umbrella.

"I think he is hungry," Claudia said rolling her eyes.

As they approached the restaurant Umberto was walking towards them shaking his head.

"No, they don't have a table. Let's take a look up here,"

he said nodding his head in the direction of the main street. "We can graze on the way and see what else we can find, *no?*"

They all nodded in agreement and were soon seduced by the wine and food on offer at the various stalls. Kate was enticed from one stall to another by her friends insisting she must taste this or that local delicacy or wine.

By the time they reached the top they were all ready to sit down out of the sun's glare.

"Ah, I had forgotten this place," Giancarlo said with a smile. "Look there's a table here, out of the sun. Let's see if it's free." He rushed through the open door into the bar and returned with a huge grin waving his arm in the direction of the table. "It is waiting for us, let's sit down."

As soon as they were seated a young man wearing a long white apron brought menus, one for food, the other for wine. Kate looked at the lengthy wine list and the short food menu. They each asked Kate questions in turn as to whether she liked this or that, followed by a brief discussion in rapid Italian. They just managed to reach a consensus before the waiter returned to take their order.

First came the antipasti and large glasses containing a selection of chianti wines.

"*Buon appetito,*" they said in unison, raising their glasses in a toast.

"Oh, this is good," Kate said as she took her first sip of wine.

"Yes this is the real Chianti," Umberto assured her.

They continued their lunch amid sounds of appreciation for the delicious food and wines. Claudia talked about the history of Radda; of how it used to be an important town, because of its position between Florence and Siena and the continual conflicts between these two city states.

"And, of course, it is famous for its wine," Claudia said raising her glass with a smile.

Kate, for a short time, was able to forget about the recent upheavals and stress as she listened to her friends talk enthusiastically about the food and wines typical of the area and their memories of previous visits. She wondered what her father would make of it after all these years.

"Let's see if we can find something special for this evening, maybe one of the stalls ….." Umberto suggested.

"*Eh,* for Simonetta, a good idea." Claudia said.

As they stood Claudia linked arms with Umberto and set off down the hill leaving Kate and Giancarlo to follow behind.

"I hope this is not too much for you. My friends they like to entertain and want you to see everything," Giancarlo said.

"Er no," Kate shook her head. "It's good to be distracted."

"*Bene,* but you must say if you need time to yourself."

"Thank you," she smiled, grateful for his thoughtfulness. "I will."

They followed the others down the hill pausing occasionally as Giancarlo pointed out a local delicacy or special wine they had missed on the way up. Whilst she enjoyed being in his company, Kate was still apprehensive about his sudden presence in her life and the feelings it stirred. So many unexpected things had happened in the last few weeks that she was having difficulty assimilating it all. Through jumbled thoughts and emotions she struggled to maintain conversations or determine whether Giancarlo was merely being friendly or, a thought she kept pushing to one side, was actually interested in her romantically. Memories of when she first met John would float to the surface as she tried to make sense of conflicting immature emotions. Had she felt like this when she had first met him and, despite the pain of recalling her feelings for him so long ago, she recognised the similarities which made the whole situation more disconcerting than she liked to admit.

The Diarist

As she turned away from yet another stall she was aware of Giancarlo observing her and she hoped the rising blush she felt did not show. They had almost reached the bottom of the hill and Kate was annoyed that Umberto and Claudia were nowhere to be seen. She began to wonder about their intentions of walking off and leaving her with Giancarlo and hoped it was just her imagination.

"*Eh,* there you are," called Umberto as he and Claudia emerged from a nearby shop. "If you are ready we can go and maybe have a rest before Simonetta arrives."

Kate, embarrassed by her thoughts merely smiled, suppressing any annoyance she felt with them or herself.

Simonetta arrived full of apologies for not being able to join them earlier. Umberto waxed lyrical, teasing her about the wonderful day they'd had and before he could go into too much detail Claudia interrupted him.

"*Scusami caro,* we have things of much more interest to tell Simonetta," and she led Simonetta by the arm through to the *cucina.*

They settled round the large table where Claudia offered bread and olives and Umberto poured wine.

"*Allora* Kate," Simonetta said, turning to her. "Tell me what has been happening."

The others sat silently eager to hear Kate's story again.

"Well," Kate began and went on to recount what had happened since she had returned to England. The unearthing of Hettie's son, meeting him and learning more about Hettie and her diaries. Then, how only yesterday, through Giancarlo and his family, she had met her father's sister, her aunt. "And now my father knows his sister is alive he can't wait to see her and will be arriving with my mother as soon as he can get a flight."

Exhausted by the telling Kate leaned back in her chair.

"*Eh, mamma mia,* you have been busy," Simonetta said letting out a quiet whistle between her teeth. "So you will be here a little longer?"

"Yes, depending on how long my parents stay."

"Hm, a great reunion after so many years," Simonetta smiled and placed her hand momentarily over Kate's.

Kate relaxed into an unexpected sense of peace and knowing that whatever happened now was as it should be, that there was no need to worry. She looked, with a brief frown, at Simonetta who merely smiled and, aware of an unspoken conversation, Kate returned her attention to the table unsure as to what had taken place or if it was merely her imagination.

"We are all looking forward to it," Umberto said with enthusiasm. "I think Kate is a little tired and overwhelmed by it all though," he said smiling at her.

Before Kate could respond Claudia had placed dishes of pasta and salad on the table and was now encouraging everyone to help themselves.

"*Buon appetito*," she said but before she could sit down the phone rang. "*Scusami.*"

She picked up the phone. "*Pronto* .... *si, si* ..... of course ..... a minute." She turned holding the phone out towards Kate. "Kate it's for you."

"Oh, thank you," Kate said taking the phone.

"Hello ...... oh, of course .... hold on ...." She turned to the others. "It's Luc, he says my parents have booked their flight and will arrive tomorrow evening at 7.30 ..."

"Do not worry Kate, we will be there to meet them," Umberto interrupted.

Kate confirmed to Luc that they would meet them and after promising not to let their father take over and do too much she ended the call and returned the phone to Claudia.

"*Bene,* so that is settled." Claudia said. "Now, let's eat and enjoy the evening."

There was a chorus of "*si*" and "*certo*" and raised glasses as Umberto called a toast to Kate's parents.

As they each expressed their desire to meet them

Claudia sounded a note of caution.

"I think we must remember that they are elderly, is that not so Kate?"

"Er yes, in their early nineties."

"So we must be careful not to overwhelm them …."

"I don't think there's much chance of that, Claudia, after all he is Italian," Kate laughed at the thought of her father being overwhelmed, "but thank you for your concern."

They all laughed with her and Kate began to realise she was actually looking forward to her parents being there with her in Italy. So much had changed since her first visit and she now felt more at home, not only in the place but also within herself. How could she have known when she first saw the photo of the cottage that it would lead her first to Hettie's diary, then new friends and a reclaiming of her Italian heritage and family.

Simonetta observed Kate processing her thoughts and was pleased she had followed her intuition and held her counsel. Kate had come a long way since their first meeting in Florence.

"I imagine your father will want to see Adelina as soon he can," Giancarlo said.

"Oh, if it is up to him he will go straight there." Kate said. "It's probably a good thing that he's arriving in the evening. Maybe we can arrange something for the following day."

"Why don't I take you over there," Claudia offered. "I'm here anyway and I'm sure Adelina won't want a whole party of us turning up. It is a special time for her and for your father."

"Thank you, Claudia."

They all nodded in understanding and agreement as Claudia stood to clear away the first course and bring in more aromatic, steaming dishes to the table.

"How do you do it Claudia? When did you have time to

prepare all this?" Kate asked amazed by the sight and smells of the food now on the table.

"Ah, that would be telling," Claudia teased. "*Eh,* I took it out of the freezer this morning before we went out so there really was very little preparation."

"It is a gift," Simonetta said with a slight laugh. Turning to Kate she added, "She has no idea …."

"What do you mean?" Claudia said, raising an eyebrow at Simonetta.

"*Eh,* only that, you do it so well, *cara.*" Simonetta said with a smile and a tilt of her head. "You are a lucky man, Umberto."

"That I know," he said smiling at his wife.

5

It was Claudia who drove Kate to the airport to meet her parents. It had been decided the previous evening that she would be a more calming influence than her husband. Kate watched the countryside speed by and Claudia respected Kate's need for her own thoughts. Very soon Kate recognised the approach to the airport and tried to quell churning emotions..

They made their way to Arrivals and waited at the barrier. Kate's breath caught in her throat as she saw her parents walk slowly towards them, both pushing a trolley holding their luggage, and her father waving his stick in recognition. She waved back and grinned widely, relieved they had arrived safely.

There were hugs, kisses and introductions to Claudia who welcomed them and asked if they would like anything before they set off for the villa.

"No, no, we're fine my dear. *Andiamo*," her father said, now eager to get to his destination.

Kate smiled at him amazed by his enthusiasm after the journey.

"Not to worry Kate, we're good, aren't we Bella?" he said using his shortened version of her name, Isobel, and looking at his wife.

"Och, of course we are."

A little more than an hour later they arrived at the villa where Umberto greeted them in his usual enthusiastic way.

"Let me show you to your room then you can take your time to settle in and join us for supper when you're ready." Claudia took charge and, before Umberto could overwhelm them, guided them to the annexe where they would be staying.

Kate went to go with them but her parents both assured her they could manage and would be with her in a short while. Feeling a little lost she followed Umberto into the *cucina* where he poured two glasses of wine.

"They will be alright. I think it can be difficult as our parents age and the emphasis shifts as we begin to feel responsible for them, *no*?" He said as he handed her a glass of wine. "I don't believe you need to worry ...."

"I know, it's just that I don't see them that often as they live so far away and .... I suppose they seem older and more fragile each time I see them and yet I know *babbo* is as tough as old boots and *maman* also ... "

"*Bene*, let's drink to them enjoying their stay."

They each raised their glasses in the toast as Claudia joined them and asked what they were toasting. Umberto explained and poured her a glass of wine.

"You should not worry Kate. My parents are a similar age and they would not hear of us worrying about them. Fortunately they have their good health as I think your parents also have."

"Yes, yes of course. Maybe I also feel a bit guilty about not visiting them more often."

At that moment her parents made their entrance and Umberto poured more wine and proposed another toast to them having an enjoyable stay. Claudia asked everyone to sit at the table as she filled it with her usual effortless flair.

"This is very kind of you," Isobel said, "to invite us to stay."

"*Eh, niente*," Umberto shrugged his shoulders. "You are

very welcome. We have become very fond of Kate and have enjoyed being part of her quest."

"And what quest would that be?" her father demanded, raising an eyebrow and looking Kate in the eye.

"Oh, it's quite a story, is it not Kate?" Umberto intervened.

"Yes, I suppose it is," Kate smiled and again told the story of the diary and the ensuing events that unexpectedly led her to meeting Adelina, her aunt.

"Hmph, I see," was all her father said.

"Darling, it's quite an adventure you've had," her mother said, giving Kate an affectionate smile.

"Bella," Kate's father addressed her mother.

"Yes?"

"Nothing," he said shaking his head.

Claudia encouraged everyone to eat more before saying that Adelina was looking forward to seeing them tomorrow. Kate hoped her father would be good humoured and less his irascible self and felt a little reassured when she heard him conversing with Umberto in Italian.

"It will be alright, you'll see," her mother said, squeezing her arm in reassurance.

Morning arrived in a blaze of brilliant sunshine. Anticipation filled the air as they decided who should go and who should stay. Eventually it was agreed that only Umberto and Enrico would go to Adelina so as not to overwhelm her. Claudia suggested Kate and Isobel enjoy the garden before the sun became too hot and brought a jug of lemonade and glasses to a shaded table on the terrace before she disappeared to the kitchen to make preparations for lunch.

Once alone Isobel's questions tumbled like a waterfall as she sought more details of her daughter's life since she had last seen her.

"So, you never found anything more about the brother other than he escaped from that camp?" she finally asked after Kate's retelling of how she came to be back in Italy.

"No. He could have been shot of course, but I haven't been able to find any records of his death and if he did survive, surely he would have contacted his family?" Kate replied, once again exasperated by her inability to find out more about the elusive Charlie.

"Well, I suppose he could have been injured, lost his memory or something. You never know darling, why someone might want to start a new life and be anonymous."

"Mmm, s'pose so." Kate said. "Of course, I've only read about him from Hettie's perspective …."

"Exactly. What about this man you met, her son, wasn't he able to tell you anything?"

"No," Kate paused as she saw his image in her mind's eye, "he ...er, didn't even know about his own father until he found the diaries."

"And there are no clues there?"

"Not that I could see. Hettie seemed to forget about him once she got home and then there was the baby and Edward and all that, so ….."

"Hm, I wonder if her trip was more about getting away from her mother ….."

"Oh, I don't know *maman*, she sounds so passionate about finding him and ..."

"Words on a page darling, depends how you read them," Isobel said raising an eyebrow at her daughter.

"Possibly. I wonder how *babbo*'s getting on." Kate said changing the subject.

"Och, knowing him, she won't get a word in and Umberto will have to drag him away," Isobel laughed at the thought. She looked beyond the garden to the mountains before turning to her daughter and saying, "It's very beautiful here. You know, your father never wanted to come back here and I didn't think of coming myself …... so beautiful ..."

"I know," Kate said seeing the sadness in her mother's eyes. "But we're here now, and so is *babbo*."

The Diarist

Claudia came out on to the terrace and joined them at the table helping herself to a glass of lemonade.

"I've just had a text from Umberto to say they're on their way home. It went well and everyone is tired, and I suspect that Umberto is hungry. They should be here soon and lunch is almost ready."

"Thank you," Kate said, "is there anything I can do?"

"No, no, no. Just enjoy your time here, there is nothing to do." Claudia smiled at Kate before turning to Isobel. "I hope you have everything you need and will also enjoy your time with us. It must be a little bit strange for you and your husband."

"Thank you Claudia, you're very kind." Isobel paused in thought before saying, "I'm not sure it's strange, maybe more unexpected. I imagine there is more to come."

"What do you mean, *maman*?" Kate asked, a frown creasing her forehead.

"Och, it's …. well, it's bound to have an impact on quite a few people, don't you think?"

Before Kate could answer Umberto and her father arrived and joined them on the terrace. Enrico sank into a chair and she thought he looked tired. There was something else but she could not quite find the words to describe it. It was more a feeling of empty and full at the same time.

"Well, I have a sister again," Enrico announced cutting off any questions that hung in the air waiting for the best moment. "Who would have thought it after all these years. You know, she never gave up on me," he added nodding his head.

"How …." Kate began but was interrupted by her father as he reached over to pat her hand.

"And it's all thanks to you, *amore*," he said through tear-filled eyes.

Unsure how to respond to her father's unexpected display of emotion and vulnerability, she placed her hand over his and smiled.

Claudia and Umberto quietly retired to the kitchen and Isobel watched her husband and daughter as tears of her own brimmed to the surface.

Enrico turned to his wife. "So, not only a sister but nieces, nephews, cousins ..... she, Adelina wants a lunch, for all of us .... everyone ..."

As his words tapered out Isobel smiled, it was not often her husband was lost for words.

"That's wonderful, and when and where is this to be?"

"*Eh,* they have to contact everyone first," he said with a shrug, and a more familiar tone returning to his voice. " She said we should all go over next time. She wants to meet you." He said looking at this wife.

Isobel nodded and wondered how this newfound life was going to play out.

Kate, aware of her mother's thoughtfulness, placed her other hand over her father's before taking both her hands away. "That's wonderful, *babbo.*" She stood and went through to the *cucina* returning a few minutes later to say that lunch was ready, happy to see that her parents were busy discussing the practicalities of extending their stay.

Lunch was a simple affair of *antipasti* followed by *ravioli con spinaci e ricotta* and salad. Enrico commented on the wonderful flavour of the ingredients and how different they tasted here even though he had tried to source the best he could in Edinburgh. There followed the usual discussions about coffee, the best beans and how it should be made and, as they all laughed at one another's stories, it was as if they had known each other for years.

By the time they finished their coffee Enrico had regaled them with details of his meeting with Adelina and the long lost extended family he had yet to meet. His voice then dropped as he repeated the account Adelina had given of the fateful day so long ago.

Kate knew a little of the history from her visit to the

Sala della Memoria at Civitella and her own limited research on the internet, but this was more intimate in its telling as she listened to her father speak.

He began. "This is how she told me what happened that day." His eyes glazed as if trying to remember her words before speaking again.

"It was early in the morning and I was at home with our mother getting ready to go to church. Babbo had gone to the woods looking for funghi. About seven o'clock we heard shots and went to the door to see what was happening. Outside frightened people were screaming 'the Germans are killing the men' and we ran back inside and locked the doors before running upstairs. We could see through the window a group of Germans point their rifles at some of the villagers and shoot them. We were absolutely terrified and could hear explosions which we thought were hand grenades going off downstairs in the house. We stood still, too frightened to move, waiting for death.

After a couple of hours or so, about half past ten, we left the house and went outside where we saw a scene of devastation. Houses had been set alight and there were bodies in the street. I saw a wall covered in blood where people had been shot but there were no bodies, they had been thrown into the burning houses.

We found the courage to walk up the steps by the wall and run for the woods but we were worried that babbo would return and find the house empty so we returned only to find him in the street with his face down in the blood soaked earth.

Another woman who had also found the body of her husband joined us and we washed the dead bodies, found a cart and took them to the church ...."

He coughed, as he hid rising emotions. "I think that is how it went .... hm."

After a short pause he continued.

"It seems it all started a few weeks before when some

partisans went into a bar where some German soldiers were having a drink. I'm not sure what happened but two German soldiers were killed and another was wounded who later died at the hospital in Montevarchi. Of course the villagers were frightened there would be reprisals, as was often the case, and most of them left the village. After a week or so, they heard that the Germans had shot the partisans they believed to be responsible and said there would be no reprisals. Thinking it would be safe, they returned and ….. well, you know the rest."

A thoughtful silence followed wherein they each tried to absorb the meaning of Adelina's experience and what had happened

Enrico broke the silence. "So, the family I thought I had lost is now here and …." His voice faltered and Isobel reached out and touched his arm as his eyes met hers he asked, "….. and what to do now?"

"We do whatever you want to do," Isobel said giving him a reassuring smile.

Enrico placed his hand over hers and, in a quiet voice, said, "Thank you."

The air was heavy with unspoken words and Kate felt her heart fill with love for her parents and the love they felt for each other. She wondered what would happen now and how long they would want to stay. There would be practicalities to deal with and as if reading her thoughts, both Umberto and Claudia offered an enthusiastic invitation for them to stay as long as they needed, followed by endless suggestions of places they must visit while they were there.

"Of course, you do not need to do any of this and are very welcome to relax here," Claudia said with a shrug as she realised their enthusiasm may be overwhelming.

"Whatever you decide," added Umberto, "we are happy to be your guides and if we are busy then Kate can borrow the little car."

"Oh but ….." Kate began.

"No buts, Kate. It is our pleasure. The insurance is, how do you say, universal ... *no,* comprehensive."

Once again Kate thanked them for their generosity but it was Enrico who raised his hand to slow down their enthusiasm.

"*Grazie mille,*" he said to Umberto and Claudia, "but Adelina and Rosa have asked us to stay with them for a few days and I would like to do that, if you don't mind, Bella?" he said turning to his wife.

"Of course, of course," she said.

"It makes sense. I'd like to spend time with them and get to know them. I thank you for your generosity," he said returning his attention to Umberto and Claudia. "And you, *amore,*" he added looking at Kate, "I don't know your plans and hope this is alright with you."

"Oh, I don't know *babbo* I hadn't really thought but you must do whatever is best for you. When will you go?"

"We thought tomorrow and ….." his words tapered out as the emotion of it all began to take its toll.

Kate realised that, in the turmoil of the last couple of days, she had forgotten to change her flight and would now have to decide when to rebook. She tutted, annoyed with herself for missing it, not because of the money but more for the loss of control of her affairs.

"What is it, dear?" her mother asked.

"Oh nothing really, just something I forgot to do. Nothing to worry about." she replied, hoping to dispel any concern. "I just need to check a couple of things, that's all."

She went through to the *cucina* and took her mobile from her bag and sent a text to Annie explaining that she would be staying on another day or two. She wondered how long she would need to stay. She would like to stay for the family lunch and hoped it would not take too long to organise. In the meantime she felt at a loss as to what to do now her parents would be staying with Adelina.

When she returned to join the others Claudia explained

that her parents had gone for a siesta and suggested they all do the same and meet again about four o'clock. Relieved to have some time to herself, Kate thanked her and Umberto and went to her room.

She closed the shutters and enjoyed the coolness of the shadowy light as she stretched across the bed. She thought of her parents and what had been her small nuclear family until a couple of days ago and the new extended family she had yet to meet. Caught between being Italian and English she felt included and excluded at the same time. Her thoughts turned to George and she wondered how it must have been for him discovering he was in fact half Italian but with no knowledge of his Italian family whatsoever. He had not seemed curious about it but it may have been something too personal to share with her. Maybe when she got back...... *when* was the question. Whilst she knew she could stay as long as she wished she did not want to outstay that welcome and what would Luc say? Probably accuse her of abandoning their parents. She should speak to him.

Her mind flitted here and there until eventually she surrendered to the quiet pause of the afternoon and to sleep. When she woke it was four thirty and she quickly freshened up and went in search of the others.

The evening passed quietly. Kate walked through the olive groves while her parents sat peacefully on the terrace in leisurely conversation with Umberto, and Claudia prepared supper. A subdued atmosphere gently embraced them as they ate and it was not long after they had finished the meal that Enrico and Isobel surrendered to an enveloping exhaustion and said goodnight.

6

Kate woke early, tired after a disturbed night. Sleep came and went as her mind intruded upon the peace she sought. What sleep she managed to find was pervaded by strange dreams, tentacles that lost their hold as consciousness took over. Fractured images dissolved as she orientated herself, gradually gaining a sense of time and place.

Showered and dressed she joined Umberto and Claudia in the *cucina* for the usual breakfast of coffee and pastries that she thought must stop when she got back home if she was going to keep any semblance of a waistline.

"No sign yet of ….." Kate asked.

"Your parents?" Claudia completed the question before adding. "No, I imagine they are tired after all the excitement yesterday. We didn't want to disturb them."

Kate looked round as she heard footsteps approaching to see her mother walking towards them.

"Good morning," she said with a smile directed at each of them in turn. "I'm sorry we're so late. I don't know what happened, we don't normally wake so late but …."

"Oh do not trouble, you needed it, *no?*" Claudia reassured Isobel.

"Thank you. Enrico is on his way, just a little slow this morning." Isobel sat down at the table next to her daughter.

"Please, help yourself, I will make fresh coffee." Claudia got up and filled a second coffee pot and put it on the stove.

"And you darling, did you sleep well?" Isobel said to her daughter.

"I'm fine *maman*, thanks." Kate said not wanting to say otherwise.

Another set of footsteps announced Enrico's entrance.

"*Buongiorno a tutti,*" he said, his voice still gruff from sleep, as he joined them at the table.

The coffee pot bubbled declaring it was ready and Claudia brought it over to the table, offering it to Enrico and Isobel.

There followed musings over the impending lunch party and a discussion of how and when Isobel and Enrico would leave to go to Adelina's. It was finally agreed that Umberto would drive them over while Claudia and Kate would go to the supermarket to catch up with some shopping.

An hour or so later there were many hugs and farewells as Enrico and Isobel loaded themselves and their luggage into Umberto's car. Shortly after their departure Kate and Claudia set off towards Arezzo, passing below the hilltop village of Civitella where Kate had first made the discovery of her long lost family. She briefly replayed in her mind the moment she stood in front of the display case and saw her family name next to the photograph of the man who would have been her uncle. She remembered Giancarlo standing next to her, concerned and supportive, and her confusion around his presence in her life surfaced once again.

"*Tutto bene*?" asked Claudia, aware of Kate's change of mood.

"Yes, yes," she said contrarily shaking her head. "I was just remembering the day I visited Civitella and …. I don't know, Claudia, so much has changed and …."

"*Davvero,* much has happened since we first met, for you and your family."

"Mmm, I suppose if I'd not met Simonetta when I first

arrived none of this would have happened," Kate said, realising the strange woman's pivotal role in her journey.

"*Eh*," Claudia gave a small shrug of her right shoulder while still focussing on the road. "She does seem to know where to be at the right time."

"Have you known her long?" Kate asked, suddenly curious.

"Yes, many years. Through Umberto of course. They have each worked at the university for a long time and I don't know anyone who knows more about Florence than Simonetta. *Ecco,* we are here," Claudia said as she drove into the car park.

Kate would have liked to ask questions, know more, but as they pulled out a trolley the business of shopping took over.

About half an hour later they arrived at the checkout, the trolley filled with the delights of fresh vegetables and regional delicacies that Kate could only dream of at home.

Claudia pulled her phone from her bag to answer a call and stop the increasing volume of a popular salsa tune.

"*Pronto ...... eh, si, si .... va bene .... a dopo.*" She returned the phone to her bag and explained to Kate that Umberto was staying to have lunch with Adelina and her parents. Suddenly inspired, she remembered a *pizzeria* not far from her home and suggested they go there.

"It's simple food but very good. I think you'll like it."

Kate, swept along in the wake of Claudia's enthusiasm to entertain, happily agreed.

They soon arrived at the restaurant, situated off the road alongside the river. Kate wondered how it survived considering its isolated position. Once inside though, she was surprised to see it was busy and, again, Claudia was greeted as a long lost friend. They were guided to an outside table shaded by a large umbrella.

They ordered pizzas and salad and Claudia assured Kate

that even though she rarely ate pizza, these were the best. A waiter brought a carafe of red wine and a bottle of water and Kate hoped she might glean more information about Simonetta. However, the business of eating overrode her curiosity as the pizza proved to be as delicious as Claudia had promised.

"Claudia, this is soooo good," Kate enthused, "what a great idea to come here. It's a good thing we don't have pizza like this at home, I'd be the size of a house!"

"Now you know why I rarely eat pizza," Claudia laughed, "and when I do, it has to be worth it."

By the time they returned home, Umberto had also finished lunch and followed them up the drive to the villa.

"*Ciao amore, tutto bene?*" Claudia asked as they got out of their cars.

"*Si, si.* Everyone is settled in and the lunch is arranged for the day after tomorrow."

"Friday?" Claudia asked, more as confirmation than question.

"*Si*, Rosa has been busy. It's all organised and will take place at Luigi's. Remember Kate, the friend of Giancarlo's uncle?"

"Of course, he was the one who told me about Adelina. None of this would have been possible without him."

"*Eh, davvero.*" Umberto nodded.

As they walked inside Kate was aware of a sense of loss now that her parents had gone, the lunch arranged and nothing for her to do. Her reason for being there had gone and she was, once again, not sure what to do, how to fill her time. She excused herself to take a siesta and went to her room.

As she stretched out across the bed, she contemplated how finding the diary had inadvertently given her a sense of purpose and wondered what she would do between now and the family lunch. Her parents were at the beginning of a new journey getting to know her father's extended family while it seemed to Kate that she had come to the end of hers. What had occupied her life over the past few months now had no momentum leaving an emptiness she did not know how to fill. A kaleidoscope of images flitted through her mind, people and places she had come to know since moving to the cottage, but still the void remained, reminiscent of her feelings following John's death. How did I get back here, she asked as tears welled and fell sideways into her hair.

She turned, curling into a ball against the renewed sense of loss. Finding comfort in her turning inward, she drifted into a brief but deep sleep.

7

The day of the lunch arrived sooner than Kate had anticipated. Umberto had elected to drive and she took a deep breath before getting in the car behind him and Claudia.

"*Allora*, today is the big day, *eh* Kate?" Umberto announced. "You are ready to meet your Italian family?"

"As ready as I'll ever be I suppose," Kate replied trying to inject her voice with some enthusiasm when in fact she felt something more akin to trepidation and uncertainty. Now the day had arrived it was more an anticlimax after everything that had led to it. She returned Umberto's smile as she caught his eyes in the rear view mirror.

They soon arrived at the villa where most of the guests had already arrived. The first half hour passed in a blur of introductions to faces and names that Kate thought she would never remember. Glasses of prosecco were passed round before Adelina clapped her hands and called everyone to the long table that had been set up in the shade of a loggia at the side of the villa.

Enrico had place of honour at the head of the table with Adelina on his right and his wife on his left. Kate was seated next to her mother and sandwiched on her left by Giancarlo. The table was soon covered with colourful dishes of *antipasti*, bottles of red and white wine and jugs of water. Once everyone was seated Rosa raised her glass in a toast to the return of Enrico to his family. Enrico reciprocated giving a slight nod of his head in acknowledgement and Kate thought how relaxed and happy her father looked, more so than she had ever known him to be. In fact, she realised how little she did know him, only the part he had been prepared to share when so much of him had remained hidden, stopped in time when he had been taken from his home and family.

"You are deep in thought?" asked Giancarlo, turning towards her with his head tilted to one side.

"Oh, er, sorry, yes I suppose I was," Kate tried to recover herself to the present, confused by the face in front of her and the feelings she had for her father.

I believe your father will stay for a while. And you Kate, what are your plans?"

"Erm, I'll ..er … go home as soon as I can, now that I know he's alright."

"So soon, what a shame, there is so much for you still to see."

"Kate, darling," her mother interrupted, "thank you so much for making this possible, see how happy he is."

"I know, I was just thinking ….."

"Kate, *cara,*" this time it was Adelina who interrupted, "*grazie, grazie,* for bringing my brother home. I always knew one day he would return."

It was at this point that Simonetta arrived and was directed to take the seat opposite Kate. They nodded in acknowledgement.

"Well actually, it wouldn't have happened if I had not met Simonetta. It was she who introduced me to Umberto, Claudia and Giancarlo who each in turn led us to you, Adelina."

"*Eh,* so I must also thank you, Simonetta," said Adelina nodding in her direction with a broad grin of gratitude as she repeated, "*grazie, grazie, grazie.*"

"*Eh,*" Simonetta shrugged. "It was meant to be I think."

Kate shivered with a feeling of unease. Was that true? Her thoughts raced back over the last few months and what had led her here. Not just the diary but that first meeting with Simonetta and the events that followed. Who had set what in motion she wondered. She was shaken from her thoughts again by the sound of Giancarlo's voice.

"I am trying to persuade Kate to stay a little longer," he was saying to Simonetta and Adelina.

"*Si, si,* you must stay Kate," encouraged Adelina.

"Thank you, but ……" Kate began.

""I think Kate has other matters to deal with, is that not right," Simonetta said with a knowing smile.

"Well, I ……"

"At least give it some thought," pleaded Giancarlo.

Kate forced a smile and picked up her glass wondering what these other matters could be that Simonetta referred to. She took a sip, then another before putting down her glass. She looked down the table to where Umberto and Claudia sat a few seats away from Simonetta. She wished they were closer to be part of the conversation as they had also played a big role in her journey.

"Yes Kate, do you really have to go so soon?" her mother asked.

"I think so, *maman.* You and *babbo* are fine and I can't be on holiday forever." Kate said through forced smile.

"Well, it is up to you ……" Isobel began but was interrupted as plates were cleared and the next course of pasta arrived in large brightly coloured bowls that were placed at intervals along the table. People helped themselves and served each other, eager to eat the pasta while it was still hot. A bowl of grated *parmesan* was passed round, though not a traditionally Tuscan, and glasses refilled with wine.

"Maybe you will allow me to show you a little more of this beautiful area before you leave?" Giancarlo said between mouthfuls of pasta.

Kate thanked him and agreed she would like that depending, of course, on when she would be able to book a flight.

The Diarist

"*Va bene,* I hope there will be time then."
Simonetta observed the exchange taking place opposite her and, again, decided to hold her counsel. She knew it was not for her to say anything that might influence either Kate or Giancarlo and they each needed to follow their own course, wherever that may lead. She sighed, raised her glass to her lips and took a large sip of wine.

A couple of hours and several courses later people moved around the table to enjoy conversations with friends and family who had been seated too far away. Adelina and Rosa took great delight in introducing Kate to near and distant aunts, uncles and cousins. It seemed nearly everyone became an aunt, uncle or cousin whether related or not and Kate was soon caught up in the bonhomie. She knew she would never be able to remember all their names or how they were meant to be related. However, one face stayed with her. A young man who, not directly introduced to her, seemed familiar yet she was certain she could not have met him before. She asked Giancarlo who said he did not know him well. His family were from a nearby village where they had settled after the war. In fact, little was known about them before then. It was said his grandfather was not Italian and his father had married a cousin and that was how they had become part of Adelina's extended family but that was all he knew. Before Kate could give it any further thought she was whisked off by Adelina to meet yet another distant relative.

Her father was clearly enjoying himself basking in all the attention. Maybe it was the combination of the sun, good food and wine but she also felt happy and relaxed and did not even find Giancarlo's attentiveness disturbing.

By four o'clock people began to leave for a late siesta and Kate noticed the day was taking its toll on her father who was almost nodding off in his chair. She went to say goodbye to him.

"*Babbo*, it's been a wonderful afternoon, so many relatives, I'll never remember all their names."

"*Eh,* not to worry. *Maman* tells me you're leaving soon."

"Yes, I'll check flights and let you know. You're going to stay on a while?"

"*Si, si,*" he said nodding his head. "I'd like to spend more time here. It's been a long time, so much to remember ……"

"Of course, *babbo.* Let me know if you need anything."

"*Eh,*" he said shrugging his shoulders as if to say what could he possibly need.

Kate turned to her mother who had just returned to her seat next to him.

"And you *maman*? Is everything alright with you?"

"Of course darling. Now, you'll let us know when you're leaving, won't you? And give our love to Luc when you get back."

"Of course. I'll try to get a flight in the next couple of days." Kate paused before adding, "I don't know why but I have a strong feeling that I need to be at home."

"In that case darling, you must follow it," her mother said and, reaching out, squeezed Kate's hand.

As she swallowed rising emotions and unspoken words, Kate kissed each parent on the cheek and said she would be in touch once she had booked her flight.

She walked towards Umberto and Claudia who were talking with Simonetta and Giancarlo.

"Ah Kate, there you are." Umberto called to her. "We were just thinking of leaving. You are ready?"

"Yes, yes."

"I can take you later if you wish to stay longer," Giancarlo offered.

"Thank you but no, I'm ready to go now."

"*Va bene,*" Giancarlo said in a quiet voice, nodding his

head in acceptance.

Kate immediately wondered if she had been too abrupt and maybe should have accepted his offer. The flux of feelings he stirred confused her. Was she being overly self-protective or intuiting something she had yet to understand. She took a breath and sighed inwardly.

"I hope we will see you again, Kate," Simonetta said. "Especially as this is also your home now."

"I hope so, and yes I suppose it is," Kate said with a smile as she absorbed the words and their meaning. "I must thank you Simonetta, none of this would have happened if ……"

"*Eh, aspetta,* wait a moment," Simonetta said with a shrug of her shoulders and outstretched hands, "it was not just me, as you know. It was meant and now, well now, you have a lot to take in so please, be gentle and take your time."

Kate suddenly wanted to hug this diminutive yet seemingly formidable woman but simply melted into a big smile. Simonetta nodded in recognition of the silent connection that passed between them.

"*A presto*, see you soon, Kate,"

"I hope so," Kate said as they exchanged the usual goodbye kisses.

As she walked away towards Umberto's car, Kate felt an unexpected freedom and a confidence that had recently escaped her. She was now ready to go home secure in the knowledge that she would soon be returning.

ENGLAND

1

It did not take Kate long to book her return flight and say a fond *arrivederci* to the people and places that had become so much part of her life. As she waited to board the plane she ran through a mental checklist to ensure she had not forgotten anything. By the time she was seated and the plane was ready for take-off she took a last look at the mountain that overshadowed the airport and, as the plane climbed and soared away, she watched the coastline disappear as they headed north.

She had promised Umberto and Claudia, not only would she phone them on her return, she would visit them again very soon. Her parents had been non-committal about how long they intended to stay. Her father did not seem to have any plans to return in the foreseeable future and her mother was content to go along with whatever he chose to do. In a way she could understand. There must be so much he wanted to know, believe that he had missed, but she could not help but worry about their health and what might happen if either of them became ill. When she raised this he had merely waved an arm dismissively, telling her that Italian healthcare was the best in the world and he was, in fact, Italian. She smiled at the memory and, turning to look out of the window, took in the still frozen white beauty of the Alps thousands of feet below.

She noticed how the light became less intense as they

flew further north. Clouds gathered as they crossed the Channel and she stepped off the plane into a grey mizzled afternoon.

By the time she had collected her car and reached home the high sun-filled skies and the flight were a distant memory. The cottage felt cold and empty as she entered the hall and collected a pile of post from the mat. Leaving her case in the hall she took the post and put it down on the kitchen table before filling the kettle and putting it on. She had become accustomed to the noise of having people around and now a strange silence embraced her.

It had been a long day and she was tired and hungry. Deciding against the tea, she used the boiling water to fill a pan for pasta, opened a cupboard and found some spaghetti and a jar of pesto and olive sauce. That would do. She could be sitting at the table eating in less than a quarter of an hour. She put the pasta in the boiling water and turned on a timer then opened her laptop to check her emails while she waited for it to be ready. While the laptop started up she opened a bottle of wine and poured herself a large glass.

As she sifted through the emails she sipped the wine. So many emails in such a short time. She would delete them in the morning. Ping. The pasta was ready. After checking and draining it she added the sauce and emptied it into a bowl, sprinkled some parmesan and returned to the table and her emails. Scanning them she opened a couple that raised her curiosity, the rest could wait.

The first was from Bernard, sent the day before and wishing her a warm welcome home and hoping her trip went well. He said he had some news for her and asked that she call him once she was ready.

The second, which stirred her curiosity more, along with a flutter in her abdomen, was from George. He echoed Bernard's good wishes and also asked her to call. She finished her pasta, leaned back in her chair, and taking a large sip of wine contemplated the two emails. Maybe it was the soporific effect of the food and wine but all Kate could manage was to put the dirty dish and pan in the dishwasher, open her case to take out essential toiletries and get ready for bed.

Kate woke the next morning feeling refreshed, relaxed and appreciative of her own bed as she snuggled into her duvet and considered how she would spend the day. She remembered the pile of post that was sitting untouched on the kitchen table, her suitcase standing in the hall, the empty fridge. She pushed the duvet further away with each thought until a surge of energy catapulted her from the bed.

Thankfully the post was either uneventful or junk mail and, after a second cup of coffee, she dealt with the suitcase. Finally she wrote out a shopping list but before she could leave for the supermarket there was a knock at the door. Annie or Bernard?

It was Annie.

"Hi, welcome back," she grinned. "Thought you might like a coffee."

"I've just had two, so best not, but come in. How are things with you? Would you like a coffee?" Kate asked.

"No, it's ok thanks, I'm fine. I was just curious."

"Ah well, I don't know where to start. Can we save it for later? What about you?" Kate could not think what else to say.

"Oh, you know, much the same. If you mean Ben, there's no change there and I'm sort of getting used to the idea ….."

"What do you mean, Annie?"

"Erm, not sure really ….. I suppose I'm getting used to being on my own and I kind of like it. I'm not saying I don't want him to come home but I do like being able to do what I want when I want and not have to fit in with him all the time."

"Hm, I know what you mean."

The Diarist

"I feel as if I'm being disloyal in an odd way but …. well, I've decided to make the most of it and not worry about what may or may not happen."

"That's great, Annie," Kate said enthusiastically and was abruptly interrupted by the phone ringing. "Excuse me, Annie," she said as she reached to answer it.

"Hello …… yes …….. ok ……..... on my way."

"Sorry Annie, that was Bernard. Said could I go over. Can we catch up later?"

"Of course, come and have supper?"

"Ok thanks, I'll give you a call later."

Kate walked along the road to Bernard's cottage and wondered what could have happened that he needed to see her so soon after her return.

He welcomed her with an eagerness that piqued her curiosity further and her patience was stretched while he retreated to the kitchen to make tea. He returned, as usual with a tray laden not only with china, but with cakes and biscuits.

"Please, help yourself, Kate," he said, as he poured then passed her a cup of tea.

"I'll just have the tea if you don't mind Bernard, thanks," she said hoping not to offend him. "Now, what's all this about?"

"What?" he asked indignantly. "I saw you were back and wondered how you got on."

"Oh Bernard," Kate said, giving him a withering look. "Come on, what have you been up to?"

Bernard, realising there was no point in protesting further, sank into his chair opposite Kate and capitulated.

"Well, I … er … I wanted to be the first to tell you, that's all," he blustered.

"Tell me what, Bernard," Kate prompted as she tried to imagine what it could be and holding on to any patience she could muster.

"I've ….. erm, asked Betty to marry me," he said nodding his head in satisfaction.

"That's wonderful, Bernard!" Kate exclaimed. "You kept that very quiet …..."

"Er, yes I suppose I did. It sort of took me by surprise as well."

"When's the happy day?"

"Oh, we haven't set it yet. I think we have to get over the shock first," he chuckled.

"Well Bernard, thank you for telling me. Maybe I will have a biscuit."

"Well, I think, in a way, it's me who should be thanking you. I mean, all this business with your cottage and the diary……. it, er, sort of brought us together," Bernard said, finishing with a satisfied, "humph."

"Oh ……. now you mention it, I suppose it does seem to have had an effect on the lives of anyone who's been involved with it," Kate said, thinking of herself, her parents and, of course, George. Even Annie, though she wasn't sure that had anything to do with it.

"Now, I want to hear all about your trip," Bernard insisted.

"Ok," Kate said relaxing into her chair as she recounted the salient points of the last few days.

"Oh my, I see what you mean now about that diary and the effect its had. What will you do now?"

"Now?" Kate frowned. "In what way, Bernard?"

"Well, it seems to me that you now have two homes and …... and maybe there's something you're not telling me?" Bernard said looking quizzically at her with his head inclined to one side.

"I don't know what you mean," Kate said defensively.

"Hm, in your own time then."

Unsure where Bernard was heading with the conversation, Kate made her excuses and got up to leave. They said their goodbyes and Kate pondered on what

The Diarist

Bernard could have meant as she walked back to the cottage.

The rest of the day disappeared in a whirl of shopping, phone calls, washing and other chores around the cottage and garden until it was soon time to go next door to Annie's for supper.

She had not had much time to think more about her visit to Bernard's or much else for that matter and, picking up a bottle of wine, made her way to Annie's front door. Annie gave her an effusive welcome, thanked her for the wine before sweeping her into the kitchen.

"Now, make yourself at home," she said as she poured two glasses of wine. "Supper's almost ready ….."

"It smells wonderful, Annie."

"Hope so. How was your day? Oh, and how was Bernard?"

"Oh, he's ok," Kate said unsure whether she should tell Annie about his proposing to Betty but decided she could hardly keep it to herself and would feel awful if Annie heard it from someone else then found out Kate knew all along. "Well, more than ok in fact. He's proposed to Betty."

"What!"

"Yes, he's asked Betty to marry him," she assured Annie.

"Well, that's ….. er ….. that's wonderful," Annie said struggling to find the words before raising her glass and adding, "a toast to them and may they be very happy."

"To Bernard and Betty," said Kate raising her glass to meet Annie's.

"Ok, I think supper will be ready now so let's eat and you can tell me all about your trip."

Annie opened the oven to reveal a steaming dish of moussaka and ladled out two large portions which spread across the plates in a mix of tomato, aubergine, lentils with a bechamel sauce and cheese topping. "It's a veggie one. I had some the other day in that little restaurant, oh, what's it called? Anyway, I really liked it so thought I'd have a go ...." She retrieved a large bowl of salad from the fridge and set it all on the table. "Now, I'm all ears," she added as she sat down and looked expectantly at Kate.

"Ok, ok," Kate surrendered and between mouthfuls of moussaka gave another account of her visit to Italy interspersed with enthusiastic comments and exclamations from Annie.

As Kate reached the end of her narrative and her meal, she leaned back into her chair and Annie replenished their wine glasses.

"So, what will you do now?"

"What do you mean, Annie?" Kate asked looking puzzled.

"Oh, I don't know ... there's so much. I mean, there's your new family, your parents are still there and then there's this .... er, whatshisname .... Gian .."

"Giancarlo, and there's nothing to tell."

"Really?"

"Really," Kate emphasised. "He's very charming and I admit that I may have been momentarily smitten but it is just his way, nothing more. And anyway, not what I need right now."

" Hm." Annie smirked.

"What do you mean, hm? I'm not looking for ...."

"For a handsome charming Italian? Just saying," Annie said with a shrug.

"Oh Annie, that's not it and you know it."

"Ok, I won't say another word about it. But what about all your new relatives, will you go back soon?"

"To be honest Annie, it all happened so quickly and it's a lot to take in. I really don't know."

Before eventually saying goodnight they continued to chat for an hour or so, around the changes in their lives and what the future may hold.

Back in the cottage Kate felt unsettled by her

conversation with Annie. Lying in bed she found sleep elusive as her mind revisited their words. Why had she been so eager to come home? How did she really feel about Giancarlo. Why was George asking her to call him. Oh John, why aren't you here? These questions and the resulting thoughts continued to torment her until, exhausted, she eventually fell asleep.

2

Kate still felt unsettled the following day as she went through the motions of showering, dressing and having breakfast. It was a beautiful sun-drenched morning but it did nothing to permeate Kate's enveloping cloud.

Unable to settle to anything she decided to go for a walk hoping this would lift her mood but she had not made it as far as the front door when the phone rang.

"Hello."

"Ah Kate, you're back. It's George, I hope you don't mind but I rang on the off chance that you might be home. I've got a meeting this morning not far from you and wondered if I could entice you to have lunch?"

"Oh ….. George, well yes, thank you, that would be lovely."

"Great, pick you up about 12.30?"

"Ok, see you then." Kate put down the phone somewhat puzzled by the brief conversation and determined not to overthink it.

The rest of the morning passed quickly. Kate forgot about going for a walk and instead wandered into the garden where pulling up one weed led to pulling up another, then another and so on until she was satisfied that few had escaped her eagle eyes. Happier and replenished by the sun and the joy of being in the garden she went inside to be ready when

The Diarist

George arrived.

He was on time and Kate was surprised by her immediate thought of how attractive he looked, and there was something else she could not quite put her finger on. She fumbled with her keys as she locked the door before taking a gathering breath and following him along the path to his car.

"I thought we could try the pub just outside the village, I've heard the food is very good, if that's ok?" he asked as he opened the car door for her.

"Mmm, I think Annie mentioned she'd been there," she replied finding his proximity unsettling.

It only took a few minutes to reach the pub during which time George again explained that he had a meeting nearby and hoped she did not mind him calling out of the blue. Kate reassured him she did not mind at all. In reality though she was not sure what her true feelings were.

Lunch itself was less challenging. Maybe it was the table between them that distanced Kate from any compromising feelings. George wanted to hear every detail of her trip and as Kate told it for the third time in two days and was once again caught up in the people, places and emotions, she was able to accept and embrace a little more of her new self. It was only after she had finished talking that she had an unidentified sense of something she could not explain. As she looked at George there was a subtle recognition that immediately eluded her and was soon lost in conversation.

"It seems your journey has come to an end and yet is just beginning. What will you do now?" George asked after ordering coffee.

Kate frowned. "I don't know, George. I thought I'd see if I can pick up some freelance work again."

"And Italy? Your new family?" he prompted.

Her frown deepened as she shook her head. "Er, I think it's more my father's journey than mine. Of course, I shall visit but ... well ....."

"You don't know them?"

"Not exactly," she said pursing her lips.

George raised an eyebrow.

"I suppose so, in a way," she capitulated, uncomfortable with the turn in the conversation.

"I'm sorry Kate," he said picking up on her change of mood. "It's none of my business but if you do want to talk I'd be happy to listen."

"Thank you, George," she said relaxing into a smile. "There's no need for apologies. I think I just need time to take it all in."

"Of course."

"And what about you? You've also had your own family revelations ....."

"Hmm, it's still a bit odd realising that I'm actually half Italian after believing I was English for such a long time. And no, I don't feel like rushing over there either."

Kate liked the way he included his understanding with her own realising, whereas she knew her immediate family, he had no idea who his father was and was unlikely to ever know. Remembering her own reluctance to talk about her experience she restrained from asking him anything about his. A step too far in intimacy maybe.

Later, once she was in the sanctuary of her own home her thoughts returned to torment her. That familiar sense of recognition she had felt with George. The young man at the family lunch she had asked Giancarlo about. There was something she couldn't quite grasp as an image of one then the other flitted in and out of her mind. What to think ...... could it be .... isn't it a bit far-fetched, and in a way too convenient. She detested it when people put two and two together and made five or worse, ten. Whilst it would be wonderful if it was true, she did not want to raise false hopes. Maybe if she had a photo of George she could send it

The Diarist

to Giancarlo, he had, after all, been there and knew something about the family. How would she get a photo though? She did not want to ask George for one, so how? Inspiration came in the form of a thought suggesting she look on the internet.

She opened her laptop and typed George's name into the search engine. From the list that appeared on the screen she saw that he had a website so she clicked on the link which took her to the homepage. No photo of him though, only of his projects. She looked along the menu bar and clicked on the 'About' button and there it was, George's head and shoulders looking out at her.

Faced with the reality of taking the next step Kate pushed the laptop away from her and looking out of the window asked herself if this was something she could, or should, do. If she did nothing no one would be any the wiser. However, if she took this step, and she was joining the right dots, then George would at least know more of his maternal family.

She stood and walked over to the window and looked out on to the garden and fields beyond. She momentarily wished John was beside her to confide in and guide her. If he was, of course, none of this would have happened and this dilemma would never have been born. She sighed and decided ignoring it was not an option she could live with. Now she not only had to work out how to send the information to Giancarlo, but also overcome her reluctance to contact him so directly.

She opened a new email and entered his address and after the usual pleasantries she explained why she was writing, asking whether he thought there might be a link between George and the young man they had discussed at the family lunch for her father. She typed in the details of George's website, sent her good wishes and, before she could change her mind, pressed send. Collapsing back into her chair she hoped she had done the right thing.

Kate did not have long to wait for a reply. Yes, Giancarlo agreed there was a strong resemblance between the two men and was there anything she would like him to do? Suppressing a rising panic, she immediately replied saying no, she would first speak to George, thanked him and would be in touch again soon.

Again she wondered if she was doing the right thing. Despite the confirmation offered by Giancarlo she still had doubts about sharing it with George. Eventually she decided to sleep on it. Another day, another perspective.

The next day arrived and Kate was still filled with doubt and devoid of any clarity she had hoped a new day might bring. She sat at the table with her coffee unable to escape the ensuing thoughts of what to say to George. She retrieved her memory of the previous day in search of confirmation.

It had been at the end of their meal when she'd had that sense of recognition. The family lunch for her father had flashed into her mind. Sitting at the table, turning, noticing the young man, a sense of familiarity and now having that same feeling. As she had looked at George she had seen the young man's face overlay his and then it was gone. She had closed her eyes to clear the image, make sense of it, but then it was as if it had never been there. George had driven her home and the memory of the image had lingered as they said goodbye. It was after he had gone that she began to make connections between the two men.

It was uncanny, not just the physical likeness but also, now she thought about it, how they shared similar mannerisms. Again, the doubts surfaced. Was she making it up? Creating something from nothing? Would George want to know? Was it any of her business?

No …. no ….. she shook her head, freeing herself from them. She knew and, in acknowledging that knowing, she also knew she must tell George. This, of course, presented her with another dilemma. Both George and Giancarlo had been kind and attentive friends whom she had kept at a distance and the thought of anything that might change that gave rise to more anxiety. She tried to remind herself she was not a naïve teenager but it did nothing to allay the trepidation she felt.

She was saved from further torment by a knock at the front door. She opened the door to meet the postman who asked if she would accept a parcel for her next door neighbour, Annie. After taking and signing for it she determined not to get further entangled in her thoughts and went out to the garden hoping to regain a sense of equilibrium.

Kate walked round the garden inspecting the flower beds as the warmth of the sun across her back and shoulders calmed and reassured her. She was about to start dead heading the roses when she heard the sound of the phone ringing through the open door. Putting down her secateurs and gloves she returned to the kitchen.

"Hello?"

"Hi Kate, it's Annie. I had a card through the door saying you have a parcel for me, is now a good time?"

"Yes, of course. See you in a minute."

Kate replaced the phone. Odd, she thought, frowning at it. It was not like Annie to phone first, she was usually more spontaneous.

Kate opened the door to greet Annie as she walked up the path towards her.

"Hi," she said, noticing how pale and tired Annie looked.

"Er hi," Annie mumbled. "Sorry to be a bother, I er …."

Kate interrupted, inviting her in and guiding her by the elbow to the kitchen.

"I won't stay, I mean …."

"Annie, whatever's wrong, you …."

"Look awful I know. It's just that, oh, I don't know ….."

"It's ok, take your time," Kate encouraged, pulling her chair next to her and placing her hand over Annie's.

Annie looked up into Kate's face and took a deep breath. "It's .... er ....," another deep breath. "I had a call from Ben and .... well, he wants to come back and I've been up most of the night ..... and Kate, I don't know, it all keeps going round in my head and I can't make sense of any of it."

Kate listened as Annie related her conversation with Ben and her subsequent conflicting thoughts before suggesting a cup of tea.

"Thank you," Annie said, managing a half smile. "I'm sorry I didn't mean to ....."

"Don't give it another thought," Kate made the tea and returned to the table. "Look you don't have to decide anything right now, do you? Why don't you take your time and wait until you're feeling stronger?"

Annie sighed.

"Of course, you're right," she said, managing another half smile. "It's just I don't know if I can go through this again ..... I mean, how can I trust him?"

Kate thought how fortunate she had been. Even though John was no longer there, the time they had together had been happy. Of course there were ups and downs but she had always trusted him and could only imagine what Annie was going through. Although she had hardly known Annie and Ben as a couple she got the impression they were happy and comfortable together so was shocked when Annie said he had gone. She looked at her friend as she searched for the right words.

"Thanks Kate," Annie said hugging her mug of tea. "I do feel better, well a bit anyway."

After Annie had left, Kate's thoughts returned to her own dilemma of whether to tell George that it was possible his uncle Charles survived the war, married and had children and that she, Kate, may have met members of his family.

The Diarist

She knew that he was working on a project nearby as they had mooted the possibility of him calling by when he was in the area. So, should she wait until she heard from him or call him? No, email would be better, and confirm the suggestion. That was it, she would email him to thank him for lunch and at the same time suggest he call in next time he was nearby as there was something she would like to run past him.

She opened her laptop, typed out the email and, releasing a sigh, pressed send. There, it was done.

3

The email arrived that evening although Kate did not see it until she switched on her laptop the following morning. George suggested he could call in about 11.30 as he had a lunch meeting nearby. Kate checked the time to find it was already ten o'clock. She quickly replied saying yes that was fine and hoping she had caught him in time. Almost immediately his reply pinged on to the screen confirming he would see her then.

Kate's thoughts soon gathered speed as she looked around the kitchen wondering what she was going to say to him. Her eyes fell on the dresser and the events since finding the diary fast forwarded through her mind in a kaleidoscope of images of the people and places that had brought her to this moment.

She closed her eyes, took a deep breath, then released it. It was done and he would be here soon, she told herself, and she just had to get on with it. However this did not stop the mounting anxiety she felt as the hands of the kitchen clock approached 11.30.

By the time George arrived, although still apprehensive, Kate felt calmer if a little ridiculous.

She made coffee and suggested they sit in the garden. There was something about sitting outside, Kate thought, that diminished the potential intensity of the conversation.

The Diarist

After the usual pleasantries about the weather and each other's well being George turned to Kate with a look filled with expectation.

"So, what is this about, Kate?"

Kate took a deep breath which she held momentarily as she searched for the words which now eluded her.

"Well, I'm not sure where to begin really …."

"Oh dear, this sounds as if it could be serious," George said as he raised an eyebrow.

"In a way it is," Kate tried again. "It was when I was in Italy recently. Remember I told you about the family lunch given for my father ..."

"Yes, of course."

"It ...er … it didn't seem important at the time, it was only when I got back and ……" she paused as she gathered her thoughts. "At the lunch there was a young man who seemed familiar and yet I knew I had never met him before. I asked Giancarlo about him and he told me about his family, which I'll come to in a minute. It was when you and I had lunch the other day, we were talking and I had that same sense of recognition but at the time I didn't understand it."

"I'm not sure what you mean, Kate?" George said as his forehead creased in a frown.

"It was only when I got home that I made the connection. Oh dear, it all sounds a bit strange now. Anyway," Kate paused, then continued, "it was then it hit me…… I mean the familiarity, the resemblance …. it was you. Sorry, I mean the man I saw at the lunch seemed familiar because he …."

"What are you trying to say, Kate?"

"Er, that there were similarities between him and you. I mean it wasn't just looks, there were certain mannerisms that you share and ….. well, getting back to his family. It seems his grandfather was not Italian and arrived in the village before the end of the war, married a local girl and stayed."

Kate tried to judge how George was taking it but his

expressionless face gave nothing away, there was only a tension that was filling the space between them. Eventually he spoke.

"I'm not sure what you're implying."

"I'm not sure myself, George, and I've been over it again and again but always come back to the same ….."

"The same what?"

"That maybe, maybe you and he are related." Kate shrugged her shoulders. "Maybe, just maybe it's possible that this young man's grandfather was your uncle, the brother Charles that Hettie wrote about in her diary …." Kate's voice trailed off as she became aware of a growing chill emanating from George as he stood up from his chair.

"I don't think it's really any of your business and fail to understand why ….. I think I'd better go."

Kate scrambled to her feet and followed him into the kitchen.

"George I'm sorry but I agonised over whether I should tell you or not and …."

"Well, maybe you shouldn't have and …... thank you for the coffee." George turned abruptly, walked down the hall and let himself out of the front door leaving Kate standing in the kitchen unable to move. When she heard his car pull away and disappear down the lane she went out to the garden to collect the now empty coffee mugs and, sitting in the chair she had occupied a few moments ago, reflected on their conversation. There was an emptiness where the words had been and regret seeped in to fill the void. How could she have so misjudged it, misjudged him and how he might react.

The more she thought about it the worse she felt. What had she been thinking? But she had been sure it was the right thing to do. She must have sat there for some time wrestling with her doubt-filled thoughts before she came to a decision. She could not spend the rest of the day cogitating all the ifs

The Diarist

and buts. As she walked back into the kitchen there was a knock at the door and when she looked at the clock she saw that she been sitting in the garden for over an hour. She checked her hair with her hands as she walked along the hall to open the door. When she did she was greeted by a large bunch of roses and lilies being held out towards her.

"Oh," she exclaimed as George's head poked round the floral display.

"I hope you'll forgive my dreadful behaviour earlier, I ...er ...."

"Oh," she repeated, still surprised. "George. Come in."

She took the flowers and they walked through to the kitchen.

"I don't know what came over me," he said. "I think it was the shock. I really shouldn't have ...."

"It's ok George, I probably shouldn't have ...."

"No, no. You should, of course you should."

They stood awkwardly then Kate pulled out a chair and invited George to sit in a chair the other side of the table.

He remained standing. "I, er ...... I was wondering if you'd like to have lunch somewhere and we can talk?"

Kate's first thought was to suggest they have lunch there but immediately dismissed it as inappropriate, the memory of their earlier conversation still in the air.

"Well, there's no .....," she stopped herself mid sentence before adding, "that would be lovely, thank you."

"Good," he said nodding to himself. "Do you know the fish restaurant in town?"

"No," Kate said shaking her head, wondering at the turn of events.

"Ok, shall we go? I mean, if you're ready?"

"Yes, er, could you give me a couple of minutes?" Kate asked as she checked the windows and locked the back door before disappearing to the bathroom to use the toilet and scan her appearance. She reapplied her lipstick and satisfied with what she saw she returned to the kitchen and confirmed to George that she was ready.

The restaurant was busy and Kate was relieved when they were led to a window table overlooking the garden, a good distance from other tables. They had not discussed their morning conversation on the drive over and she felt it hang in the air between them.

They gave their orders, she for sea bream, he for dover sole, and agreed on a glass each of chenin blanc. The wine arrived quickly and George raised his glass towards Kate, and thanked her for coming.

"I hope you'll let me explain a little ...." he said taking a sip of wine.

Kate did likewise and relaxed a little as the wine coursed its way to her head, which she nodded in reply.

"Ok."

"When I left I didn't know what to think. I started to drive but had to pull over. I think it was shock. As I went over it in my mind I realised I was being totally irrational. It struck me that it reminded me of how I felt when I found my mother's diaries and .... well, you know all about that. Anyway, I felt terrible about the way I had just walked out so I cancelled my meeting and ..... here we are. Do you really think it's possible that Charles survived the war and stayed in Italy? I mean, you'd think he would have got in touch with his family in London – let them know he was alright."

Kate smiled, relieved that he was expressing an interest in the possibilities and that, after all, she had done the right thing.

"I know, that was my first thought too." Kate said rising to the conversation. "I don't know, but if this is his family maybe someone would know what happened."

"Hm, possible I suppose. You said you spoke to one of them?"

"No, I didn't speak to him. It was just that he seemed

familiar so I asked Giancarlo who was sitting next to me if he knew him. I was certain I'd not seen him before and all Giancarlo said was something about the grandfather arriving in the village during the war and marrying a local girl. I think he said he wasn't Italian but you know how it is at these occasions, it all became lost in conversation. It was only when I saw you the other day that I made the connection and ….."

"I see." George said sitting back in his seat as the waiter removed his plate, then Kate's and asked if they would like dessert. Kate declined but accepted George's offer of coffee.

"I'm sorry, I didn't realise at the time that it might be important ……"

"No, no, how could you have known," George said shaking his head. "Do you think this Giancarlo …. I mean is he someone you could ask if he knows the family or more about them?"

Kate thought of her email to Giancarlo which she had not mentioned to George. "I could email him and see what he says," she said with a slight shrug indicating she did not know how helpful it would be. "I'll do it when I get back," she added with an encouraging smile.

"Thank you," George said returning her smile. "It's all …. I don't know. I'm not sure if I want to know more or not. Do you mind me asking, how did you feel when you found out about your father's family?"

"No, I don't mind," she said hesitantly, "I ….. at the time it was a shock and it all happened so quickly I didn't really have time to think about it, to take it in if you know what I mean."

"Is that why you came back so quickly?" George ventured.

Kate looked into her small cup of coffee as she considered this.

"Hm, I suppose so," she replied looking up to where he was gauging her response. "In a way it doesn't seem to have anything to do with me. I feel on the outside of it."

"Maybe you need time to take it in, find your way with it?"

"Mmm, we'll see." Kate said, as she considered how much she wanted to say on the subject. "I don't know George, it seems part of my life has been turned upside down and yet nothing has changed and I'm sorry if I've ….."

"Turned my life upside down?" he said, finishing her sentence and hoping that was what she intended to say.

"Yes, I suppose so."

"Then don't worry. Let's see what happens. If it turns out this is part of my family then we'll go from there. Ok?"

"Ok," Kate reciprocated with a smile behind which she hid the realisation of a new awareness, the resistance she had to accepting the new part of her own family.

After George had dropped her off at home Kate sent the email to Giancarlo explaining she had spoken to George and, yes, she would like him to make enquiries about the family that could possibly be the descendants of the long lost Charles Forbes, George's uncle.

She did not have to wait long for a reply, less than two days, and during the intervening time she tried to avoid any thoughts of George, Giancarlo or Italy. Instead she focussed on settling back into the cottage and her life there.

Annie was noticeable by her absence and Kate missed her popping in for coffee and a chat. She decided not to call her, sure that Annie would contact her when she was ready.

She was about to go out when the phone rang. She hesitated for a moment and then answered it to be greeted by an animated Giancarlo.

He enthusiastically told her how he had spoken to Luigi, the one who knew everyone, and he had shown the photo of George to the young man who Kate had noticed at the family lunch and had set this whole thing in motion. He

The Diarist

had then shown the photo to his father who had in turn shown it to his brother, and they had then compared it to old photos of their father.

"They couldn't believe it, Kate. I mean, the likeness is ……," he paused to take a breath, "it's extraordinary. They are all very excited and want to meet George and hear all he can tell them about his uncle. It seems they know very little as he didn't talk about his life before Italy."

"Oh," Kate said thinking that sounded familiar as memories of her father's silence about his early life flashed into her mind. "Do you really think it could be him?"

"*Certo, certo* ….. I've seen the photos, Kate, and truly, you wouldn't believe the likeness. I'll email a copy of one of them and you'll see. It may take a day or two but when you see it you'll ………." His voice was so full of enthusiasm she could almost see the photo in front of her.

"Thank you, I'll show George and ….."

"Yes, it is quite remarkable. We have another reunion."

"Er, ok, I'll call him now and let him know," Kate said as her mind raced ahead considering the logistics of who should contact who. "And the photo, I'll forward it to him as soon as I receive it."

They said their goodbyes and Kate, exhausted by the exchange, released a long held breath.

It was all moving so quickly and here she was, once again, drawn into someone else's world and someone else's Italy. Well, there was nothing she could do until she heard from Giancarlo with the photo.

She decided not to call George until she received the photo. In the meantime she would focus on her own life and consider her options now she was home. Whilst John had left her well cared for financially she needed to do something. To be useful. But what? She had already sent a couple of tentative emails previous clients but had, as yet, not received a reply. The more she thought about it the more she realised she did not know what she wanted to do.

No longer defined by her marriage Kate peeled away the layers, first of wife, then of widow, and her role as mother with dependent children. Now free to follow her own path she wondered what that might be. Whilst this was not the first time she had reassessed her life, this had a different flavour, a sense of a broader horizon, pregnant with fresh potential and opportunities. Her world opened and expanded before her and she grabbed a pen and paper to capture any ideas.

After a few minutes and a blank piece of paper still in front of her she gave a sigh and wandered into the garden. Was she being foolish thinking she could start again? Should she be content with what she had? After all, she was fortunate in having a lovely home, no financial worries, two children who were making their way in the world and seemed happy. Still, there was an itch that she could not quite reach. Her thoughts turned to her parents and she smiled at how they were embracing the changes in their lives. Maybe it was not too late for her to do something new after all and she berated herself for such morose thinking.

She would start by getting the local paper and going to the library, find out what was happening locally. Now that her Italian adventure had come to a close she did not want to sit around and do nothing.

Giancarlo's email arrived earlier than expected. As soon as Kate saw the photo she understood his enthusiasm and the family's eagerness to meet George. Whether George would share their enthusiasm she did not know.

Well, the only way to find out was to forward the photo to him and wait. As she wrote the short email she felt a strong reassurance wash over her and an image of George with his Italian family flashed before her eyes. It was gone in an instant, hardly memorable, yet the clarity of it remained.

The Diarist

George replied within the hour asking if he could call in later that afternoon on his way home. Kate replied confirming she would see him then. Restless and eager for the time to pass, she imagined different conversations they might have. Would he be happy, would he want to go to Italy, meet them, or, maybe would he close down again and not want to know more.

She flitted from room to room tidying this and that, unable to settle to anything just periodically checking the time, willing the hours to pass.

He arrived shortly before four o'clock and, to her relief, sooner than she expected.

"Come in, can I get you anything, tea, coffee, something stronger?" she offered.

"No, no thanks. Can we just sit down?"

Kate led the way to the kitchen and they sat at the table facing each other. There was a brief silence as they adjusted to each other and the potential conversation.

"Kate," he began, "first I want to thank you for all this. To be honest, I'm still trying to take it in but the one thing I am sure of is that I must go to Italy and meet these people, find out more. Be sure."

"Of course," Kate said, having followed every word intently. "If there's anything I can do ..... put you in touch with my friends there .... anything at all."

"Well I've been thinking. In fact I've thought of little else all day. I'd like," he paused and cleared his throat. "I wondered if you'd come with me?"

"Oh," Kate said, momentarily lost for words.

"It would mean so much to me if you did and ..."

"Yes," Kate blurted, unsure where the word had come from and what she had just agreed to. "Er, when were you thinking of going?" she added trying to find a sense of normality.

"As soon as I can get away. I'll have to take a look and

see what's possible. I mean that's wonderful and ...." George said, fluffing his words. "Look why don't I go home, check a few things and come back. We could go for a meal somewhere, if you're free of course?"

Kate let out another, "Yes."

"I know it's all a bit sudden but ...."

"That's ok, seems to be sort of normal," Kate said eventually finding her voice. "What time?"

"How about I pick you up about 7.30?"

"Ok."

After he had gone, Kate returned to sit at the kitchen table rerunning their conversation in her mind. Had that really happened? Had she really agreed to go to Italy yet again and, with George? Just when she thought life was ..... when life was what? It certainly had not been normal since she moved into this cottage.

Despite Kate's retrospective misgivings she enjoyed her evening with George. He enthusiastically told her he had been busy looking at flights and seeing how he could rearrange his work schedule. He seemed charged with a new energy and Kate was soon caught up in his exuberance as they discussed possible places to visit and where to stay.

"I thought we might as well make a holiday of it, what do you think?" George asked.

"Erm, I suppose so," Kate shook her head, wondering how many holidays she could have in such a short time. Also she could not help thinking on what basis they were making these plans. What was George expecting?

"Don't worry, Kate," he said as if reading her thoughts, "I'm not suggesting anything improper," he added with a smile.

"Oh, I er ..... "

"I mean, we'll go as friends, separate rooms etc., but I'd like it to be my treat. A thank you for all you've done."

"But I haven't done anything," Kate said, wide-eyed.

"Well, if it hadn't been for you, you know, not just finding the diary and going to Italy, but making the enquiries for me ..... "

"Oh, but that was nothing George, just a couple of emails and I think ...... "

"Please Kate, no thinking and no buts, I'd like to."

Torn between wanting to maintain her independence and honour George's wishes, Kate nodded her head and smiled as she said, "Ok."

George went on to talk about possible dates and flights and how he would like to spend a few days in Florence before going to meet his family. How he wanted to follow in Kate's and Hettie's footsteps as it were. How they would take the diary and Kate could show him the places she had visited and tell him how her journey of discovery had unfolded.

By the end of the evening Kate had relaxed and was more accepting of the whole idea. She agreed to email her friends in Italy to arrange a meeting and to leave the booking of the flights and hotel in Florence to George.

However, when Kate woke the next morning following a night of erratic dreams, she was once again filled with apprehension about her trip to Italy with George. As she worked her way through the myriad of feelings that rose to the surface, she realised the two overriding ones were fear and guilt.

She remembered how flattered she had been by Giancarlo's attentiveness and had even been a little seduced by him and how, out of fear of making a fool of herself, she had retreated into herself, hurrying back to England, convincing herself it was just his way and meant nothing more than that. Was she doing the same thing with George?

She liked George but had not thought of him romantically, or was that something else she was avoiding? Yes, he was an attractive man, and yes, she felt relaxed in his company. Yes, she found him kind and considerate and yes, there were shared similarities in that they were both half Italian and had discovered long lost families in Italy.

The more she thought about it the more she saw how guarded she was, not only of herself but also protective of her memories of John and how she used this as a shield that prevented her from taking the risk of moving forward emotionally. She curled the duvet around her in a futile attempt to hide from the thoughts and feelings that now pursued her.

She turned onto her back, stretched the length of the bed and decided the best way forward was to get up, shower and make a list for the day. Concentrate on that.

By the time she had finished breakfast and settled at the kitchen table with pen and paper she felt her resolve gain strength.

So, she was going to Italy once again and although she had only just got back she could see no reason not to go again. She just had to wait for George's email with the details of flights and hotels. Maybe that was part of her discomfort as it had been John who would have made these arrangements in the past and it seemed strange for someone else to be doing that now. There was also the matter of George wanting to pay for the trip; Kate was not at all sure about this. Whilst she was sure he was offering with the best of intentions she questioned her ability to accept his generosity without feeling obligated in some way.

As she wondered where this next trip might take her, she hoped it would be less of an emotional roller coaster than her last two visits. She had come a long way from her prison of grief and knew she now had to embrace these changes if she was going to find happiness again. Returning to Italy would give her the opportunity to do this. To be open to getting to know her family, to deepen her relationship with her father as she got to know the part of him he had held hidden for so long. Whilst she did not feel ready to welcome another man into her life, she could appreciate the attention offered by Giancarlo and George and who knew where that might lead as her defences softened.

She half blushed at the thought and was about to go out to the garden to escape such ideas when the phone rang. It was Luc.

"Hi, you're back then."

"Yes, a few days now, how are things with you?" She asked, unsure about the tone of his voice.

"Hm, good question, sis," he paused. "I mean, you're back and you just left them there."

Kate took a breath before responding unsure whether he meant his words as an accusation or a question.

"Luc, babbo wanted to stay and ..."

"And what about maman, what about her ..."

"She's fine, Luc. They're both having a wonderful time and ....."

"Great, but what ...."

"Look, there's no need to worry, they're both well and happy and anyway, I'm going back again soon."

"Oh, quite the little gadabout these days ...."

"Stop it, Luc," Kate said becoming exasperated with his sarcasm. "Why don't you go yourself, they'd love that."

Silence. Kate wondered if they had been cut off.

"Luc?"

"Yes, I'm here. Just thinking. Look, I don't want to get into it being much easier for you but you know how it is here and ...."

"Of course I do but," Kate began, now hearing a softer more amenable tone to his words. "But can't you get someone to look after things or, even close for a few days?"

"I don't know, Kate."

"Y'know, they'd love it if you did and there's a whole new family waiting for you."

"Ok, ok, I'll think about it. When are you going?"

"Not sure yet, depends on flights, probably next week." Kate said and wondered how she was going to explain that she was not going alone this time but decided such explanations could wait.

They finished the call on better terms with Luc saying he would call her again soon.

Meanwhile, sitting in a kitchen not far from the Boboli Gardens in Florence, Simonetta's thoughts were of Kate, her imminent visit and the events that had led her there. Whilst she was used to using her gifts to help others her relationship with Kate was different.

She had learnt to trust her intuition and 'nudges' for many years now and found it to be beneficial for all concerned. She came from a long line of healers and, despite her mother's attempts to deny it, it had been her grandmother who had nurtured and supported her in realising her abilities.

However, with Kate she had held her counsel in the knowledge that Kate had to find her own way through the unexpected encounters and make her own choices as she found her authentic voice again. Whether that be in a new relationship or independently she was certain that it was not her place to influence her.

Simonetta withdrew her thoughts knowing the webs that could be woven from such simple meanderings. She merely wished Kate well and looked forward to seeing her again on her return to Florence.

Back in England, Kate shivered despite the heat. The feeling disappeared as soon as it had arrived and shaking herself she moved from the table towards the front door. Locking it behind her she walked along the lane to Bernard's cottage and found him in the vegetable garden where he was collecting an abundant harvest of courgettes.

"Ah Kate, it's good to see you. You're just in time, would you like some courgettes?" he asked as he slowly eased himself to his full height rubbing his back as he did so.

"Oh, thank you Bernard, if you're sure you have enough."

"Enough? There's more than enough my dear. More than I know what to do with anyways, so you'd be doing me a favour," he said as he picked up the trug in which he had collected them. "Come inside, let me find you a bag."

Kate followed him into the cottage and hoped she could avoid any offer of tea and cakes.

Bernard headed to the kitchen after first offering her a seat in the living room and the usual cup of tea which Kate politely refused by saying she could not stay long but just wanted to have a quick word.

Intrigued, he quickly returned from the kitchen carrying a large bag of courgettes and joined her in their usual chairs.

"So, what's all this about then?" he asked, rubbing his chin.

"Oh, I just wanted to bring you up to date really," Kate responded and went on to relate what had happened since she had last seen him.

"Well, well, well, who would have thought it," Bernard said shaking his head. "And you're going to go back to Italy again then with this, er, George?" he added with a mischievous glint in his eyes.

"I suppose I am," Kate said with a frown, and in a remonstrative voice added, "but it's nothing like that, Bernard."

"Of course not, if you say so."

"Bernard!"

"Look Kate, I think it's wonderful and of course you should go. You're not having second thoughts are you?"

"Well, not exactly, it's just ......"

"That's good then. Just think, who would have thought that little book would have changed so many lives."

"I know, I've been thinking that as well."

"And, of course, that woman you met when you first

went to Florence, what was her name?"

"Oh, Simonetta. Yes, I know. If it wasn't for her I expect I would have come back none the wiser from what might have been a very nice holiday."

The both sat for a moment or two in a companionable silence, each ruminating on the events that had brought them to this point. However, not one to be silent for long, Bernard asked what plans she had for her next trip.

"I'm not sure yet, I just hope it's less eventful than the previous ones."

The Diarist

4

She returned home to find an email from George with potential dates for flights to Pisa. Kate closed her eyes and took a deep breath as she absorbed the deepening reality of the trip. She did not have any appointments or arrangements so replied leaving the final dates to him, but before she pressed send she paused, changed her mind wanting to maintain her newfound independence and rewrote the email confirming a date the following week.

It was not long before George wrote again with the flight confirmation. This was the catalyst she needed. First she grabbed a pen and paper and began to make a list of what she needed to do between now and then. First, she emailed Umberto and Claudio informing them of the date of their arrival and their plans to spend the first few days in Florence. Next, she called Annie and left a message inviting her to supper. Then she emailed Emma as she was not sure when she was due back from Thailand but hoped it would be before her own trip to Italy.

After what felt like an eventful morning she made a simple avocado salad and took it out to the garden where she sat in the shade and mused over the upcoming trip. She was soon pulled from her thoughts by the sound of her phone ringing. She considered ignoring it but after a couple of more rings ran to the kitchen to answer it.

" Hi, mum, how are you? Have I missed much?"

"Oh," Kate paused as she thought about it. What could she say? She had not yet told her daughter about the diary and vowed to do so very soon. Emma was therefore unaware of the catalyst it had been in not only Kate's life, but also the lives of others who came within its aura. How could she explain how it had been so incremental in her going to Italy where she had followed in Hettie's footsteps leading her not only to new friendships but also to a family she had not known existed. How this little green book then led her to George, more diaries and the possibility that Charles, his uncle and the reason the diaries were first written, had survived the war, married and fathered children.

Were she and George really going to Italy together to meet this family?

And then, of course, there was Betty and Bernard whose curiosity about the history of her cottage had brought them together and they were now soon to be married.

All that had taken place since she moved into the cottage. She thought it was more the stuff that novels were made of than real life and merely smiled before replying.

"No, not really love. Did you have a nice time?"

"Fantastic, it was amazing. Can't wait to tell you all about it. How about lunch?"

The agreed to meet a couple of days later and Kate felt happy that she would finally be able to tell Emma about finding the diary and subsequent events.

Emma was captivated by it all and lunch went on well into the afternoon.

Kate listened as her daughter regaled her with details of her holiday. She was happy to hear that Emma had met with her brother and he sent his love and hoped to be able to visit soon.

Kate then explained what had been happening since she had moved to the cottage and her upcoming trip when she would be returning to Italy again.

"This is amazing mum," she enthused. "It would make a great novel ….."

"Hang on a minute …." Kate stopped her, remembering her own thought from the other day.

"No, I mean it. You can change the names and …. well, say you'll think about it."

"Hmm, I don't know, but ok." Kate said with a shrug, hoping that would be the end of it.

Relieved now that she had been able to tell Emma the truth about the diary and her trips to Italy, Kate was almost ready for her next visit. There was just Annie to see before she left. She wondered why she had not heard from her and had sent a text to which Annie had replied saying she was spending a few days with Ben and would be back tomorrow. Kate hoped this meant that they were working things out.

She hardly saw or heard from George in the remaining days as he worked to organise the smooth running of his business during his absence. In fact, she did not mind this as it gave her the chance to get used to the idea of spending more time with him once they were in Italy. She was still struggling with the pros and cons of the trip. There was not only a strong pull of a loyalty to past memories but also a quiet excitement about a future she had not expected. How she was going to reconcile this conflict she did not yet know but tried not to dwell on it.

Annie breezed in the following day full of news about her visit with Ben which initially overshadowed Kate's news of her upcoming trip.

"Oh Kate, I feel I've been so stupid and yet at the same time don't know what else I could have been, if you know what I mean." Annie's words streamed from her as they sat at Kate's kitchen table with mugs of coffee. "I mean when he finally explained it to me I could see the sense in it …... not that I think it was right to just go the way he did but if only he had said all this sooner …. though I suppose he couldn't. Anyway, I'm not rushing into going back to how we were …. I mean I think this time on my own has made me think more about what I want and well, I'm not sure any more what that might look like....." Annie paused for breath and took a slurp of coffee.

"So …...," Kate began.

"I don't know, Kate. I mean I was very hurt and then there's this thing called trust and while it was lovely to be with him and talk more than we have for a long time I'm not sure how …. if I can trust him, or maybe ….. maybe in time.... I really don't know. But right now I've suggested we take it very slowly and see what happens. Now, what about you, what have you been up to?"

"Oh," Kate paused wondering where to start now the focus had changed to her. "I er, I'm going back to Italy again in a few days ….."

"That's fantastic, but you've only just got back, what's happened?"

"Well," Kate tried to remember when she had last seen Annie and once she had it clear in her mind she told her about the resemblance between George and the man in Italy and how, with a photo of George from his website and Giancarlo's help, they had discovered that there was the possibility he was descended from Charles, Hettie's long lost brother.

"Wow," Annie fell back into her chair, "you have been busy, but why the trip?"

"Oh that, yes well, George has asked me to go with him. He wants to follow in the footsteps of his mother's diary before meeting this potential family. All a bit daunting really and …....."

"Kate, how exciting. Ooo, do I smell romance in the ….." Annie bubbled.

"No, now stop right there, Annie," Kate said indignantly. "I'm struggling enough with the whole idea as it is."

"But ..."

"But nothing. It's all arranged, separate rooms and ….."

"And what about this Gian ….."

"Giancarlo? Nothing Annie, there's nothing," Kate said with a firmness that surprised her.

"Ok, ok," Annie raised her hands in surrender. However, she could not contain herself for more than a few seconds. "But Kate, I mean not just one good looking man of interest but two, and you say there's nothing?" She leaned forward on the table looking at Kate with an highly arched eyebrow.

"Annie please, there's nothing to tell but as soon as there is you'll be the first to know," Kate said hoping that would be the end of it.

"Ok, ok," Annie sat up straight again. "I won't say another word. How long did you say you're away for?"

"Just a week. So, we'll spend half of it in Florence and the rest of the week with Umberto and Claudia. George will be able to meet his …. er, not sure …. cousins I suppose, and I'll be able to spend some time with my parents."

"You know, if you want to stay longer that's fine with me, I can keep an eye on things here." Annie offered.

"Thanks Annie, that's good to know but I don't think…..."

"Well, you never know and just saying so you can if you want to."

"Ok, thank you."

"Well, I'd better get going, but remember what I said and have a fabulous time." Annie grinned as she made her way to the front door.

5

The day arrived and Kate was in a whirl of last minute checks before George came to collect her to go to the airport. She had only seen him once in the last few days when they had met for an early evening drink. It had been brief and mainly to discuss and finalise arrangements. Although Kate felt relaxed in his company she still had reservations about the trip and spending so much time with him.

How many times had she examined her thoughts and feelings about George, and also Giancarlo. Both were attractive men who, she had to admit, had had an effect on her despite her resistance. There was also her loyalty to John's memory and she knew it was indeed time to start letting this go. He would not have wanted her to spend the rest of her life on her own. In her mind's eye she could see him standing there, smiling and nodding his head in a familiar way, confirming it was time. Tears pricked her eyes as she felt she could reach out and touch him, though those tears were not of sorrow but of love, both received and given. In that moment, as his image faded, she knew it was time, time to move on and now, with the embrace of John's blessing, she was ready.

Any doubts she may have had soon dissolved and were overridden by a mixture of excitement and trepidation when she put her case down in the hall and simultaneously heard a car pull up outside. She gave a last minute glance round the downstairs rooms before greeting George at the door.

"Ready?" He asked with a smile she could not help but catch and return.

"Ready," she affirmed.

A MATTER OF TIME

When successful art journalist, Lucia Walker accepts an assignment to interview reclusive art collector, Giacomo Martinelli, in Florence, the home of her maternal family, she is haunted by a recurring dream and other disturbing experiences that disrupt her ordered life, and cause her to doubt her own sanity. Supported by her family she meets Tom, her aunt's landscape gardener and Simonetta, an enigmatic academic and psychic and is forced to confront the possibility of a previous life at the time of the Cathar communities in Florence. As other feelings rise to the surface and her relationship with Tom deepens, she is stretched beyond her usual boundaries, opening her to new ideas and love.

Praise for A Matter of Time

'A thoroughly enjoyable read; a real page turner! A delightful story of love and intrigue, 'A Matter of Time' is a beautifully-written and well-paced mystery which, as it gradually and gloriously unfolds, grips the reader's attention from beginning to end. Highly recommended!'

'This is a great read and one I didn't want to put down. With a tightly crafted plot and an easy style I was drawn in and lived through the intriguing narrative. If you love Italy or want to know more about it then this book has an extra level of interest for you, The location and life of Florence is totally real and the style, what can I say? It's like a mid-morning glass of wine on the Via Veneto or wonderful Italian ice cream being enjoyed in the shade while walking in the park. Read it, you won't regret it.'

'What a wonderful read and beautiful story. "A Matter of Time" has a real sense of place, which together with the narrative kept me reaching for the book until the very last page. You find yourself not only caring about the characters and what's happening but longing for Florence and Italy! I highly recommend.'

'This was a great read from start to finish - once I started the book, I didn't want to put it down. It was totally absorbing and the sense of Italy created was so very strong that I had trouble working out that I wasn't there each time I stopped reading. The story was gripping with many twists and turns. A highly recommended book!'

Read the first chapter at
www.essentially-art.com

ABOUT THE AUTHOR

Themah is a writer, artist and dancer. She has a BA in Related Arts and Dance. Her love of Italy began many years ago when on holiday in Liguria. More recently, she lived in rural Tuscany for several years, the source of inspiration for both her novels and visits whenever she can. She now lives in Somerset where, when not writing and dancing, she loves to spend time in her garden and on her allotment.

ACKNOWLEDGMENTS

So many people have been part of making this book a reality and I thank you, each and every one, for the parts you played. All those who patiently listened to my ideas, my readings and re-readings, who read through various stages of the manuscript supporting and encouraging me to continue. You know who you are, thank you.

None of this would have been possible without the years I spent in Italy inspired not only by its beauty, but also by its people and the stories they hold, deserving to be heard and told.

Printed in Poland
by Amazon Fulfillment
Poland Sp. z o.o., Wrocław